Clarity

By Jocelyn Powers

CLARITY
© 2009 BY JOCELYN POWERS

ISBN 10: 1-935216-07-4
ISBN 13: 978-1-935216-07-0

First Printing: 2009

This Trade Paperback Is Published By
Intaglio Publications
Walker, LA USA
WWW.INTAGLIOPUB.COM

CREDITS
EXECUTIVE EDITOR: VERDA FOSTER
COVER DESIGN BY SHERI

Dedication

For Sheri Payton, thank you, my dear friend, for your
support and enthusiasm. You are the reason I put pen to paper.

Acknowledgments

A special thank you to Kate Sweeney and Becky Arbogast for helping me get to the heart of this story one night in Provincetown. You girls rock!

To my editor, Verda Foster, who had almost no time at all to guide me through the most challenging part of the book process. You are a gem, thank you so much.

For Sheri the artist, Thanks mate for a gorgeous cover.

To my dear friend Kevin Griffith, thank you for supporting me through everything that has transpired over the past year, including the rise and fall of my estrogen.

And to Julie Greenspoon, who came into my life near the end of the creation of this book, thank you for your encouragement and love. You mean everything to me and my life is better with you by my side.

In memory of Allie, the best little dog a girl could ever have.

"Clarity of mind means clarity of passion, too; this is why a great and clear mind loves ardently and sees distinctly what it loves."

~Blaise Pascal (1623 – 1662)

Chapter 1

Andi Connelly peered out the door of the apartment and scanned the interior of the dimly lit, narrow stairwell. When she was satisfied that no one was there, she dragged a large canvas bag across the worn, dirt-stained, green carpet of the small landing to the top of the stairs. The oversized brown duffel bag was too heavy and bulky for her five-foot-five-inch frame to carry down from the second floor of the four-family flat, which left her no choice but to drag it down the steep flight of rickety wooden stairs, covered in the same ugly green carpet.

She stepped over the bag, grabbed the end, and pulled. The contents of the duffel made a loud thud and a crack as it hit each step on the way down. She moved slowly so as not to draw the attention of the other tenants with the noise. When she reached the landing at the bottom of the stairs, she leaned against the wall and wiped away the beads of sweat that had formed along her blond hair line. She took a deep breath and reached down to continue her manhandling of the duffel bag. At the same time, the heavy wooden door of the building swung open and a gust of cool early morning Chicago air rushed into the musty stairway.

Andi sprang to an upright position and grabbed her chest. "For Pete's sake, Phillip, you nearly scared the life out of me!"

"Sorry, Andi. I was just coming back in to see if there was anything else that needed to be loaded."

"Shh, keep it down, you'll wake the neighbors." She yanked

1

the bag out the door and into the breezeway that divided two apartment buildings. "This is the last of it."

"Here, let me get that." He reached down, and in one fluid motion, the big Irishman with wavy hair the color of rust flung the bag over his shoulder. "Jesus, Andi, what do you have in here, a frickin' dead body?"

She gave her cousin a playful shove from behind. "No, chucklehead, it's the memory foam mattress topper from my bed. I paid a lot of money for that, so be careful where you put it in the storage container. Make sure it lays flat."

He waved her off as he started down the sidewalk to the alley.

She went back inside for one last pass through her apartment in search of any forgotten items. As she ascended the shaky stairs, she looked up to find Tinker, her three-year-old Australian shepherd mix standing at the top wagging her tail.

"Tink, are you ready to go?" She scratched the top of the dog's head as she walked by.

The gray and black-speckled pooch continued to wag her tail and followed Andi into the empty apartment.

Andi walked through each room and opened closet doors looking for anything she might have forgotten. She placed her keys on the counter in the kitchen, as instructed by her landlord, and headed for the door one last time. She stopped in the living room and looked around.

The space that had been the center of her universe for the last six years held many memories, some good and some bad. The worst, however, came six months before when her girlfriend left her for hotshot columnist Ariella Leblanc, whom they had met a few months earlier at a cocktail party.

The woman wrote the society column for the Chicago Sun-Times and was invited to all of the swanky parties and events of the Chicago affluent. She used them as much as they used her. She got to hang with the rich and they got their names in the paper. Andi's ex, Elisha, was a tall, slender, beautiful woman drawn to designer clothes and the glamorous life of the Chicago rich and famous. Coming from one of the most influential families in Chicago, Elisha and her trust fund were the perfect target for someone like Ariella. Andi liked the clothes but had almost no taste for the glamour. Ariella offered plenty of both.

The night Elisha left, Andi came in from work exhausted and found her bags packed and sitting in the middle of the living room floor. When Andi asked for an explanation, Elisha couldn't even look her in the eyes. She told her she was leaving for both their benefit. She would be moving into Ariella's condo on the North Side, in what Elisha referred to as a lovely brownstone in the Gold Coast neighborhood.

Andi could have easily afforded a condo in a brownstone on North Dearborn Street with the salary she received from the television network. She elected to remain on the less-glamorous south side of Chicago to stay close to her grandmother's younger sister and her family. Her Great Aunt Noleen and Uncle Jimmy were four buildings down on the same block, and her cousins all lived nearby as well.

As Elisha rushed to get out the door, she told Andi there was a full explanation in a letter she left on the dresser. Their relationship had begun to sour long before the reporter interfered, but it was still an unexpected jolt. Being told to read the explanation for their breakup, rather than Elisha having the guts to explain it to her face to face, stunned her.

Andi smiled to herself. She knew something about Ariella, thanks to her best friend Desi and her brother the cop, which by now Elisha surely knew, too. Ariella was a phony. Her real name was Norma White and she was not the Ivy League-educated trust fund baby she claimed to be. The truth was, she was raised near a small town in Alabama, where her family ran a commercial catfish farm. Her history hardly made up the pedigree of the socialite she boasted of.

That was all in the past now. Andi was about to start a new job and a new life in the heart of Colorado ski country.

"Girl, I don't know why you insisted on having those movers here at the ass crack of dawn. Nobody gets up this early." Desi, a tall slender African American, stood in the doorway of the apartment with one hand on her hip, a large Gucci bag dangling from her shoulder, and a Starbucks venti cappuccino in the other.

Andi jumped. "Why is everybody sneaking up on me today?"

"Huh?" Desi looked puzzled.

"Never mind. It's not the ass crack of dawn. It's seven thirty in the morning, and you should be on your way to work."

Desi walked over to the large plate glass window and looked out on to the tree-lined street below. "I told Sal I'd be in a little late. Didn't get his Italian knickers all bunched up in a knot this time because I told him I was stopping by to see you off. Besides, it's Friday. You know how laidback it gets around the office at the end of the week."

Andi smiled. "You so manipulate that man."

"I know. It's a gift." She turned and looked around the room. "We had some really good times in this old flat. Lord, girl, I am so gonna miss you. I know I've told you about a hundred times, but I still can't believe you're leavin' Chicago."

"You know I tried everything not to have to do this, but since Epstein continually passed me over for promotion, I had to look elsewhere. I just needed more of a challenge, something new." Andi slipped her hands into the pockets of her jeans and walked over to the window beside Desi. "I know KCOR is a small fledgling station, but the growth Resort TV is promising is phenomenal, and I'm really excited about this opportunity Mr. Redmann has given me. It doesn't hurt that it's part of Vantage Point Media. Who knows, I could end up at the big house in New York battling CNN and Fox for the breaking headlines of the day."

"This will be good for you and a path to bigger and better things." Desi put an arm around Andi's shoulders. "Epstein is a jackass, not a station manager. Hell, I don't think I could have passed up that executive producer job you took, either, and I've never been to Colorado."

Andi smiled. "You'd never leave Chicago, especially not for a job. Your entire life is here in the Windy City, always has been."

Desi wrinkled her nose and smiled. "Yeah, you're right, besides Mama would kill me. She expects the whole family to be right here at her beck and call." She brushed a caramel-colored curl off her forehead and turned to face Andi. "If you have to make the move, I guess this is the best time. You're completely unattached at the moment and free to go."

Andi leaned down on the window sill and pressed her forehead to the glass, contemplating Desi's words.

"Speaking of your freedom…" Desi took a deep breath. "Did you read Norma's, I mean Ariella's, announcement in her column yesterday?"

Andi spun around and sat on the window frame. "You mean the one that read, 'And finally, this reporter is pleased to announce that she will be taking a short break from her duties here at the Sun-Times to get married. On Saturday, Elisha Nichols and I are to be wed in a private ceremony in Provincetown, Massachusetts, followed by a honeymoon at Club Olivia in beautiful Cancun, Mexico.' Is that the announcement you're referring to?"

Desi's mouth hung open. "Yeah, that would be the one. Please don't let the Wicked Witch of the Magnificent Mile and her poisonous gossip column get to you, okay?"

Andi took the cup from Desi's hand and swallowed a mouthful of cappuccino. "Good luck to them. They deserve each other." She scowled and waved her hand in the air. "I was the one that took Elisha to Cancun first." Then a devious grin crawled over her face. "I hope they have a fun-filled week in the sun…and burn."

"Andrea Connelly!" Desi said with fake surprise as she snatched the coffee cup back.

"Kidding, I'm just kidding," she said with that same devious grin.

"You think Elisha knows Norma is living large and deep in debt?" Desi asked.

Andi shrugged her shoulders. "She's been with her six months now. Elisha's not the brightest bulb in the box, but she's not totally oblivious, either."

Desi laughed. "You're right about that bulb thing."

Andi grinned again. "Yeah, but she made up for it in other ways."

Desi cupped her hands over her ears. "Oh, dear, Jesus. I do not need to hear about that. "

Desi looked Andi in the eyes with all seriousness. "You need to get back into the game. It's time. Six months is long enough to grieve over that cold-hearted, social-climbing bitch and what she did to you."

Andi folded her arms over her chest. "I'm not grieving. I'm just more cautious these days. Besides, I'm moving to an area of the country where I don't know anyone. I seriously doubt I'll be dating again anytime soon." Andi thought for a moment over what she just said; it sent a sting down her spine.

"That's a damn shame." Desi wagged a manicured finger at Andi. "You should be out having a good time with some sweet young thing."

"Desi, really, can we please just drop this for now—"

"Hey, Andi, truck's here!" Phillip's booming tenor voice echoed in the stairwell.

Andi dropped her arms to her side and shook her head. "I can't believe I'm related to that man." Secretly, she was relieved that Phillip had interrupted their conversation concerning her current dating situation, something she was still not ready to discuss.

By the time they reached the alley behind the apartment building, the two men had Andi's packed storage container locked and loaded on their truck. She confirmed the address in Frisco, Colorado, where the container was to be delivered and signed the release form so the men could start their journey.

They watched the truck, with almost everything Andi owned on it, roar down the alley on its way west. When it was gone from sight, they made their way back to the entrance to the building.

Phillip threw his big arm around Andi's shoulders. "You going by Gran's to say goodbye?"

"Yeah, it's gonna be so hard to leave them." Andi rubbed her face with her hands.

"They're gonna miss you."

"I'm going to miss them, too. I'm going to miss all of you."

They stopped in front of the door to the building. "Will you walk over with me?"

Phillip pushed his ball cap down on his head. "Can't, I gotta run back by the house before work."

"Well then, I'll just say goodbye now." She reached up and wrapped her arms around his thick neck.

He circled his arms around her and lifted her up. "You take care now, girl, ya hear?" His voice cracked as he spoke.

"I will," she said as he lowered her to the sidewalk.

He turned to Desi. "Don't you be a stranger. Stop by Gallagher's some Friday night and I'll buy you a drink."

She flashed him a coy smile while she toyed with her designer bag. "You can bet on it. Best offer I've had in a long time."

Andi grabbed Phillip by the collar. "I better hear from you, mister, a phone call, e-mail, something," she said with tears forming at the corners of her light blue eyes. It was hard to say goodbye to him. Of her great aunt's ten grandsons, he was her favorite. He had become more like a little brother to her than a cousin since she first moved to Chicago to attend college.

Phillip swallowed the lump in his throat. "You can count on it." He turned away from the women, afraid they might see his own tears forming, and started down the sidewalk toward the street. "I gotta go. You take care, Andi. Bye now."

"Tell your brothers bye for me. I love you," she called after him.

"Love you too." He waved as he rounded the building.

She wiped her eyes and looked at Desi, who also was dabbing at her eyes, trying not to smear her perfect makeup.

"I guess I better get to work, too," Desi said, clutching a handkerchief to her breast.

Andi held up her arms and embraced her best friend. They clung to each other for a long time. She finally let go. "Remember I'm only a phone call away."

"I know, but it's not the same." Desi sniffed back tears. "Still, I want you to find your happiness."

"I won't quit looking until I do."

Desi straightened the jacket of her suit. "All right then, I gotta go. You call me when you get there, ya hear?"

Andi rolled her eyes. "Yes, Mom."

Desi slapped her arm playfully. "I mean it. I won't rest till I know you're there in one piece."

"Don't worry, I'll call."

Desi set off down the sidewalk in the direction Phillip went. "Love you and be careful."

"Love you too." Andi shook her head at the motherly display of her friend. She stood for a moment alone in the breezeway and thought about the journey she was about to embark upon. At thirty-four, she would be starting over a thousand miles away in a new place with a new job and no familiar faces. The sting returned, this time in her gut.

She pushed it all out of her mind and ran up the stairs to her empty apartment. She attached the leash to Tinker, grabbed her backpack, and closed the door behind them.

They walked down the street to the building where her aunt and uncle lived. She knocked before opening the door to the ground floor apartment. "Hello, Aunt Noleen? Uncle Jimmy?"

"In here, dear," the elder female voice with an Irish accent answered.

Andi set her backpack next to the door and let go of Tinker's leash. The dog dashed ahead into the kitchen.

"Oh, gracious, aren't you full of it this morning." The white-haired woman patted the speckled dog on the head as Tinker jumped up on her.

"Good morning, Aunt Noleen."

"Good morning to you, too, dear." Aunt Noleen wiped her hands on her apron that protected her simple floral print dress, then cradled Andi's face with her hands and pressed her cheek to Andi's with a small kiss. "All ready to go, are you?"

"Yes, ma'am. The truck just left and I closed up the apartment for the last time."

"'Tis a sad day, your leaving and all. Phillip will be lost without you."

Andi laughed. "He'll be fine. It's about time he learned to make his own coffee."

Aunt Noleen laughed. "You must be joking. He'll be down here now in the morning looking for a mug full."

Tears welled in Andi's eyes again. "Thank you for everything, Aunt Noleen. For looking after me when I moved here, all the free meals, the going away party…"

"Stop now, young lady. That's what family is for. I made a promise to your Nan that I would fill in for her. You've been like a granddaughter to me, so enough said." The stout woman held steady, not a tear shed.

Andi smiled. "I hope I'm not making a mistake."

"Now we've been through all that enough times, too. You know you have to go and look for your life, create it for yourself because it's not going to come find you."

"You're right. I have to do this."

"You never know what you'll find now. There might just be some pretty young lady waiting for you to find her out there in the mountains." She winked at Andi.

Andi blushed at her aunt's suggestion.

She looked at Tinker. "Little girl, I guess we better go if we want to be at Mom and Dad's in time for dinner."

The dog answered with a soft woof and a shake of her head.

The Irish woman wrapped her arms around Andi's neck. "Be safe, child, and remember we love you." She kissed Andi's cheek.

"I'll call you when I get to Mom and Dad's."

"That will be just fine, dear." She turned to face the hallway. "Jimmy Long, come in here and say goodbye to Andrea."

The tall, slender man with a full head of gray hair made his way into the kitchen slowly. "Are you leaving already, girl?"

"Yes, Uncle Jimmy. I promised Mom I'd be there for dinner tonight."

"We're sure to miss that smile of yours. Lights up the whole place." He leaned down and Andi hugged his neck. He gave her a light kiss on her forehead, scraping her skin with his stubble.

"Love to your ma and dad," Noleen said as she adjusted Andi's ball cap lovingly.

"Anything for Grandpa?" Andi picked up her backpack.

Noleen's jovial face turned bitter. "I have nothing to say to that old goat!" She crossed her arms over her chest.

It was a mystery to the family why Noleen and her brother-in-law had an ongoing quarrel. When asked, neither one could explain the particulars for their distaste of each other that started as teens back in Ireland.

"I have one message. You tell that old fool I'm still waiting on me bottle of brandy."

Andi laughed. "I'll tell him. I think he has a new batch ready. I'll make sure myself that he sends it."

She patted Andi's cheek. "You're a good girl."

"Come on, Tink, we have some driving ahead of us." She kissed her aunt and uncle one more time before she walked out of the apartment. With a wave, she was off.

Andi tossed her backpack in the passenger's seat and opened the back door of the white Ford Escape hybrid so Tinker could hop in. Once she settled into the driver's seat, she took one more look at her building.

Again she wondered if she made the right decision taking a job so far from everything she knew. She tried to think of the positive—advancement, new experiences, and being far from bad memories. She started up the SUV and headed out of town.

Chapter 2

The sign at the entrance read: "Welcome to Chateau Le Poer, home to the Connelly Family Vineyards." Andi maneuvered the white SUV up the horseshoe gravel driveway toward her parents' old farmhouse and felt a warm feeling rush over her.

When she got closer, a large gray dog with floppy ears and a stubby tail appeared from the side of the house, barking ferociously, alerting everyone who could hear him that an intruder was on the property.

Andi brought the vehicle to a stop and opened the door, but before she could get out, Tinker vaulted over the seat and out the door. She immediately jumped on the big gray dog, and the two wrestled playfully in the grass.

Andi got out and stood with her hands on her hips. "Great, we're not even here thirty seconds and you're already dirty." She shook her head and laughed.

The large dog managed to break away from Tinker and jumped on Andi, licking her face.

"Hello, Ernie." She hugged her father's beloved Weimaraner and scratched the top of his ears. When he was done saying his hello, the two dogs ran off to play.

Andi walked to the back of the vehicle to get her overnight bag and was met by a small but sturdy elderly gentleman with short, thick wiry gray hair, wearing an off-white Henley, the sleeves stained by grapes and soil, faded baggy jeans held up by leather suspenders, and a pair of tall dark green Wellington boots. He was carrying a thermal coffee mug. "Well, the saints be praised, it's me own granddaughter come home for a visit," he said with a crooked smile.

"Hey, Grandpa." Andi threw her arms around his neck and kissed his cheek. He smelled of Old Spice and pipe tobacco. She breathed in the familiar scents.

"You're a sight for sore eyes, girl." The Irishman squeezed her.

"It's good to see you, too." She hugged him with a smile.

"How was the trip down?"

She released her hold on him. "Long and boring."

He took a long look at his granddaughter. "Geez, girl, you're tiny. Your ma needs to fatten you up some."

"The last few months have been rather stressful, guess food just wasn't high on my list of priorities. I'm sure Mom's got something cooking in there that'll fix that."

"Yes, she does indeed, even sent me down to the cellars for a few bottles of the estate red." He took her bag as they walked toward the big porch on the front of the house.

Before they reached the steps, the front door swung open, and an attractive, slim woman in her late fifties appeared on the front porch. She wore a pink T-shirt and brown Capri pants, her blond hair loosely pinned up in a bun. "Andrea!" she called out and rushed off the porch.

"Hi, Mom." Andi could barely get the words out with her mother's arms wrapped around her neck so tightly.

Katharine Connelly's voice was giddy. "My baby girl is home. I'm so happy to see you." She planted a motherly kiss on Andi's cheek and rocked her daughter as she embraced her.

Katharine loosened her hold and looked her daughter up and down. "You look pale, are you feeling all right, sweetheart?"

"Yeah, Mom, I'm fine. I've just been sitting in the car too long."

Katharine looked her in the eyes with sympathy.

At that moment, the two dogs came bounding around the side of the porch, and Tinker, in her excitement, slammed into

Katharine's leg.

She bent down to greet the dog. "There's my precious grand-puppy. It's good to see you, too."

Tinker greeted her with licks on the nose.

Katharine stood back up and put her arm around Andi's shoulders as they walked. "I hope you're hungry. I've been cooking all afternoon. I made your favorites—beef stew and Grandma's Irish soda bread, topped off with cherry pie for dessert."

"That's exactly what I need, Mom, some of your wonderful home cooking."

Katherine squeezed her shoulders. "Yes, you do, you're a little on the thin side, dear."

"I was telling her the same thing. The girl needs to eat," Grandpa said and shook his head. "Geez, what would your Nan say?"

Andi walked up on the white porch that wrapped around the lower level of the farmhouse. To the left was the old wooden swing that held many memories and to the right sat her grandmother's wicker furniture with its floral print cushions. She opened the wooden screen door and walked into the foyer with a staircase in the center and a hallway on both sides giving access to the rooms on the lower level. The look, the smell, she was home again.

"Everyone will be here for dinner shortly, and I still have a few odds and ends to take care of," Katharine said as she walked in behind her and headed down the hall to the kitchen. "Your father should be here any minute. He finished in court early today."

"I'll just take this up to your room, girl." Grandpa started up the stairs with her bag in hand.

"Thanks, Grandpa."

A scratch and a whimper at the door reminded Andi that she had forgotten someone. She opened the screen door and stepped to the side. "Come on in, you two."

The dogs darted through the door and headed down the hall behind Katharine. They landed at the water bowl next to the back door and began lapping up its contents.

Andi walked into the kitchen. "Is there something I can help you with, Mom?"

"You just got here, wouldn't you like to rest?"

"I'd rather keep moving. I'm afraid if I sit, I won't get up."

"If you'd like to finish setting the table, that would be fine, sweetheart."

"I can do that."

"Andi, dear, use the large, stemless burgundy glasses."

"Yes, ma'am."

The house was abuzz with activity, and Andi's smile was big as she placed the glasses around the table. The house would soon be out of control when the rest of the family arrived.

First in was her father. He was greeted at the door by Tinker and Ernie. Both got their backs scratched and, in usual Weimaraner fashion, Ernie followed his master around with a squeaky toy in his mouth.

"There's my girl." Michael Connelly, a distinguished man of about sixty with thick, light brown hair mixed with gray, appeared in the doorway of the dining room wearing a dark gray business suit and tie.

"Hi, Dad." Andi practically leapt into her father's arms. She greeted him with a hug and a kiss.

"Welcome home, Andi Panda."

"It's good to be home. I missed you." Her father's hugs always made her feel like a little girl again. His arms were safe and reassuring.

The dogs were having a tug of war with the squeaky toy at their feet.

"You two need to take that in the other room before you knock into the table and break something. Then you'll both be in real trouble," Andi said. The two dogs ran off down the hall.

"Looks like Tinker's happy to be home, too."

"Yeah, she has lots of room to run and Ernie to keep her entertained."

"He's a big clown, isn't he?"

Andi smiled and nodded.

"I'll just go kiss your mother and get out of this monkey suit, then we'll all have a glass of wine. How does that sound?"

"That sounds wonderful, Dad. I think I'll go clean up, too,

when I'm done with the table."

He disappeared into the kitchen. The next thing Andi heard was a utensil hitting the granite countertop with a clang and the shriek of her mother's voice. "Michael Patrick Connelly, you should know better than to sneak up on me when I'm in the kitchen."

The sound of her father's laugh resonated out of the kitchen into the dining room.

Andi smiled to herself at the playful banter of her parents as she went to her room for a hot shower, with the dogs trailing behind her. They jumped on the bed and watched as Andi opened her bag and got out the things she needed, went to the bathroom, and closed the door.

When she emerged showered, blow-dried and with fresh makeup on her face, she found the canines asleep in the middle of the bed. She finished snapping the pearl buttons on her brown faux suede blouse, then checked her jeans in the mirror. She gave the footboard a nudge at the same time she sprayed herself with perfume. "Wake up, you lazy hounds. It's almost dinner time."

They both jumped up and paraded to the kitchen behind her.

She found her mother still trying to finish last-minute preparations for the family dinner. Her grandfather was seated at the island in the middle of the room, freshly pressed in a crisp white oxford shirt and tweed slacks with brown loafers. He was opening the wine he brought from the cellar and ever so gently pouring the ruby liquid into an aeration decanter.

Andi took a seat next to him. "Grandpa, before I forget, Aunt Noleen asked me to remind you about the bottle of apricot brandy you were supposed to send her."

He sneered. "That old battle ax can just keep waiting."

"Finbar Connelly!" Katharine scolded. "Honestly, you and Noleen are too old to keep up the bickering."

He grumbled like a little boy being made to stay after school. "Geez. All right, I'll have it sent out to her first thing tomorrow."

He reached for a glass sitting next to the decanter and poured a small amount of wine. His face brightened when he turned to Andi and held out the glass. "Here, me darling, tell me what you think."

Andi took the glass and, as she was taught, put her nose to the rim and breathed in the wonderful essence, swirled it, then put it back to her nose before taking a sip. "Let's see, the bouquet is black cherry and there's bittersweet chocolate, oh, and I got a hint of cinnamon. It's bold on the palate, but the tannins are soft. Good aeration. It's nice." She tapped the glass. "This one's a blend, isn't it?"

Grandpa Fin delighted in his granddaughter's evaluation. "Aye, girl, you're every bit as good as Nicolas at identifying your wines."

Andi took another sip and winked at him.

"Your brother combined Syrah grapes with the Norton's, makes for a better balance and spice. We aged it in the old oak barrels we got from that bourbon distillery in Kentucky."

Michael walked in and stood behind his father. "If it meets with my daughter's approval, what you say you pour us all a glass?"

"Aye, son. This girl knows her wines."

Michael set four glasses on the counter in front of the decanter, and Finbar filled them with the Chateau Le Poer Norton Estate Reserve.

"Katharine, put that spoon down and come have a drink," Finbar said.

"Yeah, Katie, everything looks and smells great. Stop for a minute and enjoy having Andrea home." Michael held out a glass to her.

"Some dinner this will turn out to be if I get drunk. It will be entirely your fault for tempting me." She accepted the glass with a smile and put her arm around Michael. "I'm delighted and relieved to have my beautiful daughter home. My only wish is that I could keep her here."

"Your daughter is a grown woman with a life of her own, Katharine." Fin winked at her.

"I can't help it. I'm a mother and wife first and foremost." She took a sip from her glass.

"And you're the best, Mom," Andi chimed in.

"Thank you, dear."

The creek of the hinge from the screen door was followed by the excited screams of two little voices calling out, "Andi, Andi."

The sound of the children caused the dogs to run barking toward the front of the house. The children sprinted by the dogs and into the kitchen. Before Andi could get out of her chair, Abby and Riley were jumping on her for hugs.

Abby had Andi around the neck and Riley wrapped his arms around her leg.

"Hi, you guys. Boy, am I happy to see you two." She squeezed them tightly and kissed their round cheeks.

"Well, kill the fatted calf, Mother, your prodigal daughter has returned." Nick was standing in the doorway with his usual big easy grin.

Andi let go of her brother's children and went over to get a much-needed embrace from her eldest sibling. "Shut up and give me a hug, ya big dork." She wrapped her arms around his six-foot-two-inch frame.

Nick hugged her back and kissed her forehead. "It's about time you came home, Shrimp. I almost forgot what you looked like." Right behind him was Rebecca, his wife. Andi moved from her brother and greeted her sister-in-law with a hug and kiss on the cheek also.

"It's good to have you home, Andi. It's been too long in between visits," Rebecca said.

"I know it's been way too long. Work just kinda got out of control."

A small hand grabbed Andi's. "Andi, I Jack Spro," Riley proclaimed, pointing a small plastic sword in the air with a twinkle in his blue eyes and a delightful grin reflective of his father's.

Andi looked at Rebecca with a questioning expression.

"Somebody gave him the Pirates of the Caribbean DVD." Rebecca shot a look at Grandpa Fin. "And now he thinks he's Jack Sparrow, long hair and all. I tried to cut it, but he would have none of it, so I just let it grow. I figured he would move on to his next obsession soon enough, but this pirate phase seems to be sticking around longer than Thomas the Tank Engine did."

Andi gave a hardy laugh at her three-year-old nephew and ran her fingers through his almost shoulder-length blond, wavy locks as he poked the sword at the imaginary pirates who surrounded him.

"Andi, Mommy is taking me to riding lessons." Abby was jumping up and down with her hands clasped together.

"All right, kids, give your aunt a break. There's plenty of time to catch up." Rebecca smiled at Andi. "They have so much to tell you. It's been Andi, Andi, Andi ever since Nick told them you were coming for a visit."

Andi smiled with delight as Nick and her father herded the little ones off to the family room to wait for dinner.

Andi and Rebecca helped Katharine finish with the dinner preparation and brought everything to the table. Grandpa Fin carried the decanter with the wine into the dining room and poured it into the glasses Andi had set on the table earlier.

Just as Katharine was about to call the family to the table, a distinctively male voice called out, "It sure does smell good in here."

The sound sent the dogs running and barking toward the kitchen. Andi recognized the voice right away; it was her younger brother Timothy. She hurried into the kitchen and found him at the back door with Tinker and Ernie jumping on him for attention.

He stood his six-foot frame up straight and shook his brown hair back off his face, revealing a smile similar to Nick's. With one hand on his hip, he pointed at her and said, "Hey, don't I know you?"

He was a sight for sore eyes in a leather jacket, T-shirt, and blue jeans. Andi flung her arms around his neck. He squeezed her tight and lifted her off the ground. "Welcome back, sis." He loosened his hold on her and set her down.

"Look at you, your hair is getting so long." Andi gently pulled at a lock of his hair.

"Yours is too." He laughed and ran his fingers through his shoulder-length mane. "It drives Mom crazy, so I thought I'd just let it grow for a while."

"I see you haven't changed. You're still doing everything you can to yank her chain. You and Riley are two peas in a pod."

Katharine stood in the doorway to the kitchen, delighted to see her youngest child. "Well, you finally found your way here. I'll never know where you get your timing, Timothy Joseph. I'm just now putting dinner on the table."

Tim walked over and kissed her forehead. "Then I'm on time for the shindig, right?"

Katharine reached up and lovingly stroked his hair. "I wish you'd get a haircut, love."

"Aw, Mom, chicks love long hair, especially the hot ones, right, Andi?" He flipped Andi's blond ponytail.

Andi held her hand up as she headed for the dining room. "I'm staying out of this one." She stopped just shy of the door. "But he's right, Mom, the hot chicks do dig the long hair." She left the room with a chuckle.

"Andi," Katherine said, "don't encourage him." She handed him the basket of warm bread from the counter and pointed him toward the dining room. "Put this on the table, then go wash your hands, young man."

Once everyone was seated, the prayer said, and the dinner served, Katharine sat at the end of the oval dinner table flanked by Andi on one side and Tim on the other. She smiled approvingly at her family as they enjoyed the meal she prepared.

"What is it, Katie?" Michael asked in between bites.

She picked up her fork. "I'm just thrilled to have my entire family together in one place, even if it's only for one dinner."

"And it's not even a holiday," Fin added.

"We still have plenty of room at the table to add more as our family grows, right, Timothy?" Katharine took a bite from her fork.

Tim stopped in mid-chew and looked at her with surprise, then swallowed hard. "Hey, I'm not the only single adult here at this table." He pointed his fork in Andi's direction.

Andi stuck her tongue out at him.

"Timothy, leave your sister alone. She's still nursing a bruised heart." Katharine patted her daughter's hand.

"That's right. Besides, my life is in transition at the moment." Andi took a sip of wine. "You know every available female within fifty miles of here, Tim, surely there's one that suits your fancy," Andi teased.

Tim rolled his eyes and drained his wine glass.

"Here, boy, I think you need another drink, the women are ganging up on you." Fin filled his glass.

"Thanks, Grandpa. We single men need to stick together." He put his hand on Fin's shoulder.

Fin nodded in agreement and everyone laughed.

"Speaking of expanding, did Dad tell you about the Bauer place?" Nick asked.

Andi shook her head. "No, the last I heard, Mr. Bauer had passed away. That's been what, four or five months ago?"

"Yeah, about that. Anyway, we've put together a proposal to buy the vineyard from Mrs. Bauer. We're just waiting on the bank for the financing."

"Wow, that's big news and no one bothered to tell me?"

"We had to act quickly, honey," Michael said. "Last week, we found out Mrs. Bauer's kids talked her into selling the property. They had no interest in maintaining the land or paying the taxes."

Fin interjected, "Ole man Bauer let the vines go when he got sick with cancer a couple of years ago. Me and Timmy went over last week and had a look at the grounds. The vines are a bit tattered from neglect and the weeds have grown up, but the roots are hardy and show some new growth."

"We worked it out with Mrs. Bauer to purchase the vineyard, barn, and the tool shed," Nick said. "Mrs. B gets to keep the house and the grounds around it, and we'll do the land maintenance for her. She's also getting a fair market price for the deal."

"So that means Chateau Le Poer will expand across the entire valley, right?" Andi asked.

"That's right, sis."

"That'll add thirty acres of the beautiful little blue Norton's to our harvest once we get the vines healthy again. Just need a little TLC and some good ole fashion blood, sweat, and tears to whip 'em back into shape," Fin said.

"We're also looking into hiring a marketing firm to help us with expansion," Tim said. "Nick wants to add to our line of wines, and Rebecca is in the process of expanding the menu for the restaurant with plans for additional weekend events."

"That's wonderful, guys. I'm so proud of all of you," Andi said. Deep down, she felt a little sad that she wouldn't be there to be a part of it. Her life was taking her in a different direction.

After dinner and dessert, everyone retreated to the family room where Abby and Riley demanded Andi's attention. Abby shared her excitement over riding lessons while she and Andi worked on a puzzle together and Riley explained the thrills of a life as a pirate. Andi's heart filled with joy.

Rebecca sat in the rocker next to Andi and clipped her auburn hair back in a loose ponytail. "Are they wearing you out yet?"

Andi contemplated the placement of a puzzle piece she held in her hand. "I love it. I miss them so much, and they're growing so fast." Andi stroked Tinker's fur as she leaned against her leg.

"Tell me about it. They're outgrowing their clothes at an alarming rate, and they miss you, too. We all do."

Andi smiled in appreciation.

"So," Rebecca said, "how are you getting on? Mom told me about everything that happened at the station, and I imagine you're still stinging over the breakup with Elisha."

Andi looked down and shuffled her feet on the Persian rug. "I'm okay." She looked up at her sister-in-law. "I couldn't stay there any longer. I was being taken advantage of by my boss and his old boy's club. He passed me over three times for a promotion, and each time, it was given to a man with inferior credentials. I had to stand up for myself and let them know I was worth more than they wanted to give me credit for."

"Good for you. We Connelly women are strong and independent, and the rest of the world needs to know it." Rebecca reached over and put her arm around Andi.

"My only regret was leaving everybody in Chicago." Andi paused a moment. "As for Elisha, I think I knew all along we weren't going to last. We didn't want the same things from life.

She definitely didn't want kids." Andi placed the puzzle piece in its proper grooves. "We had our problems, but I never expected her to cheat on me like she did. And not with that old wind bag, Ariella."

"You know the old saying, what goes around comes around." She squeezed Andi's shoulders. "One day, you'll find that special relationship you're looking for." Rebecca looked over at Nick sitting on the floor Indian style with a pirate patch over one eye, pretending to lose a swordfight to Riley. "And when you do, you'll wonder how you ever got along without that person."

"You and Nick are certainly blessed."

"And I believe you will be, too. You know what? You're going to make a wonderful mother someday." Rebecca kissed her forehead and gave her another reassuring squeeze.

Andi laid her head on Rebecca's shoulder and smiled at Abby, who was holding a puzzle piece up for her.

Andi got plenty of quality family time, something she dearly needed. After everyone had said good night and gone their own way, she found herself in the kitchen with her mother. Katharine was drying the last of the utensils and pots that remained in the sink.

Andi leaned across the counter of the island. "Dinner was spectacular, Mom, thank you."

"You're welcome, dear. If you're still hungry, I think there's some pie left in the fridge."

"Thanks, but I don't think I can eat another thing tonight."

Katharine returned the pot she dried to its cabinet. "Are you doing anything with your painting, dear?"

Andi rubbed her hands together. "No, I haven't," she said sadly. "I don't know how to explain why." She thought for a moment. "It's…it's as if the fire has been extinguished, and no matter how hard I rub the sticks together, I can't seem to generate enough friction to start it up again. It's always been about passion that has driven me to create." She folded a towel sitting on the counter. "I find myself still searching for something to inspire me to put paint to canvas again."

"Maybe you're trying too hard. From your very first crayon

masterpiece on the bathroom wall at the age of three, your talent has always come natural to you." Katharine put her towel down and sat next to Andi. "It will come again. That something you need will find you, and your passion will soar to new heights."

A lump rose up in Andi's throat; she forced it back down. "Thank you, Mom, for believing in me."

Katharine hugged her. "I've always believed in you, all of you. Each one of my children has their own special place in this world, and I'm so proud of my three babies." She let go of Andi. "Nick was always the protector and perfectionist. Tim was, and still is, the epitome of the baby of the family. That boy would try the patience of a saint."

Andi giggled. "It's a wonder we didn't kill one another growing up."

"True, there were enough trips to the emergency room to go around." Katharine laughed, then reached over and gently fingered a lock of Andi's blond hair. "I never wanted you to feel like a middle child, like you were ignored or not as important, but how could you? You were my first girl. I fell in love with you the moment Dr. Rice laid you on my chest, wet and crying."

Andi wrinkled her nose at the image in her head.

"Your father bawled his eyes out when he saw those big blue eyes of yours open up and you grabbed his finger. He sat and rocked you for an hour." Katharine's own light blue eyes twinkled as she spoke. Then she held up a finger. "You did, however, get the one most important middle child trait, and that's the creative, artistic side of you. You have a gift of expression, and I think you need to use it to feel complete."

Andi could not deny her mother's statement. She knew there were pieces of herself missing.

Katharine rubbed Andi's back. "I do wish you could stay longer. It's been so long since you were home last and there's no telling when you'll get back to visit with the new job and all."

"I wish I had more time, too, but Mr. Redmann wanted me to start as soon as possible. Sounds like the work has really gotten behind since the last EP left."

Katharine wrapped her arms around Andi. "If anyone can get

things sorted and organized. it's you. They're going to love you out there."

Andi smiled. "Thanks, Mom. Your opinion isn't biased now, is it?"

"Maybe a little, but you're good at what you do, don't kid yourself."

Andi hugged her mother, then went off to bed.

The next morning, she slowly packed her bag while Tinker watched. "Tink, we're halfway there, little girl. By tonight, we should be in Frisco."

Tinker just stared at her.

"Looks like we should have good weather for the drive." She carried the bag down the stairs and set it by the door. Tinker ran off to find Ernie.

She had breakfast with her parents and Grandpa Fin before she left. Tim stopped in to say his goodbyes as did Nick and his family.

Abby raised her innocent face to her aunt. "When are you coming home again, Aunt Andi?"

"I'm not sure, sweetie. I'm starting a new job and I'll have to get a lot of work done before they let me have vacation. In the meantime, we'll talk on the phone and send lots of e-mails."

Abby wrinkled her nose in displeasure.

"I promise the next visit will be longer and we will have plenty of time to do things."

A smile replaced the scowl on Abby's face. "Like ride horses?"

Andi's rear end hurt at the thought of getting on a horse. "Yes, we'll go riding and you can show me what you've learned."

The little girl squealed with delight.

Rebecca instructed the two little ones to give Andi a hug and a kiss so they could get to the church field in time for Abby's soccer game.

Andi experienced a ping of sadness as she stood on the porch with her mother, waving goodbye and watching Rebecca maneuver the minivan down the driveway toward the road.

Andi turned to her mother. "I guess Tinker and I should be getting on the road, too."

Katharine touched her hair and gave her a look of distress. "I wish you had more time, honey."

"Me too, Mom, me too."

They returned to the kitchen so Andi could say goodbye to her brothers before they went off to work, then her father carried her bag to her SUV and put it in the back. Andi followed with her mother and grandfather.

"Call us as soon as you get there," Katharine said.

Andi rolled her eyes jokingly. "Yes, Mother."

Katharine hugged her tight, and before she let go, she kissed her check. "I love you, sweetheart."

"I love you, too, Mom."

Andi hugged and kissed Grandpa Fin.

"Listen, girl, I wrapped up a few bottles of the good stuff for you and a box with a mix of red and white, as well. Can't go off to a new home without something to celebrate it with."

Andi laughed. "Thanks, Grandpa. Did you put a bottle of your apricot brandy in there, too?"

He looked at her with astonishment. "Well, of course, I did. Those nights will be cold up in the mountains and you'll be needing a little something to help warm your bones."

"That's very true." She hugged his neck again.

Michael closed the hood of the SUV. "Your fluids look fine, sweetheart."

Andi wrapped her arms around her father's neck. "Thank you, Dad."

He held her tight. "You be careful, love." He kissed her forehead.

"I will." She let him go and moved toward the vehicle.

Andi looked around for Tinker, who was nowhere in sight, then whistled.

Tinker immediately appeared on the porch with Ernie.

"Come on, little girl, we have to go."

Tinker jumped off the steps with Ernie behind her and ran for the SUV.

Andi gave Ernie a hug and scratched his head. "We'll see ya soon, big guy."

Her mother got one last hug in, then Andi opened the door so Tinker could jump in, ready for the continuation of their journey. A final goodbye and the two travelers were off.

Chapter 3

It was after six in the evening when they arrived in Frisco. Andi went south on North Summit Boulevard along Lake Dillon toward Main Street. She held the directions her new boss Thomas Redmann mailed her in hand as she made her way into town.

When she finally found 6 Hunters Hollow Circle, the blue and orange glow of twilight was nearly gone. She spotted her storage container in the driveway as she approached the town house and pulled in next to it. With keys in hand, she opened the front door of the corner unit. Before she could take a step in, Tinker ran passed her. "Welcome to your new home, Tink." Andi looked around. "At least it'll be home for a while."

The town house was beautiful. The paint was fresh and the wooden floors and carpet freshly cleaned. The colors were earthy and very Colorado. The front door opened into a large room with a high ceiling. On the left side of the room was a staircase rising up to the loft area and the master bedroom. To the right, the living area with a floor-to-ceiling, river rock fireplace and hand-carved wooden mantel. Next to the living area was a large kitchen with enough room for Andi's dining room table. A sliding glass door at the back of the kitchen opened to a small patio overlooking the common ground of the complex, lined by Douglas firs and aspens along a stream. Across the room from the front door was a hallway with a bathroom and small bedroom.

Andi found a fruit basket wrapped in yellow cellophane and a red bow on the island in the kitchen. The card attached read:

Ms. Connelly,
Welcome to Colorado.
Warmest Regards,
Thomas and Wendy Redmann

Andi smiled at the gesture. She pulled a banana from the basket and ate it on her way out to unload the SUV. She called her parents as she brought her things in. When that was done, she unlocked the storage container. Thankfully, she had Phillip and his brothers pack the furniture in first and the boxes last. She was sure she could move her favorite big red chair and ottoman on her own with the furniture dolly. She and Tinker would sleep in the chair that night, and the next day, she would hire help to move the big pieces.

She was moving the last of the boxes into the town house when an old green Jeep Cherokee pulled into the driveway next door. A young man in his twenties wearing a tan insulated corduroy jacket, T-shirt, tattered jeans, and work boots got out and walked toward Andi. Tinker jumped behind her and gave the man a warning bark.

"You must be the new neighbor. I can tell by the box in your hands," he said.

"Yeah, that would be me. Don't mind Tinker the Terrible, she's just out of her comfort zone." Andi shifted the box under her left arm and extended her right hand to the young man. "I'm Andrea Connelly, the new executive producer at KCOR." She liked the way that sounded.

He shook her hand firmly. "Leo Montgomery, welcome to Frisco, Andrea," he said with a naturally perfect smile.

"Thanks, Leo, it's nice to meet you, and please call me Andi."

Tinker poked her head between Andi's knees and growled.

"The ferocious attack dog hiding behind me is Tinker."

Leo laughed and bent down so Tinker could sniff his hand. After she deemed him acceptable, he was allowed to pat her on the head.

"Thomas told us he'd rented to a new employee, and I must say, you're much prettier than his last tenant."

Andi blushed. "He didn't really neglect to tell you. We haven't actually met face to face yet."

"Well, he'll be pleasantly surprised when you do." He smiled at her again. "Here, let me help." He reached for the box under her arm.

"Thanks, it's been a long day, and I still have so much to do."

Leo looked into the container. "Ya know, my roommate and I can carry the rest of that in for you."

"Oh, I don't wanna bother you. I planned to arrange for help to move the big stuff tomorrow." Andi grabbed another box.

"Nonsense, Vince and I can move that stuff for you." He followed her in through the front door and set the box on the floor with the others. "I'll just run over and get him. I'll be right back."

Before Andi could say a word, Leo was gone.

He returned with a dark-haired, stocky man about the same age. He was slightly taller than Andi and looked like he had been sleeping.

"Andi, this is my roommate, Vince Donatello."

She shook his hand. "Hi, Vince, nice to meet you."

"Hey, Andi." He had a hint of a New York accent in his voice.

"You don't have to do this, guys. I don't want to impose on you."

Vince gave a reassuring grin. "It's no imposition. We're just helping a neighbor. So where we going with everything?"

Andi laid out the floor plan for the guys, and they went to work. An hour and a half later, the storage container was empty and the furniture was in its respective rooms. It was a chore getting the bedroom furniture up the stairs, but they managed to move it all without causing any damage.

"I don't know how to thank you guys for all the help. I really appreciate this. I wish I could at least offer you a beer, but I haven't been to the store yet. I do have a nice fruit basket and the water is on."

Vince perked up. "We have beer. I'll be right back." He returned with a six-pack, and they sat at the dining room table for a chat.

"You guys haven't told me what you do."

"Ski patrol over at Breck during the season and construction in the off-season," Leo said.

"We came out here after college to be ski bums for a season and ended up staying. This is our fourth year." Vince pealed the label from his beer bottle.

"That's so cool that you're living your life the way you want to," Andi said.

"It's a fun life. Our parents aren't too happy about it, though. They keep asking why they paid all that money for us to get college degrees if all we're gonna do is ski all day and chase women every night." Vince high-fived Leo.

"What about you, Andi? What brings you to the mountains?" Vince asked.

"A new start, I suppose. I was caught in a dead-end job by a boss that didn't see women as equals." She paused. "And I had a long-term relationship that ended roughly. I just needed to move on." She looked out the glass door into the night. "The mountains are so beautiful, maybe I'll find some peace and inspiration here."

"So your boss was a pig and your man was an even bigger pig. That sucks." Vince shook his head.

"My boss was definitely a pig, but my girlfriend was more of a shallow narcissistic socialite." Andi took a long drink from her bottle and eyed the two men as the dust settled from the bomb she just dropped.

Leo and Vince looked at each other with blank expressions, then Vince smiled in Andi's direction. "Girlfriend? You gay?"

"Yep, card-carrying lifetime member of the homo club."

The boys looked at each other again.

Finally, Leo spoke with a smile. "Rock on, girl, that's cool."

"Hell, yeah, it's cool. I'm from Brooklyn, it'll take more than that to shock me," Vince chimed in.

"Really?" Andi looked at them with surprise.

They both nodded in agreement.

"But I gotta ask you…" Vince started.

Leo interrupted his roommate with an elbow to the ribs. "Dude, don't be disrespectful and get all up in the lady's business."

"I'm not. I just wanted to know if this means we got more competition or what?"

"Relax, boys. Your girlfriends are safe. I don't mess with straight girls. I'm too old for those games." Andi smirked and finished her beer.

Vince looked relieved.

After the beer was gone, the boys said good night. They refused to take any money for their work, so Andi promised to make dinner for them one night after she got her house in order.

Once alone in her new home, she unwrapped the six-by-twelve-foot canvas she titled "Her Temptation." The painting depicted two young women scantily clad with loose cloth draped around them, their shoulders exposed, passing an apple between them. She lovingly protected her masterpiece with extra packing blankets. It survived the trip splendidly. She stood back and looked it over for a moment. The high ceiling and the sheer size of the room made the painting look smaller. It still commanded the central focus of the room.

The gripping sensation in her stomach sent her to the kitchen in search of something for herself and Tinker. She opened the box marked pantry and found a microwavable bowl of ravioli for her and the bag of chow for Tinker. She heated the ravioli and had an apple from the basket for dessert. Tinker gobbled down her food and followed it with almost an entire bowl of water. Andi noticed she too was more thirsty than usual. Must be the long trip, she thought.

Andi was so tired she barely had the energy to climb the stairs and make the bed. She was thankful for the help of her new neighbors. The thought of sleeping in the chair that night, as tired as she was, wouldn't have been very restful. She carried her toiletry bag into the master bath to brush her teeth and change into her night clothes. When she flipped on the lights, she discovered a large bathroom with beautiful muted green walls and a green marble and glass block shower stall. In the corner was a Jacuzzi tub big enough for two people. The tub and toilet were a cream color that matched the doors and trim.

"Wow." She scanned the room a second time, and her gaze stopped at the tub. "Can't wait to try that out."

When she was done in the bathroom, she dug the alarm clock out of one of the boxes in the bedroom. She set it for six and placed it on the nightstand, then climbed into bed next to an already sleeping Tinker. In a matter of minutes, she too was sound asleep.

Chapter 4

Andi opened her eyes a little before six Monday morning and stretched her limbs. She was excited to start the day and a little scared of what it would hold; new people, new places, new life. She pulled herself out of bed and turned off the alarm on her way to the bathroom to use her new shower. She emerged in a matching navy blue silk bra and panties with her hair blow-dried and done up stylishly in a ponytail. She spent more time doing her makeup that morning, so it was flawless. Next she dressed in the business suit and jewelry she laid out the night before. She looked smart; she thought this is what an executive producer looked like.

Tinker followed her down the stairs and into the kitchen. Andi filled a bowl with dog chow and another with fresh water. The shepherd was standing at the glass door and looking back at Andi.

"Do you need to go out?"

The speckled dog answered with a wag of her tail.

Andi looked around the back of the building before she opened the door. It was beautiful and relaxing, but she was mindful of the wildlife that called the forest home.

She stepped out into the crisp Colorado morning first, then let Tinker out. The dog darted past her with her nose to the ground. Andi filled her lungs with the cool, dry, fresh air while she kept a watchful eye on Tinker. The sound of the water in the stream running over the rocks gave her a moment of peace.

When the canine was done, they returned to the kitchen and Tinker went for the water bowl. Andi rummaged through the pantry box for something to call breakfast. There was a box of cereal but no milk to go with it. She had plenty of tea but wanted something more. She closed the box and decided to try to find a bakery or coffee shop on the way to work.

She left the kitchen in search of her backpack containing her laptop and handbag. Tinker of course was right on her heels.

"I'm sorry, little girl, I have to go to work and you have to stay here for now, but I'll run home at lunchtime to check on you."

Tinker's ears drooped and she held them back; she knew she was about to be left behind in a strange place. Andi couldn't even leave a radio on for her for noise this time because she hadn't hooked up the home theater system yet.

Tinker jumped on the red chair and curled up in a blanket that Andi laid out. The look the dog gave her sent guilt shooting through her body. She kissed Tinker on the head and promised to be back in a little while. Then she put on the black trench coat that she brought downstairs with her, picked up the backpack, and out the front door she went, on to the next step to her new life.

She drove a short distance to Main Street looking for someplace to get a quick and easy breakfast to go. Seeing the town of Frisco, Colorado, in the light of day showed off its Old West mining town charm.

She spotted a bakery next to a real estate office and found a parking space in front. The sign painted on the window read, "Griffin's Main Street Bakery." Andi stepped onto the wood plank sidewalk, which lined the row of businesses, and walked past a dirty mountain bike chained to the post that supported the overhang. A tiny bell dinged as she opened the door. The smell of fresh baked goods filled the shop. The décor in the small shop emulated that of the town. The use of hanging blown glass light fixtures and brushed metal trim around the pastry case and counter gave a modern twist. The walls were a terra cotta color with a mix of black and white photos of historical scenes of Frisco and bakeries from the 1800s. Six small tables along the walls and window of the bakery offered seating for twelve patrons to socialize and enjoy the shop's fare.

There were two people in the shop when Andi entered. An older gentleman dressed in a fleece jacket and canvas pants, with his glasses resting low on his nose, sat at a table in the window reading the paper with his morning coffee. He paid no attention to her when she walked in. Behind the counter near the cash register was a tall, slender woman in her mid-twenties. Andi's gaydar went off the moment she saw the cute, butchy woman with short, spiky, platinum hair. She wore jeans and a white long-sleeve T-shirt with the sleeves pushed up to her elbows. Her black apron was streaked with the white dust of flour. Andi could hear the clanging of the bangles around her wrists as she pushed a broom back and forth. The woman looked up with a smile and gave Andi a nod while setting the broom aside.

"Morning. What can I get you?"

"Can I get a protein smoothie and a banana nut bagel?"

"Sure thing." The girl turned to the blender behind her and began adding the ingredients for the smoothie. "Beautiful day, isn't it?"

"Yes, it's a lovely morning," Andi said while digging in her handbag for some cash.

The young woman kept turning around to look at Andi while she worked on the smoothie. "You in town for the pharmaceutical conference?"

"Conference?" Andi was still trying to find her money in the bottom of her bag. "No, I just moved here. I'm the new executive producer for KCOR."

"Really? That's so awesome. I was on 'Sunrise Summit' last season when Chip and Buster broadcasted live from the board park in Breck," she said with excitement.

Andi nodded as if she understood but had no idea what the girl was talking about. The board park in Breck?

The girl finished mixing the smoothie and poured it into a large plastic cup and put a lid on it. She set the cup, with a small white bag, on the counter and punched the items into the register. "The total is $2.86. The bagel's on the house, a little welcome to Frisco," she said with a soft smile.

Andi handed her the money. "That's very kind of you, but I don't want you to get in any trouble."

The girl leaned toward Andi as if she had a secret to share. "No trouble, my folks own this place."

Andi smiled back. "Well then, thank you very much for the bagel."

"I'm Bonita Griffin, my friends call me Bo," the girl said as she handed back change.

Andi extended her hand. "Nice to meet you, Bo, my name is Andrea Connelly and my friends call me Andi."

Bo shook Andi's hand. "Andi," she said, "I like that."

Andi picked up her breakfast and winked at Bo. "I'll see ya 'round, Bo. I'm off to the station. Oh, and thanks again for the bagel." She held up the bag as she turned toward the door with a flirty swing in her step.

"Yeah, see ya 'round, Andi."

Andi sat on the bench outside the shop and enjoyed a few quiet moments in the brisk mountain morning air while she ate her breakfast.

When she was finished, she drove down Main Street to the station, following the directions Mr. Redmann sent to her. As she drove, she noticed how small the town of Frisco was.

Her morning commute would be nothing compared to the one she had in Chicago; in fact, it would be good exercise to walk on a nice day. She wouldn't miss sitting in traffic or the road rage of the other commuters along Lake Shore Boulevard. This place was small, quiet, and clean. No horns or loud trucks belching exhaust into the air, just a pretty town surrounded by mountains and a lake, and residents who didn't seem to rush to get where they were going.

She turned into the parking lot shared by two large buildings. The gray building to the right housed the offices of the local newspaper. On the left stood the white metal-sided building of the television station. The letters KCOR were illuminated in blue over a tinted plate glass window and door on the front of the building. She parked the Escape and took a deep breath before getting out. She grabbed her bag and walked to the front door with her head held high. This was her new beginning, and she was going to make the most of it. She was now an executive producer, and she looked forward to all the challenges that would come with her new position.

Inside the reception area was a pair of stuffed easy chairs with a table to one side of the room and a large white desk along the back wall. Behind the desk sat a young woman in her late twenties with long curly brown hair she had pulled up loosely on top of her head. She was cute with her small rectangular glasses, light makeup, and simple yellow cotton blouse. She greeted Andi with a smile. "Good morning, ma'am, how may I help you?" She had a lovely English accent.

Andi set her backpack down in front of the desk. "Good morning. I'm Andrea Connelly, the new executive producer."

The young girl barely let Andi finish before she sprang out of her chair. "Oh, Ms. Connelly." She removed her glasses and tossed them on the desk. "I-I'm sorry I didn't recognize you. I mean, I should have known who you were, we've been expecting you." She came around the desk. "I'm Rachel Oliver, and I have the strictest of orders to bring you directly to Thomas's office the minute you arrive."

Andi extended her hand to Rachel. "It's nice to meet you, Rachel."

The curvaceous receptionist looked at Andi's hand with surprise before extending her own.

"I'm looking forward to finally meeting Mr. Redmann."

Rachel grabbed Andi's backpack and opened the door to the side of her desk. "Ms. Connelly, if you'll please follow me."

Andi followed Rachel down a hall. On the left were a row of offices, to the right was a plate glass wall that looked out over a soundstage. In the far corner was a set for what Andi guessed was a talk show, decorated to look like a log cabin. They passed a nice conference room with a large flat-panel TV screen hanging on the wall before they reached the open door to the station manager's office. Rachel tapped on the door with a knuckle. "Thomas, Ms. Connelly has arrived."

A fit man of forty with brown hair graying at the temples stood up from his desk. He looked comfortably casual in khaki pants, a light blue oxford shirt, and hiking shoes. "Thanks, Rachel." He walked toward Andi with his hand out. "Welcome, welcome, Ms. Connelly."

Andi gripped his hand and looked him in his brown eyes. "Thank you, Mr. Redmann, I'm very excited to be here." She found him to be very handsome.

Rachel spoke from the doorway. "Ms. Connelly, I'll just take your bag down to your office."

"Wait, Rachel, take Ms. Connelly's coat, too, please." Just as a gentleman would do, Thomas helped Andi remove her trench coat.

Andi handed her the coat. "Thank you, Rachel."

Rachel accepted the items and disappeared into the hall.

A young man stopped her as she headed for Andi's office. Curiously, he asked, "Hey, Rach, who's the blond suit in with Thomas?"

"That's the new EP." She looked back at the office door.

"So whadda think?"

"She's big city. I guess we'll see how long this one lasts."

The young man agreed.

"Please have a seat, Ms. Connelly." Thomas directed Andi to the two chairs in front of his desk.

"Thank you, Mr. Redmann." She straightened her suit jacket before she sat.

"Please call me Thomas. I think you'll find that we're casual around here for the most part." Thomas sat in the chair next to her.

Epstein always sat behind his desk when he addressed his employees; it was his way of letting everyone know who was in charge. This man was addressing her at the same level, which caught her off-guard.

Inside, she was relieved. "You should call me Andi since we're on a first-name basis." That too was a surprise; never would

Epstein have allowed his employees to call him Howie.

Thomas crossed his legs and got comfortable. "So how do you like the town house, Andi?"

Her face brightened. "It's beautiful, and thanks for the lovely fruit basket. I must send your wife a thank you note, too."

"You're welcome and I'm glad you like it.'"

"It's roomier than I anticipated, oh, and the two-car garage was a nice surprise."

"Do you need any help with unloading your things?"

Andi smiled. "Actually, I took care of everything last night."

Thomas looked concerned. "Don't tell me you moved furniture by yourself."

"No, no, I had help. My new neighbors popped in last night, and between the three of us, we moved every piece."

"So you've met Leo and Vince already?" He rolled his eyes.

"How did you know who I was talking about?"

"It just sounds like something those two would do. They're good guys, but they're a bit like stray cats, feed them or give them beer, and they'll never leave you alone."

Andi laughed. "I'll keep that in mind. I don't need two overgrown cats hanging around."

"So what do you say we get started? I have some papers from HR for you to look over and sign, then we'll take a tour around the studio."

"I'm ready, Thomas. Let's do it."

He reached for a folder on his neatly organized desk and opened it. Resort TV was one of several cable and satellite channels that made up the conglomerate known as Vantage Point Media Group. Andi did her homework as Thomas had suggested. She looked at everything on the Web site and checked into VPMG. Together they went through the employee handbook, the contract, and benefits. When they were done, he organized the papers and returned them to the folder and placed it back on his desk.

Thomas stood and moved toward the door. "Let me show you around and introduce you to some of your new coworkers."

Andi got up and straightened her jacket, then followed Thomas into the hall.

"Can I get you anything to drink?"

"I could really use some water, my mouth is a bit dry. I must be more nervous than I thought." She laughed it off.

Thomas led her to the conference room and retrieved a bottle of water from the refrigerator in the corner.

"The air is very dry here because of the altitude. Help yourself to what's in the fridge whenever you need something."

"Thanks, Thomas." She drank half the bottle before they reached the studio door at the end of the short hall.

He pointed to the log cabin set in the corner. "That is the set for 'Sunrise Summit,' but it's temporary. Corporate wants a more polished set but wants to retain the Colorado flavor of the show. As soon as you are up to speed with the show, I'll have you meet with a set designer and you can hash out some ideas for a fresh look."

Andi jotted down a few notes on her legal pad about the studio. As they walked through the building, she met the people who would become her crew. The group was made up of twenty-five unique individuals. Andi assured them she would learn all their names by week's end. The equipment was first rate, most of it acquired over the past year by VPMG. Andi was impressed with all that she had seen. Her only reservation was the computer system the station used. She had no experience with Mac and would have to relearn the computer all over. Even the edit suite was Mac, which meant she would have to rely on Hayley, the young female editor, to teach her how to use the equipment and software.

"Would you like to see your office now?" Thomas asked as they walked out of the edit suite.

She smiled. "Oh, yes, I would very much."

"Then follow me."

Thomas led her back to the hallway on the other side of the studio. Two doors down from his office, he stopped and held his arm out to welcome her to her very own office.

For Andi, this was exciting. She had been stuck in a noisy cubicle for so long that the sanctity of an office seemed to only be a dream for her; now it was a reality. She stepped up to the door and read the nameplate—Andrea Connelly Executive Producer. She worked to contain the giddiness inside. The room was large. She guessed it was the same size as Thomas's office. It was most definitely larger than Epstein's office. She couldn't wait to call Desi and tell her. She stood in the doorway and grinned like a child at Christmas.

Thomas stood behind her and waited for a reaction. "Well? Do you like it?"

"It's perfect, Thomas. I've had to work out of a small cubicle for so long I'm not sure I know what to do with all this space." She walked to the middle of the room.

"I'm afraid this room will shrink quickly. Once you get into the thick of things, you'll be asking for more room."

The walls were white and the wood-framed glass door to the right at the back of the room let in lots of light making the room bright. The desk sat to the left with a bookshelf behind it. Another large bookshelf sat to the right of the hallway door, and in front of that was a table with four matching chairs. The furniture was solid wood with a natural finish. On top of the desk sat a Mac laptop with an external hard drive. The office looked similar to Thomas's except for the plasma screen and theater system he had in place of the second bookcase.

"The big wigs at the home office did the remodeling of the offices not too long ago. You're the first to use the laptop, it's brand new."

Andi sat in the oversized leather swivel chair behind the desk and ran her hands over the smooth top of the desk as she continued to look around.

Thomas crossed his arms over his chest and leaned against the door frame, watching her with amusement. "If there's anything else you think you might need, Rachel will help you with the purchase order. Unfortunately, we have to share Rachel until corporate gives me more money to hire another administrative assistant."

"I don't mind. Can I have her long enough to help get me started with this Mac? I've never worked on one."

"She's a wiz with that machine. I'll make sure she's available to help you."

"Thanks, you've been very generous."

"Let me be generous one more time and take you to lunch."

Andi dropped her smile.

Thomas walked toward the desk. "Is there something wrong?"

Andi tried to smile convincingly. "No, no, lunch would be good."

"You had other plans?"

She shifted in her chair. "Sort of... I-I planned to run home at lunchtime to check on my dog." Andi's face reddened with embarrassment. "She stayed with my aunt and uncle during the day in Chicago, and I'm worried that the anxiety of being left alone all day in a strange new place might be too much for her."

Thomas gave a little laugh. "Well, if it will help to eliminate the anxiety, bring her to the office with you."

Andi's face relaxed. "Are you serious? It's all right to bring her in the building?"

"It's perfectly all right with me. I sometimes bring mine in just for fun."

"Wow, that would be great. She's very well-behaved and quiet, so she'll be no trouble."

Thomas smiled as Andi went on. "Tell you what, I'll take you to lunch, then we'll stop at the town house and get," he paused, "I'm sorry, what's your dog's name?"

"Tinker."

"We'll get Tinker, and while we're there, I'll check the filter on the water softener. I forgot to do that before you moved in."

"Thank you, Thomas, for everything. So far, the transition has been easier than I thought it would be."

He held his hand up as he turned toward the door. "You may change your mind about that when you see the mother ship's business plan and all the work I have in store for you." He stepped out into the hallway. "Meet me in the lobby at 11:30."

The tension in Andi's shoulders eased and she smiled. "Will do."

She was all alone in her office, yes, her office. A feeling of pride swelled within her as she thought about how long she had waited to become an executive producer and now, finally, she had earned the title. She would prove to those who overlooked her what a big mistake they made, and to those who gave her this opportunity she would not let them down.

Andi's thoughts were interrupted by the cell phone ring from her jacket pocket. She knew by the ring tone—Aretha Franklin's "Respect"—that it was Desi. On the screen was a picture of Desi sticking her tongue out at the camera. She flipped open the phone and answered. "Andrea Connelly, executive producer, speaking."

There was a heavy sigh on the other end. "Girl, you're all business, but you're wasting it on me. I know better."

Andi laughed. "What's up, chick?"

"Just calling to see how things are going on your first day."

"So far, so good. I got the ten-cent tour and met most of the employees. So many new faces and I can't remember most of their names."

"How's your new boss?"

"Very nice and very personable, I might add."

"Not like the tyrant we have here."

"No, not at all. Desi, you should see my office, it's twice as big as Epstein's, and they gave me all new furniture and a laptop."

"Geez, you hit the jackpot."

"They're more on the casual side here. I wore my dark gray Prada suit today and I feel so overdressed. I definitely look like the new kid at school."

Desi laughed. "Well, you are the new kid. What is everyone else wearing?"

"You know, it's like casual Friday but on a Monday."

"I have no doubt you'll fit in. You just have to wait till the newness wears off."

"You're right. Hell, I've only been here a few hours." She laughed.

"So what's new there?"

"Nothing really, but I can say you're missed tremendously. Everyone's work load has increased. Hargrove was saying the other day he didn't know how you got your projects done on time and on budget. And of course Pricilla bitches constantly about everything. Malcolm is ready to tape her mouth shut."

Andi spun back around to find Rachel standing at her door. Rachel motioned that she would come back later, but Andi held her hand up for her to wait.

"Des, I'll call you later. I have someone in my office."

Desi laughed. "La-dee-da Ms. EP, you just go ahead and take care of business."

"I will. Hey, tell Teri I said hi and I'll call her soon."

"I'll take care of it. Later, girl."

"Bye." Andi closed the phone.

"Rachel, come in please."

Rachel stepped in front of Andi's desk. "Ms. Connelly, Thomas told me you needed some help with the Mac."

"Yes," Andi wrinkled her nose, "I've never had to use one, but if you could get me started, I think I can figure it out."

"I would be delighted to get you started, Ms. Connelly."

"First of all, please call me Andi. Ms. Connelly makes me sound so old and stuffy." She smiled softly at the receptionist.

Rachel looked relieved. "Right then, Andi, we'll get going on that machine. Where would you like to start?"

"How about with the login?"

Rachel laughed. "You really do need help." She pulled a chair from the table and placed it next to Andi's.

"Rachel, can I ask you a question?"

"Sure, what is it?"

"Am I overdressed?"

Rachel cringed. "Honestly?"

"Yes, honestly."

"Just a wee bit." She sat in the chair next to Andi. "Thomas only wears suits for clients and the New York people. William is the only one that wears the suit and tie every day."

"William?"

"Yeah, he's our sales manager. He commutes between here and the Denver office. You'll meet him later this week. He's a real charming fella and very good at his job."

"What about the last EP?"

"He only wore the suits when he was with clients, as well."

Andi shook her head. "So I guess I need to tone it down, huh? I sure don't want everyone to get the idea that I'm some snobby executive."

"Oh, I don't think anyone would have such a thought. This place is most likely very different from your last post. People here are quite laidback you could say. They look beyond the clothes."

Andi contemplated Rachel's statement for a moment. "That's a good way to be."

Rachel took control of the keyboard. "Let's get started, shall we? Once I have you set up on the network, I'll show you where to find the video samples Thomas had me put together for you."

The two worked till 11:30 when Andi left to have lunch with her boss. Thomas drove her to The Dillon Dam Brewery on the other side of the lake in his black Hummer H3. Over lunch, employee and boss got to know each other better. They spoke of family and shared stories of the television industry. Andi spoke of the family vineyards and promised Thomas a bottle of wine. Thomas talked of his wife and her clothing shop in Breckenridge and about teaching his young son how to ski.

After lunch, they drove back around the lake to the condo. Tinker was so excited to see Andi when she opened the door, she let out a howl and nipped at Andi's pants leg. While Andi searched through her boxes in the downstairs bedroom for a blanket and small pillow to take to the office for Tinker, Thomas changed out the water filter. When she emerged with the bedding, she found Thomas bent down studying the large painting she left uncovered against the wall.

"This is magnificent. The brush strokes are filled with purpose and intention."

"You have an eye for art." She delighted in watching people examine her work.

He continued to study the canvas. "I had a girlfriend in college who was an art history major. A lot of our dates consisted of trips to the museums. I learned a lot while trying to impress her. Didn't get me very far, though, her Jewish mother put an end to her relationship with a gentile before it went anywhere."

"The mame protecting her tokhter from the evil sheygets."

He laughed. "I'd say that's a fair statement. Where did you learn the Yiddish?" Thomas continued to study the painting.

"Grad school. I had several friends who were Jewish. I picked up a word here and there from them."

He was taken by surprise when he discovered the signature at the bottom. "Andi, this is your painting."

"Uh-huh. It's titled 'Her Temptation.'" She stood behind him and grinned at his revelation. "You might say I have an eye for the female figure. The two women in the painting are modeled after a couple of ex-girlfriends."

"Beautiful women. Exquisite work." He stood and watched her fold the blanket. "Do you have any more?"

Andi was intrigued by his reaction. Thomas didn't flinch at her admission of being gay. His display of interest was in her talent not her orientation. "I still have a few that I did years ago. It's only been recently that I've started thinking about painting again." She finished with the blanket and walked around the red chair.

"You stopped?"

"Yes, well, a girl's gotta eat, and working full time in the broadcasting business doesn't leave much time for anything else." Her statement was only part of the story.

"I know what you mean. My wife and I thought when we moved out here from LA, things would slow down and I'd have more free time. We had no idea the enormous task I had taken on with KCOR."

She grabbed Tinker's leach. "Shall we go? I have a ton of video to look at and new projects to start planning. I want to impress my new boss, ya know."

Thomas followed her to the door. "Oh, I think you've already impressed him."

Andi locked up and Thomas drove them back to the office.

Tinker trotted happily into the building with Andi and down the hall to her office. She set the box she brought in on her desk and let Tinker free of her leash. The shepherd proceeded to inspect her surroundings while Andi laid the blanket and pillow out on the floor beside her desk. She opened the box and unpacked its contents. First, her prized Telly award. She positioned it in a place of prominence on the shelf behind her desk. Next she unwrapped the angel coffee mug Desi gave her and placed it on her desk. She continued to unpack her things and personalize her new office. While Andi was busy with her box, Tinker sat looking out the glass pane door and occasionally glancing at her master.

When Andi finished arranging her things, she sat and pressed her hand to her forehead. Her entire head was throbbing. She reached for her bag and got out the bottle of ibuprofen. With nothing to wash the pain reliever down with, she went for the refrigerator in the conference room. Tinker followed her down the hall. She got two bottles out and found a clean bowl in a cabinet for Tinker. Back in the office Tinker sat on the blanket while Andi took the medicine, then filled the bowl and set it next to the dog. Tinker immediately went for the water and drank most of it. Andi also drank down the bottle of water.

"I guess it's the dry air that's making us so thirsty, little girl. Hopefully, we'll get used to it."

Andi spent the rest of the day looking at video of "Sunrise Summit" and other programs produced by KCOR. The pain in her head was reduced to a dull ache but never went away. At the end of the day, she locked up her office, and she and Tinker headed for the parking lot. Andi's first day was officially over. She still had so much to do at home, but she really just wanted to spend the evening soaking in her new oversized tub. She loaded Tinker in the Escape and headed for the Safeway at the other end of town to pick up groceries and a few things she needed at home.

By the time she had gathered everything on her list, plus a few extras, her cart was full. She made her way to the checkout lanes and browsed through the magazines as she waited in line. The woman in front of her dropped one of the items she was holding while fumbling through her purse for her wallet. Andi instinctively bent down and picked up the box of oatmeal. As she rose up, the woman's brown eyes met with Andi's. She had a sparkle that danced and flickered in her gaze and her face was framed by shimmering light brown hair.

"Thank you," she said sweetly.

"You're welcome," Andi replied with a smile.

A red glow appeared on the woman's face and she smiled back, then looked away shyly. She watched Andi's hands intently as she set the box on the conveyor belt of the checkout counter.

Andi was intrigued by the beautiful woman and the way she looked at her, but it was a brief exchange and nothing more was said by either woman.

The woman with the dancing brown eyes paid for her things and gathered her bags. She glanced over once more and caught Andi's gaze, smiled, and made a quick turn for the exit.

She completely distracted Andi as she walked out. When the teenaged boy bagging the groceries asked if she wanted paper or plastic, she answered, "Yes."

The throbbing in her head brought her back to reality, and once she paid for her things, the only thought she had was to go home.

Leo was on the porch next door when Andi pulled into the driveway of her condo. She was glad to see the storage container had been picked up as planned.

"How was your first day, Ms. Producer?" he called out.

"That's Ms. Executive Producer, thank you. Busy and so many new faces to get acquainted with," she said, pulling her groceries from the backseat.

"Here, let me get those for you," he offered as he crossed the driveway. "Geez, you look tired."

"I've had this headache all afternoon that I can't seem to get rid of." She hung her backpack over her shoulder.

Leo smiled knowingly as he followed her to the front door. "Altitude sickness."

"What's that?" She rubbed her forehead while fumbling with her keys to unlock the door.

"Your body's not used to functioning at this altitude and in the dry, thin air," he explained. "Most people go through it when they first come up here."

"What can I do for it?" The lock finally clicked and the door popped open. Tinker ran past them for the water bowl.

"Water and aspirin is all I did for it. The doc told me to lay off the caffeine and alcohol." He deposited the bags on the kitchen counter. "Eventually, your body will adjust and it'll go away."

"And how long can I expect to suffer with this?"

Leo shrugged his shoulders. "About two or three days."

"Great." Andi wrinkled her nose.

"Vince had it bad, puked for two days and ended up in the ER."

"It gets that bad?"

"It can, but he was an idiot. He went out and got hammered." He headed for the door.

Andi shook her head and laughed. "Thank you for helping me with the groceries."

"No problem. Hey, nice painting." He pointed at the two nude females with the apple.

"Thanks. Oh, one more thing, is there a gym in the area you would recommend?"

He stopped at the door. "I work out at the Rec Center over in Breck. Nice equipment, pool, spinning classes, locker room is clean and it's not overpriced."

"Sounds good, I'll have to check it out."

"See ya later, gator." He closed the front door behind him.

Andi got to work putting groceries away, then fed Tinker. She had no appetite but tried to eat anyway. She got down about half a can of soup and some crackers before she quit. Nothing tasted good, and the throbbing was starting again in the back of her head.

She walked out onto the patio with Tinker, and while the dog sniffed around and did her business, she used the key to open the storage closet outside. Inside, she found a snow shovel that looked well used, a pair of old banged-up ski poles, and three patio chairs with a small matching table. She pulled one of the chairs out and set it on the edge of the patio so she could see the trees and creek. She watched Tinker as she snooped along the edge of the stream in the twilight.

Everything had so much beauty to it here. She felt a sense of calmness from the swish of the water tumbling over the rocks in the stream as she watched the long pine needles sway in the breeze. She noticed there were no people noises, no cars, no loud music, and no screaming voices. All sounds she was used to hearing in Chicago.

When Tinker was done, she trotted back to the patio and stood at the door. Andi moved the chair back to the closet and locked the door. She locked up for the night and grabbed her glass of water from the counter and two more pain relievers out of her bag on her way to her bedroom.

Upstairs she found her Bose wave radio, a gift from her parents, and plugged it in. She found a classical music station and turned the volume on low. She then started to look through her boxes for clean bed clothes and ended up organizing the rest of her clothes in the walk-in closet. In the bottom of one box, she pulled out an old gray sweatshirt with Vassar written across the front. It was Elisha's college shirt. A hollow feeling rose inside her, but she fought it off. She balled up the sweatshirt and tossed it in an empty box and kicked it to the side. It would go in the Dumpster with the boxes. When she was done, all the boxes marked bedroom had been emptied. The only thing that she didn't do was hang the wall decorations. That would be a chore for the weekend when she planned to get the entire place whipped into shape.

Tinker was lying on the bed watching with mild interest.

"One room is nearly done, baby girl. I got all my stuff put away in the closet and now I think I'll try to soak some of this altitude muck out of my body." She gave Tinker a hug and went to the bathroom.

She found a candle in the box in the bathroom that she placed on the counter and lit. She filled the tub with water as warm as she could stand, and once she figured out how to run the jets, she immersed herself up to her neck. The force of the jets felt good on her back and legs. She began to relax with the steam rising off the surface of the water.

Thirty minutes later, she emerged with damp hair and skin coated with lotion, feeling better. The throbbing in her head was almost gone. She turned off the radio, set the alarm, and climbed into bed next to Tinker. In no time, both were in a deep sleep.

Chapter 5

The pain in Andi's head woke her. Through blurred vision, she read the time on the clock—4:26 a.m. She pushed the covers off and clumsily walked to the bathroom in search of the bottle of pain reliever. She popped two pills in her mouth and washed them down with as much water as she could drink.

"When is this altitude crap gonna stop?" she asked her reflection in the mirror. She splashed a handful of water on her face, toweled it off, then stumbled back to bed. Tinker stretched her furry limbs as Andi crawled into bed. She gave the dog a pat on the hind leg and rubbed her forehead with her other hand.

She tossed and turned for the next hour in discomfort. The pain subsided slightly, but she couldn't get back to sleep. By 5:30, she was up and trying to eat. She pulled a box of oatmeal out of the cabinet and mixed some of the oats with water, then popped it in the microwave. While she stood waiting, she glanced at the oatmeal box, and the sparkling brown eyes of the woman in the grocery store flashed through her mind and disappeared. She rubbed her eyes and looked over at Tinker. She was happily munching on her bowl of kibble. She ignored the image from her subconscious and retrieved the bowl from the microwave.

She made it to work by 8:00 a.m. with the headache under control. After checking e-mail and reviewing her notes, she spent the rest of the morning in a meeting with Thomas, the two producers Simone and Ian, and Leigh, the assignment editor, who she would be supervising. She liked her new crew; they were full of energy and fresh ideas and looked to her for direction.

The meeting ended around lunchtime. Andi found Rachel in the video vault returning tapes to their respective shelves.

She stopped at the door and leaned against the frame. "Rachel, are you familiar with the Rec Center in Breckenridge?"

Rachel put the last on its shelf. "Oh, yes, been there many times for a swim."

"If I buy you lunch, will you ride over there and show me where it is?"

Her face lit up. "I would be happy to show you, and lunch would be delightful."

"Great. I'll meet you in the lobby at twelve," she said as she started down the hall.

"I'll be waiting."

With Tinker in the backseat, the two set off down Highway 9 for the rustic mining-town-turned-skier's-haven, promptly at twelve.

Andi took a quick look around the facility, skimmed through the pamphlet, and signed up for a one-year membership.

"Okay, that's done," Andi said. "Where would you like to eat?"

"How about The Bottom Dollar Bar on Main Street? The food is good, and they have locals' night every other Thursday," Rachel said.

"Why every other Thursday?"

"That's payday for the resorts and most of the businesses in the county. They always have special prices on food and drink for the locals on payday."

"That sounds like fun."

"You should stop in next week. There are usually a good number of us from the station that get together for drinks and a game or two of pool."

"I'll keep that in mind."

"You can meet my Charlie. He always comes with me."

"Charlie is your boyfriend?"

Rachel blushed. "Yes, he's from Texas, a real cowboy and all. He's quite handsome and very thoughtful."

"I look forward to meeting him."

The two had a quick lunch on the back deck with the mountains as a backdrop and Tinker at Andi's feet. She was astonished that dogs were allowed in places they never would have been allowed in Chicago.

By the time they returned to the office, they were becoming friends.

Andi spent the afternoon reviewing more show clips and video footage on her computer. She made it through day two feeling more confident about the way things were progressing. The altitude sickness seemed to be fading, and she felt good enough to try out the Rec Center with her first workout. She promised Tinker she would be gone only a short time and left her curled up in the big red chair.

She drove down Highway 9 into Breckenridge. The Rec Center was at the edge of town across from the firehouse. The parking lot was about half full at 5:30 on a beautiful May evening. She grabbed her bag and headed for the locker room. The young man at the desk scanned her new ID card and waved her in.

On her way to the locker room, she passed a spinning class and made a mental note to check on class times. She secured her things in a locker and moved to the gym. She decided to start with cardio to warm up since it had been about a week since she last worked out.

The room was surrounded by mirrors and sparsely populated for that time of day. She assumed everyone was in the spinning class. She had the usual choice of elliptical, stationary bike, Stairmaster, and treadmill. She started with the treadmill located in a row to one side of the room.

A man with ear plugs and an iPod occupied a center treadmill; he looked up at Andi and nodded. She gave him a smile in return. At the far end of the row in the corner of the room, a woman dressed in a pink tank top and matching running shorts ran at a swift pace while she monitored her Ironman watch. Her long, sweat-soaked, honey brown hair pulled back tightly in a ponytail bounced behind her as she ran. Sweat beaded along her jaw line and down her neck, with loose pieces of hair that had escaped the hair tie dangling to the sides of her face. Andi guessed her to be a distance runner by the way she was built. The woman was a little shorter and much thinner than Andi, and her muscle definition was visible with each stride she took.

Andi hopped on a treadmill at the opposite end of the row and started it at a slow jog. She stole a look down at the attractive woman in the pink every so often as she increased her pace, but the woman appeared to be focused on her own workout and never took notice of Andi.

About twenty minutes into her workout, Andi began to feel slightly lightheaded. She cursed the altitude as she had done several times over the past two days. She attempted to outrun the wooziness, but it was getting the best of her, turning from dizziness to nausea. She finally stopped and got off the treadmill slowly. With water bottle in hand, she took a seat on the bench near the door to the locker room. She put her head down and covered her face with her towel in an effort to hold back the nausea. She tried to concentrate on breathing, thinking that would calm her stomach.

While she sat with her head down, she heard footsteps approach, and a female voice asked, "Are you okay?"

Andi didn't move or look up. "Yeah, I'm still adjusting to the altitude is all." She wiped her mouth.

She heard the squeak of the locker room door opening and the voice replied, "I had the same thing when I first moved up here. I found that Gatorade helped."

"Thanks, I may try it when my stomach settles."

"Good luck," the voice said as the door squeaked closed.

"I must look like a real idiot. Everybody knows who the new girl in town is, she's the one bent over in the gym about to puke," Andi said to herself.

When her stomach finally calmed, she raised her head and found she was the only one left in the room. She got up slowly and went to the locker room to get her things with the promise to herself no more workouts till she was over this adjustment.

The next morning, she arrived at the station surprisingly well rested and free of the headache that accompanied her the last two mornings. Tinker ran past Andi when she opened the front door and went straight to Rachel at the front desk.

"You're spoiling her, Rach. She expects a bite of your breakfast every morning."

"Who could refuse a sweet face like this?" Rachel said as she cradled Tinker's head. She turned to her desk calendar. "William is back in the office today. I'm sure you'll be at the top of his meeting list."

"The sales guy, right?" Andi spun her key ring around her finger.

"Yes, and I happen to know he has new work coming in, I saw the fax last night before I locked up."

"You know everything that goes on around here, don't you, Ms. Oliver?" Andi winked at her coworker.

"Yes I do, it's called job security."

"We'll be in my office if anyone needs us." Andi opened the door, and she and Tinker went to her office.

With the sleeves of her sky blue blouse rolled up and a fresh cup of hot tea in hand, Andi got to work on her proposed changes for the morning show. She would have to meet Chip and Buster sooner than later, and she knew the changes VPMG outlined would not make them happy. As executive producer, it was her responsibility to deal with their egos and see to it that they understood what would be expected of them.

She scratched her head while looking at the proposal. *"Great, I walk in as the new boss to implement a new format and make the changes, and right off the bat, I'll piss off the talent."*

She got up from her desk and walked to the glass door and opened the shade. She stood for a moment sipping her tea and looking out at the base of the mountain that overshadowed the building; the view was reassuring. Tinker stood next to her wagging her tail in anticipation that Andi would open the door. She put her hand in the pocket of her brown slacks as she turned and looked around the room. She was still in awe of the office she occupied. Desi was blown away by the pictures she sent her from her phone. She showed them to all of Andi's former coworkers.

The appearance of Thomas at the door brought Andi out of her daydream.

"Are you busy?"

She set her mug on the desk. "Never too busy for the boss."

He smiled. "Good. William's here. I want you to meet him. Oh, and I think he's already got something for you."

She heard the sound of footsteps coming down the hall and a man about her age appeared from behind Thomas. His short, light brown hair was perfectly combed, and his complexion was clear and soft. He had a twinkle in his blue eyes that caught her attention.

Thomas made the introductions. "Andi, this is William Ericsson, our account manager."

William extended his hand to her.

Thomas continued, "William, this is Andrea Connelly, our new executive producer."

William greeted her with an easy tone. "I'm pleased to meet you, Andrea, I've heard a lot about you. Welcome to KCOR."

Andi shook his hand. His grip was firm like someone who was used to greeting top executives, yet his skin was soft. She thought he did not do much hard labor with his hands like the men in her family. "Thank you, William, and please call me Andi."

"So how do you like your new position so far, Andi? I hope you aren't feeling overwhelmed yet." He put his hand in his pocket and held a folder in the other.

"Altitude sickness aside, I'm adjusting quite well, and everyone has been very helpful."

"Altitude sickness, huh? The curse of the newcomer." The shiny silver-winged statue displayed on the shelf behind Andi's desk caught William's eye. "Congratulations on the Telly, it sure is a beautiful statue."

"Thank you. With a little luck and a lot of hard work from

everyone, I hope to bring one to KCOR."

William liked the confidence she displayed.

Just then, Tinker poked her head out from around the desk.

"Who do we have here?" he asked.

"This is my lovely assistant, Tinker."

William bent down and offered his hand to Tinker. She stepped toward him and sniffed his fingers. He passed the test. She allowed him to scratch her head.

Andi pointed to the table and chairs. "Gentlemen, please have a seat, let's talk."

Thomas and William waited for Andi to be seated.

William started. "I'm sure you have plenty to do, Andi, but I got a call from the marketing department over at Snow Cap Resort last week, and after months of schmoozing for their advertising dollars, they've finally come around. They usually work with a production company out of Denver, but they couldn't resist the production and airtime package VPMG authorized me to offer them. They're willing to give us a try with a set of commercials for the resort's restaurants." He pushed the folder containing a copy of the outlined contract in Andi's direction. "There are a total of six distinct food and beverage establishments throughout the resort. The contract allows for one sixty-second stand-alone spot and two thirty-second spots that can be edited with weekly updates for each restaurant.

"Sounds easy enough." Andi opened the folder and looked over the papers. "The dollar amount looks adequate."

"A word of warning about these folks," Thomas said. "Because of the competition with the other resorts, they're under constant pressure from their corporate office to maintain an image of the highest standards, so they're going to expect perfection, and that's what we shall give them."

Andi nodded in agreement. "Absolutely."

"I have a meeting set up for three o'clock Friday afternoon with Julianna Stevens, the marketing manager for food and beverage. She'll have a copy of the storyboards and menus for you so you know what you're dealing with." William folded his hands on the table. "Our meeting on Friday will be a preliminary information exchange with Julianna, but eventually, you'll have to deal with the art director."

"What's up with the art director?"

"To put it bluntly, the woman is a pain in the ass, pardon my language."

"No offense taken, I appreciate the straight talk. I need to know what I'm up against since these are all new personalities I'll have to deal with."

Thomas rolled a pen between his fingers. "Julianna is a true professional. She's as nice as she can be and smart as they come. Susan McManus, however, is your classic type A personality and will try to take control of everything if she's not kept in check. She thinks she should have total creative license on all things involving the resort and its property."

"So I should plan to bring my whip and a chair when I do have to meet with her?"

William laughed. "Yeah, that might be a good idea. Actually, I think if you can connect with Julianna on this and gain her confidence, she'll keep Susan off your back and out of the way."

"I'll be taking this one myself rather than handing it over to one of the producers. If the resort is a potential big sell, then I want to be on top of it from the start."

Thomas sat back and smiled. "See, William, that's why I hired this young lady. She's already grabbed the bull by the horns and is ready to tame it."

"I haven't met any of the bulls yet," Andi said. "We'll see how easy they are to tame."

After Thomas and William left her office, Andi got to work on her new project. She needed to do some rough drafts of her own so she wouldn't look unprepared for her first meeting with a new client. She read though everything in the folder, mocked up an itemized budget, made a list of crew names, and laid out a schedule for production with dates and places to be filled in later. She then made a new folder with everything she had done printed out neatly.

The rest of the day she spent answering questions and giving direction to the people working under her. She was slowly beginning to put names with faces and getting a feel for their personalities. In return, her employees were pleasant and eager to listen to what she had to say, which gave her a sense that maybe she was starting to fit in.

Chapter 6

Friday morning in Frisco was ushered in by the sun shining brightly over the mountain ridge to the east and reflecting off the glassy surface of Lake Dillon at Frisco Bay. Andi strolled into Griffin's Bakery with a spring in her step. There were a half dozen people in the shop enjoying breakfast. Bo stood at the register in her black apron, waiting on a customer. When she saw Andi approach the counter, she gave her a welcoming smile.

When it was Andi's turn, Bo leaned on the counter and greeted her. "Well, good morning, Andi Connelly, and how are you on this fine Friday morning?"

Andi smiled at Bo's flirtatious greeting. "I'm very well today, Ms. Griffin, and yourself?"

"Business is good and that makes me happy. What can I get for you?"

"I think one of your protein smoothies would do me fine."

"Coming right up." Bo turned to the counter and got to work on Andi's drink. "How was your first week at KCOR?"

"So far, so good. I had a bout with altitude sickness earlier this week, but I think I've survived it."

"I've heard the AS is rough. I've never experienced it myself. I was born into this altitude."

"Consider yourself lucky then. Imagine a hangover that you think is over, then out of nowhere it comes back."

"That would totally suck. I hate hangovers." Bo set the

finished smoothie on the counter and put a lid on the cup.

Andi handed her the money for her drink. "So what is there to do up here on a day off?"

"Depends on what type of activities you're into. There's the Summit Trail Running Series on Wednesday in Breck."

"Umm, no thanks." The treadmill incident flashed through Andi's mind. "I tried running earlier this week and almost puked all over the equipment at the Rec Center."

"Now that would be embarrassing to say the least."

"Tell me about it. I think I turned about three shades of green before my stomach settled."

"Okay, so the running thing is out." Bo thumped the counter with her thumb.

"I'll be there at the run anyway in a professional capacity. We're doing a summer in the mountains documentary, and I've got a camera crew covering the event. Thought I would join them and check it out so I know a little bit about the series and how it works."

"There are some hot chicks that run that series," Bo said. When she didn't get a response from Andi, she redirected her comments. "Really anything you can think to do outdoors you can find it around here."

Andi smiled. "I need to get my dog out."

"The trails aren't just for running. There are plenty around to walk."

Andi turned for the door. "I think I'm up for that. Thanks, have a good weekend, Bo."

"You too, Andi."

At noon, Andi sat at her desk, engrossed in what she was doing on the computer, when a sharp rap on the door startled her. Tinker jumped up from her pillow and barked at the man standing in her doorway.

"Didn't mean to scare you, Andi." He leaned against the door frame.

"That's okay, Justin, sometimes I get so wrapped up in what I'm doing, I just block everything else out."

"I know what you mean." Justin was one of the full-time cameramen working for Andi.

Of all the people working at the station, Justin Barnes was the one she had the most in common with. He reminded her of her younger brother Tim and, like Andi, he was also an art school graduate. Justin received his degree in photography from the Rhode Island School of Design. She liked his work. He had his own unique style, and his footage was always pretty and clean. The two hit it off from the start. With an art school background, they could relate to each other on a level no one else at the station could.

"So what's up? What can I do for you?" Andi sat back in her chair and Tinker returned to her pillow.

"You can join everybody out back for lunch." He smiled from under the shaggy hair that covered his forehead.

"That sounds wonderful. What's on the menu?"

"I think Thomas brought in hamburgers and brats. And Hayley made a bowl of her award-winning potato salad."

"It's that good?"

"She really did win an award last year at the Copper Mountain Cook Off. Her potato salad was voted best side dish."

"Wow, that's so cool." She shut her computer down, and she and Tinker walked toward the back patio with Justin.

"What's the occasion?" she asked.

"No occasion. Thomas just likes to get everybody together, usually on Friday, for some fun on the clock. Kinda relieves the stress in the office."

"He has a very different approach to management than my last boss. It's encouraging to see things get done without intimidation."

"I've never had a total asshole for a boss, it must really suck."

"Yeah, it did. The bully tactics are part of the reason I left. I'm in a much better place now."

"I'm glad you think so." Justin opened the door to the patio and they joined the others for lunch.

She returned to her office around one o'clock. Tinker landed on her pillow with a belly full of grilled burger, and Andi returned to her chair feeling overfed. She turned her attention to the folder for the meeting that afternoon. She opened it and thumbed through the pages, making sure she had everything in order. Her attention was diverted by the ring of the desk phone.

"Andrea Connelly, how may I help you?"

"Andi, it's William. Listen, I'm not going to make the meeting this afternoon. I'm on my way back down to Denver. My wife called. My son fell on the playground at school and broke his arm."

"I'm so sorry to hear that. I hope he'll be all right."

"Thanks, my wife assures me he's doing fine." He changed the subject. "About this afternoon, will you be okay to have the meeting without me? If you're uncomfortable, I can reschedule this thing for next week."

"No need to reschedule, I'll be fine. Listen, you take care of your son and I'll take care of Ms. Stevens. I have the paperwork you gave me and some preliminary work I did of my own. Is there anything else I need to know before we meet?"

"I think you have everything. The meeting is at the Lodge at Snow Cap. Go to the concierge desk in the main lobby and check in with them. I'll give Julianna a call and let her know it'll be just the two of you today. I'm sure she'll be fine with that."

"Sounds good. How will I know her?"

"She's about your height and age with long brown hair."

"I think I can find her. I'll e-mail you with notes from the meeting."

"That would be perfect. Thank you. Oh, if there's anything else you need, I'll have my cell with me."

"Thanks. Be careful and I hope everything's all right."

"Thank you, Andi. Bye now."

"Bye, William."

She sat back in her seat and clasped her hands together. It's a very simple meeting. This should be a piece of cake, she thought to herself.

Andi stopped at the front desk on her way out. "Rachel, I'll be out of the office the rest of the afternoon, I have—"

"You have a meeting with Julianna Stevens at the Lodge at Snow Cap at three. I presume you'll be dropping Tinker at home first."

Andi was amused. "Yes, as a matter of fact, I will be dropping her at home beforehand. If you need anything, you have my cell number, right?"

"Oh, yes, of course. You know, you really should get the number changed to a local one." She reached in her desk and pulled out some paperwork. "Here, take this with you when you get the phone changed. The company requires you to have a BlackBerry and a certain package plan." She handed the papers to Andi. "Make sure you read the papers carefully."

"Yes, ma'am, I'll get it done this weekend." Andi snickered at the motherly manner in which Rachel spoke to her. "Have a good weekend. See ya Monday." With that, girl and dog were out the door and on their way.

Andi parked in the lot to the side of the lodge and looked at her watch—2:50. She had no trouble finding the resort and had a few minutes to spare. She walked around to the front entrance. The main lobby opened to a large area made to look like a rustic log cabin. The check-in desk was to the left and next to it was a hallway leading to the conference center. To Andi's right was a hallway leading to the guest rooms. To the rear of the lobby sat a circular fireplace and a large plate glass window that offered a view of the resort village and the front of Snow Cap Mountain. The concierge's desk was to the left of the fireplace. Andi walked over to the nicely dressed woman with her blond hair pulled back tightly in a ponytail sitting at the desk.

"May I help you?" she asked in a pleasant tone.

"Hi, I'm Andrea Connelly. I'm here for a three o'clock meeting with Ms. Stevens."

The woman flipped through papers clipped together. "Yes, Ms. Connelly. We have a conference room reserved. Ms. Stevens has not arrived yet. If you would like to take a seat, I'll let you know when she's here." The concierge pointed at the couches surrounding the fireplace.

"Thank you." Andi took a seat across from the desk. She looked out the big window and marveled at the view. She thought it would be hard to get tired of such beauty.

Her daydream was interrupted by the text message alert of her cell phone. Andi pulled it out of her suit pocket; it was Desi. She opened the message and read it.

"Guess what? I got a date! The man is hot. Talk to you later. —Me"

Andi smiled at the news.

The bellman held the door for a woman with a large square case slung over her shoulder. She thanked him as she entered the main lobby and headed toward the concierge desk with a confident stride. When the woman at the desk spotted her, she pointed to the blonde in the dark blue pin-striped business suit sitting on the couch across from her.

"Andrea Connelly?" a voice queried.

Andi had heard the voice before, but it sounded softer this time. She looked up from her phone. Standing in front of her was a woman dressed in a white suit and black high-heeled boots with a portfolio case hanging from her shoulder. Her long honey brown hair hung loose around her face, and her bangs lay effortlessly across her forehead. She smiled as her light brown eyes searched Andi's face for a response.

Andi slipped the phone back into her pocket. "Yes. You must be Julianna Stevens." Their gazes met as Andi stood to greet her.

Julianna looked at Andi with curiosity. Then it hit her—the blue eyes at the grocery store. This was the blonde who picked up the box she dropped at the checkout.

"Yes, that would be me. It's so nice to meet you, Andrea." Julianna offered her hand to Andi and at the same time took notice of her square shoulders. She looked down at their hands clasped together and remembered how graceful and strong Andi's hands appeared. Her handshake felt the same way.

"It's nice to meet you, too, Julianna. Please, call me Andi," she said, taking Julianna's hand. "Forgive me, but have we met before?" she asked with an inquisitive tone.

"I believe our paths have crossed before, yes."

Andi looked down at the Ironman watch on Julianna's wrist. She felt her face heat up when she recognized the timepiece. "Ah, the gym. I was bent over and green with nausea while you were on the treadmill."

"Looks like you've recovered well from your bout with the altitude."

Andi laughed it off. "Yes, I think I'll survive. I had no idea it would hit me so hard."

"It took me a while to adjust when I first moved up here, too. Thank the stars above it's only temporary."

Andi agreed.

Julianna motioned toward the hallway to the conference center. "I have a meeting room reserved for us so we can lay these storyboards out and get a good look at them."

"Great." Andi nervously followed Julianna down the hall.

Inside the conference room was a long rectangular table surrounded by chairs with décor in keeping with the theme of rustic Colorado. Julianna closed the door behind Andi, then laid the portfolio on the table and opened it. She placed six storyboards along the length of the table. "This is what I have from the art department. I know they're sketchy, but I think it will give you a pretty good idea of what we're looking for."

While Andi looked over each board, Julianna removed her jacket and draped it over the back of a chair. Andi tried to stay focused on the artwork and not give away that she was aware of the sleeveless white top Julianna was wearing or the lovely bare arms and shoulders it revealed.

Julianna reached across the board Andi was looking at to point out a logo that needed to be updated and brushed her arm against Andi's. The small innocuous touch stirred something in the pit of Andi's stomach. She swallowed hard as she continued to try to stay focused on the task at hand.

Julianna hovered near Andi throughout the meeting as they went through one board after the other. The proximity of her bare arms and long soft hair made Andi uncomfortably aware of her physical presence. Her perfume drifted intermittently through Andi's olfactory senses, adding to the distraction. It was soft and subtle and decisively feminine.

For the sixty minutes they spent together, Andi managed to follow Julianna's descriptions and commentary despite the physical distraction she unwittingly created.

When they were done, Julianna gathered up the storyboards and handed Andi a smaller version to take with her. "That's about all I have right now. I hope it's enough to get you started."

"I think I have what I need." Andi had extracted the necessary information and lots of footage of pretty food and people enjoying the pretty food. The wheels were turning with what she would do next.

"I do have one other thing." Julianna shuffled the papers in her hands tensely. "The art director requested to direct these spots, and my boss has agreed to it." She took a deep breath and looked at Andi with an apologetic expression. "I'm sure Susan will be fine. The spots are simple and stylish, something she does well."

William's words on Susan McManus rang in Andi's ears. "Then I won't need to budget for a director?"

"No, her time won't figure into any of your budgets." Julianna still looked unhappy about the whole idea as she put her jacket back on.

Andi touched her sleeve. "Don't worry. I'll make sure these spots are shot correctly, you have my word."

Julianna's face relaxed. "Thanks, Andi. My goal is to get these on the air in a timely fashion with as few complications as possible. My boss is adamant about staying on budget and on time."

"I understand. We'll certainly work with you to make that happen."

Julianna walked Andi back to the main entrance. "Thank you again," she said, offering her hand.

As they shook hands once more, Andi caught Julianna's gaze. She recognized the sparkle that danced in her brown eyes and was instantly taken back to that day at the Safeway. Indeed their paths had crossed on several occasions in the short time Andi had been in the mountains.

She promised to send over an itemized budget and preliminary schedule on Tuesday and said goodbye. On her way back to her vehicle, she could still feel the softness of Julianna's hand on her palm.

She pulled out onto Highway 6 and headed toward Frisco. Along the way, thoughts of Julianna crept into the part of her consciousness not being used to navigate the route home. She was obviously a straight girl. She looked like one. She acted like one. She certainly didn't give off any signals that Andi could key in on that suggested she had any interest in her other than professional. This is a client, for God's sake. How unprofessional.

She decided to push the thoughts out of her mind and made a quick stop on her way home to pick up a case of beer. She wanted to be prepared should company happen to drop in over the weekend.

Tinker was ecstatic to see her when she came in through the door from the garage. The dog demanded attention first, then she made a dash for the back door. Andi set the beer and her bag on the kitchen table, opened the sliding glass door, and Tinker ran for the grassy area. Andi watched as she sniffed and poked around the creek.

Leo was out on the patio next door working on a well-used mountain bike turned upside down on its seat and handle bars. "Hey, neighbor," he called out.

"Hey, Leo, what's up?"

"Trying to salvage the gears on this thing. I dropped off a rock and took a dump. Looks like the sprockets got the worst of it." He scratched his scruffy jaw. "I think I'm gonna be buying new ones, these things are just too fucked up."

"Want a beer?"

"Far be it from me to turn down a cold one." He dropped the wrench in his hand and it hit the stone patio with a clang.

She tossed the key for the locker to him. "Here, get us a couple of chairs out of the locker and I'll be right back." A few minutes later, she emerged with two beers in hand. She had kicked off her heels and replaced her suit with a sweatshirt and workout pants while she was inside.

Leo looked at the label on his bottle. "Wow, local brew, cool. We usually get whatever's on sale at Safeway." He sat down and took a long drink.

Andi took a seat and drank, too. She preferred wine to beer, but that night, it tasted pretty good.

Tinker returned to the patio and made herself comfortable under the table.

"So how are things at KCOR?" he asked.

She sat back and folded her legs underneath her. "I have to say, my first week was pretty good. I like the people I work with. This job is certainly promising to be a challenge, and despite the altitude sickness, I think I'm going to like it here in the mountains."

"No homesickness?"

"Not yet, but I've been so busy I haven't had time to really think about it." Andi took a drink. "I talk to my best friend Desi at least once a day, that helps. I do miss her a lot. She's got a date with a new man, and I'm not there to check him out."

"What about your family?"

"I haven't lived in my hometown with them since I left for college, but we've always stayed close."

"Thank God for the Internet and cell phones."

The two clanged their bottles together.

"What's on your agenda for the weekend?" Leo asked.

"I'm going to work on getting the rest of my stuff out of boxes. I think Tinker and I may check out some of the trails in the area, and I brought home paperwork I really need to spend some time on." She paused and took a drink. "I had a meeting this afternoon with a manager from Snow Cap's marketing department. We're doing some spots for their restaurants."

"The manager wouldn't happen to be Julianna Stevens?"

"Yeah, you know her?" Andi tried to sound nonchalant, even though her heart jumped when he said her name.

"I met her at The Bottom Dollar. I had a couple of dates with her one summer, but they didn't amount to much. The girl is in the market for a husband with a fat bank account and social status to match. At least that's my take on her. I think she comes from money." He stretched his legs out and slouched down in his chair.

"She didn't look like a gold digger to me, but my only dealing with her has been one business meeting." Andi was eager for Leo to elaborate.

"I don't know that I would call her a gold digger, a social snob might be a better epithet." He snickered at his own sarcasm. "I'm just kidding. She really is a nice girl. I just wasn't what she was looking for, but then I've heard I have lots of company in that category."

"Really?"

He leaned toward Andi. "Rumor is she's dated the majority of single guys here in the county, but they've all turned out to be frogs, so I guess she's still looking for the well-to-do prince. Most of the young guys that come up here are like me, they just wanna be ski bums for a few years till they're forced to become responsible adults and get real jobs." Leo confirmed what Andi had already surmised, Julianna Stevens was terminally hetero and craved status much like Elisha.

"Sounds like she's shopping for the perfect man." Andi picked at the label on her bottle.

He shrugged his shoulders. "It's all just hearsay."

"We all have our ideal mate. Maybe she's just not willing to settle for anything but that."

"I suppose so."

After Leo left, Andi e-mailed William with the details of her meeting earlier in the day, including the nugget of information about Susan being appointed director of the shoot by the head of the marketing department.

"Can't wait to see how William reacts to that one," Andi said out loud.

When she was done, she called Desi. "Hey, what are you doing?"

"Hey, girl, I'm glad you called. I'm sitting on Tia's new

leather sofa with a martini in my hand."

"Life is rough. So tell me about this man."

"Would you believe my auntie set me up? He's the new deacon at the church."

"I thought you only dated bad boys."

"Ha ha, he's single, he's handsome, and he's got a good job. And are you ready for this? He's older."

"What? You with an older man? I don't believe it."

"Oh, yes, honey. Desi is stepping into new territory."

"I'll say. So how old is he?"

"Thirty-eight."

"Does this mean you might be getting serious about settling down?"

"I'm not saying anything. I'm just taking one date at a time." Andi laughed.

"What's up with you?" Desi asked.

"I finished my first week with no disasters or mishaps, so I'm feeling pretty good. I even had my first meeting with a new client." Andi's mind drifted back to the conference room and the soft flow of Julianna's hair, her smooth skin, and the gentle shape of her bare shoulders.

"That's great. And have you met anybody yet?"

"What?"

"I asked if you had met anyone yet."

"I've only been here a week and I've spent almost all of it working. When have I had time to get out and meet anyone?"

Desi laughed. "What about the girl in the gym that you almost puked in front of?"

"Funny you should mention that, she's my new client."

"No shit! See fate does have a hand in your personal business."

"It's not what you think. Her name is Julianna, she's gorgeous, and she's chronically heterosexual."

"How do you know that? Did you ask?"

"No, I didn't ask. My neighbor Leo dated her. He said she's looking for a rich husband."

"Just keep your eyes open. You never know when an

opportunity will present itself."

"Yeah, yeah, yeah." Andi paused. "Remember this is a small community in a remote area. There are a lot of nice people here, but the gay population is not exactly out and loud."

"Well, keep your eyes open."

"Yeah, whatever. Tell Tia hi and don't spill that drink on her new sofa, she'll have your head."

"It's all good. She says hi back."

"I gotta go. I need to get some dinner. I want a full report on this date."

"Oh, you'll get one."

"I'll talk to you later. Love you. Bye."

Andi spent the rest of the evening emptying boxes and trying to make the town house feel like home. The bedroom on the ground floor was perfect for an art studio with its large window facing the rear of the building. It would allow for lots of natural light during the day.

Andi sat on a stool in front of her easel while she finished tightening its bolts. She picked up a charcoal pencil from the art cart she kept her supplies in. With pencil in hand, she began to draw on the oversized pad. At first, it was just the start of a doodle, but the more work she put into it, the more it began to take on a defined identity. The figure in the drawing was a female leaning forward as if she were talking to a small child.

By the time Andi finished, the figure had become a detailed sketch of a woman clad in an oversized blouse that loosely hung from her form with one shoulder exposed. Her hair was tucked behind one ear and flowed down her neck. Her hands were clenched to her heart and the sleeves of the blouse gathered around her elbows. She was leaning over a single rose in a bud vase and appeared to take delight in its fragrance. The woman in the drawing was unmistakably Julianna.

Andi had a natural talent for working from memory. If she studied something for a time, she could reproduce it in great detail. She studied Julianna closely as she leaned over the storyboards in the conference room earlier that afternoon.

She got up from the stool and rubbed at the charcoal that stuck to her hands as she walked around the easel to get a look at the drawing from several angles. She had replicated Julianna's image flawlessly. Once she had decided she was finished with the drawing, she told herself this fascination with Julianna needed to come to an end. She was not accessible and that was not going to change.

She left the drawing on the easel and turned the lights off on her way upstairs for a shower and on to bed. Tinker, who was lounging in the red chair, jumped down and followed behind.

The weekend was very productive for Andi. She emptied all the boxes and got the condo organized and decorated as she wanted it. Tinker got plenty of exercise and fresh air on the trails around town. She did as Rachel ordered and switched her cell to a local number and upgraded her phone to the latest BlackBerry model on the market.

Leo and Vince helped Andi hang the large painting. In return, they were compensated with beer and pizza. They were bowled over when they found out Andi was the artist.

On Monday, she completed the budget and schedule for the restaurant spots with one exception. She had a question concerning a food stylist, so she dialed the number for the marketing department that was listed on the papers William gave her.

The phone was answered on the second ring. "Good morning, thank you for calling Snow Cap Marketing. My name is Liz. How may I direct your call?" The voice was cheerful.

"Good morning, Liz. This is Andrea Connelly from KCOR. I was wondering if I might speak to Julianna Stevens."

"Julianna? Sure, can you hold a moment?"

"Yes." Andi busied herself with checking her numbers while she waited. In no time, the phone was picked up.

"Good morning, Andi. What's up?" Julianna also had a happy note in her voice, but she sounded tired.

Andi's stomach muscles tightened when she heard Julianna's voice. "Good morning, Julianna, I hope I'm not interrupting anything."

"Not at all. I was just reading e-mail."

"I have a question concerning the budget."

"Okay, shoot."

"Food stylist. Do we need one or will the restaurants take care of their presentations?"

Julianna hesitated. "Yes, we'll have a stylist, but it doesn't need to come out of your budget. Originally, the chefs at the restaurants were going to take care of their dishes, but Susan demanded a stylist, and of course, my boss agreed. So to answer your question, we will provide the stylist, and it will come out of Susan's department budget." There was a hint of frustration in her voice.

"Will I need to take care of any of the arrangements for the stylist?"

"No, it will be taken care of by us."

"Okay, well, that answers that." Andi wanted to be more social but didn't know where to go with the conversation, so she stuck to her business. "I'll have everything done today, and William will bring the paperwork to the meeting tomorrow.

"That's great. Thanks, Andi."

"You're welcome. I'll talk to you soon."

Andi hung the phone up slowly. She pondered the temperament in Julianna's voice. This Susan must be a real thorn in Julianna's side. Andi could relate to a problematic coworker.

She finished the schedules and budget, printed three copies, and placed them neatly in individual report covers. She dropped them on William's desk.

Thursday evening, Andi passed Rachel at the front desk on her way out the door. "Night, Rach, see you in the morning."

Rachel put her hands on her hips and gave Andi a disapproving look. "Have you forgotten about Thursday?"

Andi stopped to think what she might have forgotten that seemed so important.

"What did I forget?"

"Thursday? Payday?"

It still didn't ring a bell. "I have direct deposit. Is there something else I need to do?"

"No, silly. Thursday night, locals' night at The Bottom Dollar." Her hands were still on her hips. "You'll join us, won't you?"

Andi squirmed a little. "That's tonight, huh?"

She tossed her glasses on the desk. "Yes, and you need to be there. It's time you do a little socializing. It'll be fun."

Andi tried to come up with a quick excuse, but Rachel caught her without one.

"All right, I'll stop in for one drink. What time will everybody be there?"

Rachel's disapproval turned to a joyful smile. "The drink specials start at seven, but everyone usually gets there 'round eight."

Andi proceeded toward the door. "I shall see you then."

She didn't really feel like spending the evening in a bar, but Rachel was right, she needed to get out and socialize. She had been all business since she arrived in Colorado. It was time to meet some new friends.

Andi slipped her black fleece jacket on over a tight white T-shirt and zipped it halfway. She adjusted the waistband on her green camouflage Capris and decided not to wear a belt. She left her hair loose in the back and pinned the sides back with a clip. Her makeup was simple but accented her eyes. The Bottom Dollar was a typical local bar and pool hall with absolutely nothing fancy about it. She finished off the outfit with a pair of white cross trainers and white ankle socks. She was comfortable and fashionable.

She arrived at the bar a little after eight. The place was filled with people from front to back. The jukebox was kept alive by the patrons' quarters as it continually cranked out a mix of country and rock and roll.

Andi weaved her way through the crowd looking for a familiar face. The bar occupied the center of the large room. Two pool tables sat to the rear with a door to the outdoor patio. A large plate glass window faced the street side of the establishment with booths and tables filling the front of the room.

Andi recognized the profile of Justin near the pool tables and made her way through the sea of people to her coworkers.

"Andi," an excited Rachel called out in her English accent and waved her over to their table. Rachel was leaning against a tall, well-built, young man in his late twenties or early thirties, who was perched on a bar stool with one arm around Rachel's shoulder and a pool stick in his other hand. He was dressed in jeans and cowboy boots with a striped western style shirt. His hair was cropped short and he wore a Stetson cowboy hat. Andi found him to be quite handsome.

"Hey, Rachel. I had no idea the place would be so crowded."

"Everyone comes out for a little fun. Thomas even shows up every now and then. Andi, I want you to meet Charlie." Rachel smiled as she looked up at the young man. "Charlie, this is Andi, our new executive producer."

Charlie set the pool stick to the side and extended his large hand. "Pleased to meet you, little lady," he said with a healthy Texas drawl.

Andi shook his hand. "Very nice to meet you, too, Charlie."

He picked up his beer bottle only to find it empty. "Can I get you ladies a drink while I'm at the bar?" He slipped from Rachel's side.

Andi said, "Sure, a glass of red wine would be great."

Rachel had him order another Bacardi and Diet Coke.

Justin walked over and put his arm around Andi's shoulders. "Hey, boss, glad to see you made it."

Andi playfully tapped him in the ribs with her fist. "I had to come and see what you all got up to after hours. If I'm gonna be a local, I wanna act like one."

He laughed. "I don't think you want to act like these characters do in public." He pointed at the crowd.

"Here you go, ladies." Charlie set the drinks on the table for them.

Andi offered to pay for her drink, but Charlie refused to take any money. She said hello to the other people gathered around the pool table she knew from the station. Then she scanned the crowd and spotted Leo and Vince sitting at the bar talking with several of the female patrons. The boys looked over at her and she waved.

They waved back with big smiles.

Sitting on the other side of Leo was a muscular athletic woman with short dark blond hair. She wore blue jeans and a hooded sweatshirt with the LA Dodgers logo on the front. She elbowed Leo and asked, "Wow, that chick is smokin' hot. Who is she?" She pointed the mouth of her beer bottle in Andi's direction.

"Who? The girl that waved to us?"

"Yeah, dumb ass, the blonde in the tight camo pants."

He looked at her distrustfully. "That's our new neighbor, Andrea. She just moved here from Chicago. She works for KCOR."

"Mama likes," the woman said with a devious grin.

"Yeah, well, she might be out of your league, Val. She's not gonna fall for any of your beautiful lies. She's a very smart girl. She's not naïve and she's certainly not an airhead like your usual marks."

"That's nonsense. I can charm my way around any obstacle a female tries to put in my way…including the straight girls." She continued to watch Andi keenly.

Leo was irritated by Val's remarks. He worked the last two seasons with her on the ski patrol and knew the kind of player she built herself up to be. For Val, it was all about quantity, not quality. She was out to bed as many women as she could, and it didn't matter if they were gay, straight, had a significant other, or spoke English. She only had two requirements—they had to be female, and they had to be of legal age.

He decided not to give any more information to his predatory coworker. He liked Andi and didn't want to see her become the target of someone only out to put another notch in her bedpost.

Andi sat talking to Justin and Rachel while Charlie finished his game of eight ball. When her glass was empty, she offered to get the next round. She hopped off the bar stool and removed her fleece jacket before going to the bar. She weaved her way through the crowd to where Leo and Vince were sitting.

"Hey, girl," Leo greeted.

"How are you guys?"

"We're great, out spending some of our hard-earned money. How's your night going?" Vince asked.

"It's good. I'm glad I came. I really did need to get out."

Val elbowed Leo again, this time for an introduction.

Leo vacillated. "Andi, this is Val, she's one of our ski patrollers."

Val quickly extended her hand around Leo to Andi. "Hi, Val Tierbrock, nice to meet you, Andi."

Andi gave her a smile as she shook her hand. "Nice to meet you, too, Val."

Their introduction was interrupted by a touch of a hand to Andi's left arm and a soft voice that diverted her attention. "Andi."

She recognized the voice immediately and turned to find Julianna standing behind her. Andi's heart skipped a beat when she saw her sweet smile. The words stuck to her tongue, but she managed to speak. "Hi, Julianna."

Val's smile instantly turned downward, and she glared at the intruder for redirecting Andi's attention.

"I didn't expect to see you here. How are you?" She acknowledged Leo with a small wave as she spoke to Andi. He waved back.

Andi thought she was radiant in the soft dim light of the bar. "I'm good. Thought I would get out and mingle with the locals now that I am one. How's your week going?"

"That's great that you're getting out." Julianna scanned Andi from head to toe quickly. "My week has been long, but it's my own fault. I over-trained for the trail run series that started last week, and I'm still trying to recover." Once again, she took notice of Andi's straight shoulders. They were better defined in the T-shirt. Julianna's eyes fixated briefly. "William delivered your budget and schedule. Everything looks good. I'm just waiting for my boss to sign off on it so we can get started."

As they talked, a drunk overweight fellow walking past them stumbled into the back of Julianna, pushing her forcefully into Andi. Andi's natural reflexes caught her as she fell against her chest.

Julianna grabbed Andi by the shoulders as she tumbled into her. Leo and Vince jumped to help while Val sat motionless. The glass of wine Julianna was holding dropped from her hand, exploding into pieces and splattering its contents on the tattered wooden planks of the floor. Andi stood with her arms around Julianna until she felt her regain her balance. Her hair brushed against Andi's cheek, and the perfume she was wearing filled her senses again. The feel of Julianna's slight body pressed against her own sent an electrical impulse through Andi's every cell.

Julianna froze in Andi's arms, resting her chin on her shoulder. Her frame was every bit as rock solid as it looked, but she was soft to the touch. Her body created a wave of heat that lapped at Julianna's breast bone. It surprised her and made her feel a little uncomfortable, but at the same time, she enjoyed it.

The drunk mumbled, "Excuse me." Vince helped steady him, then he meandered toward the door, knocking into several other patrons on his way out.

"Are you okay?" Andi asked.

Julianna stepped back and brushed her hair from her face. "Yes, I'm sorry I plowed into you like that." She sounded embarrassed.

Val rolled her eyes and silently got off the stool and walked away.

Andi bent down and picked up the pieces of the wine glass. "You have no reason to be sorry. That clumsy oaf is so drunk he can't see straight." She set the broken glass on the bar. "I'll get you another drink."

"No, that's okay." Julianna protested weakly.

"Really, it's no problem. I was up here to get a round of drinks for my friends at the table over there, and I'm buying one for these guys, too." She pointed at Leo and Vince. "What's one more on the tab?"

Julianna nodded in agreement

She motioned for the bartender and ordered three beers, a red wine, and a rum and Diet Coke, then turned to Julianna. "What were you drinking?"

"Just a glass of white wine." She didn't specify.

Andi guessed that she didn't know the difference between a chardonnay and a Riesling. "How do you like your wine? Sweet or pungent?"

"Is there such a thing as somewhere in the middle?"

"I think I know what you're looking for." She looked over the unopened bottles that sat on the back bar. Nothing jumped out at her as being exceptional. However, she did spot a nice unopened domestic Riesling and ordered a glass. Andi pushed the beers down the bar at the boys. They thanked her and she gave them a wink.

She turned to Julianna and handed her the glass of wine. "I think you might enjoy this. It's light and fruity and just a hint of sweetness."

Julianna lifted the glass to her plump soft lips. Andi watched with anticipation.

"This is so much better than what I spilled on the floor, thank you." She took another sip and smiled at Andi. "Maybe that drunk did me a favor."

She smiled back at her joke. "You're welcome and I'm glad you like it. I better get these drinks back to the table. It was good seeing you, Julianna."

She touched her arm. "You too, Andi. I'll call you next week."

"Talk to you then." Andi picked up the drinks and returned to the table. She took a deep breath as she walked away from Julianna with the sting of her touch still fresh on her arm. She reminded herself not to let the girl get under her skin.

Julianna looked back as she walked away.

Andi spent the rest of her night talking with her coworkers and playing pool. She was having fun with her new friends. Only twice she glanced around nonchalantly in search of Julianna, but she was nowhere to be found.

From a table near the front window, Julianna sat with friends. Concealed by a full house, she was able to steal a glimpse of Andi at the pool table every so often through the crowd. She was taken at the sight of her leaning on a pool stick in the tight white T-shirt wearing Charlie's Stetson. That uncomfortable feeling she got in Andi's arms crept in every time she allowed her gaze to linger on the white shirt.

Andi left The Bottom Dollar around eleven. She exited out the back and across the patio. On her way to the gate, she saw a spiky, platinum head bobbing above a group of twenty-somethings at a corner table.

A female voice from the corner called out, "Hey, Andi!" The words were slightly slurred and loud.

Andi knew right away whose voice and platinum head it was. She walked over to the table with her hands in her back pockets. "Bo, what's up?"

Bo was sitting with her arm slung around the neck of another girl with short, jet black hair and a tattoo of a geisha girl that covered her right arm from shoulder to elbow. Everyone at the table looked like they had just stepped out of a skateboard park. "Ya found locals' night, huh?" Bo raised her bottle of beer. "Hey, everybody, this is Andi. She's the new executive producer of 'Sunrise Summit.'"

In unison, the drunken group said, "Hi, Andi" They sounded like a grade school class addressing a visitor.

"Hi, everybody."

Bo pointed at Andi. "Next locals' night, I'm buyin' you a beer. Deal?"

"Deal." Andi graciously said good night and went on her way.

Chapter 7

The sun was hanging low to the west of Breckenridge as the runners gathered at the starting area of the Summit Trail Run on County Road 450 north of town. Andi parked her SUV on the side of the road, and the crew unpacked the camera equipment. She brought the two best videographers at the station, Justin and Glen, with her to cover the event.

She carried Justin's tripod to the starting line. "What time is it?"

Justin held his arm up. "According to my atomic watch, it's exactly five."

She shook her head at him. "All right, let's get some shots of the pre-race. When the race starts, Glen, I'll have you go down the trail to get some action shots when the runners pass by. Justin, I want you here at the starting line."

Justin saluted her. "Yes, boss."

She made a face at him. "Please try to show me a little respect in public."

"Yes, madam boss. Is that better?" He winked at her.

"Get out of here and don't come back without some good footage." She gave them both a shove, and they walked off laughing.

Andi mingled with the crowd as the runners warmed up and chatted amongst themselves. She spoke briefly to the run coordinator, who was excited to have the series included in the documentary, and a sponsor eager to get his sports drink showcased.

She pulled a water bottle from her backpack and cracked the seal on the lid. As she lifted it to her lips, she saw Julianna walking toward her with a confident stride. She looked so poised and sure of herself. Andi couldn't avert her stare.

"Hey, nice to see you, Andi. Are you running today?" Julianna had a huge smile on her face.

Andi swallowed the water hard. "No, not me. I'm still trying to adjust fully to this altitude. Besides, I have a knee that doesn't take well to distance running since it was repaired."

"That's too bad. It really is a lot of fun." Julianna unzipped her white warm-up jacket.

"I'll take your word for it." Andi took another drink to wet the dry mouth that suddenly developed. "So this is what you've been training for at the Rec Center?"

Julianna removed the fleece and stuffed it in her bag. She was wearing a light blue T-shirt that hugged her torso, dark blue shorts, new trail running shoes, and the Ironman watch. "This is it. Last year, I ran the short course and was second overall. I decided to step it up this year and try the long course. Last week, I came in first for the women," she said as she pulled her hair back in a ponytail and secured it with a clip.

"You're quite the athlete," Andi said.

Julianna laughed. "I don't know about that. I just have a hard time sitting still."

Across the road, Leo's coworker Val was warming up with a couple of other runners from the ski patrol. She narrowed her eyes and watched intently while Andi and Julianna talked under the canopy of a tent. They appeared captivated with each other, and she wondered if something was going on between the two.

At the bar, Julianna conveniently diverted Andi's attention with her clumsy little antic and now they were here together and looking all too chummy for her liking. Julianna was starting to get in her way at every turn, it seemed.

"Since you're not running, what brings you out today, if I may ask?" Julianna inquired.

Andi clasped her hands behind her back. "Call it a fact-finding mission. I have a side project going. It's a documentary on summer activities in Summit County." She pointed at Justin with his camera near the starting line. "I've got a couple of camera guys shooting today's run and thought I'd tag along to see what the trail run series is all about."

Julianna looked at her inquisitively. "You're all business, aren't you, Andrea Connelly?"

Andi smiled lightly. "So much to do and no time to get it done. My deadline was yesterday on most of the projects I have in the works."

Julianna put her hand on Andi's shoulder. "Well, take some time when you can and enjoy the mountains. It's a lot of fun up here."

Julianna's hand left a warm and pleasant sensation on Andi's shoulder. "I'll do that...soon."

"I gotta warm up before the start. I'll see ya later." She patted Andi's shoulder.

"Good luck," Andi said and watched her walk away.

Julianna went to the parking area on the other side of the road and put her bag in the back of her car. She closed the door and began to stretch. She crossed her legs and bent down to stretch her hamstrings. Out of the corner of her eye, she saw someone approaching.

"Hey, Stevens," Val said her in gruff fashion.

Julianna didn't care much for Val. They competed against each other in the trail run series and several times in the Frisco Nordic Time Trials for cross-country skiing in winter. Her crass manner irritated Julianna. It made her feel as if Val was trying to bully her every chance she got. She considered it payback for the deflection of the pass Val made at her a few years earlier during the Ullr fest in Breckenridge. She didn't know much about her personally, but having seen her around with numerous women, Julianna picked up on her coquettish ways and had decided she was trouble.

"Hi, Val," Julianna said unenthusiastically. Her gaze remained pointed at the ground.

Val stood over Julianna. "So you're doing the long course this year, huh?"

"Yes. I suppose you are, too?" Julianna stood and took a step away from Val.

"Nah, I like the short. I get to the party quicker," she said, fidgeting with the run number pinned to the front of her long-sleeved shirt.

Julianna bent over again and continued to stretch.

"Stevens, I was wondering…are you and that new girl in town Andi an item or what? I mean, do you have something going with her?" Val asked brazenly.

Julianna popped up and put her hands on her hips. "What makes you think I have something going with Andi?" Her voice filled with fury. "I highly doubt my boyfriend would approve of me having a thing, as you put it, with another woman."

Val held her hands up. "Okay, okay, I was just asking. You looked like you were into each other over there at the tent. I didn't want to interfere with anything, but since there's nothing to interfere with, I'm good to go."

Julianna was still fuming. "What makes you think Andi would have anything to do with you or any woman for that matter?"

Val rubbed her hands together. "Let's just say I have a hunch."

"Yeah, well, your hunch was wrong when you tried it on me. I'm sure it will be when you try it on Andi, too." Julianna walked away.

Val raised an eyebrow. "We'll see." She swaggered in the direction of the tent where Andi was still standing.

She zeroed in on Andi, who was talking to some of the other run participants and taking notes as they told their stories of past runs. She weaseled her way through the crowd and casually landed at Andi's side ready to make her move.

"Hi, Andi, how's it going?" she said confidently.

Andi looked at her, then recognition kicked in. "Hi. Val, right?"

"Yeah. You remembered me, that's a good sign." She gave Andi a toothy grin.

"I've been working on that whole face with the name thing. I think I'm finally starting to get it."

"Yes, I think you are." Val continued to ogle Andi. "So what brings you out to the Summit Run? Those aren't exactly running clothes." She pointed at Andi's jeans and lilac oxford shirt.

"Work, actually. We're including the series in a summer activity documentary."

"That's cool. Leo mentioned that you worked for KCOR. Must be a fun job, eh?"

"Yes, I've enjoyed it so far." Andi kept her answers short.

"Leo also mentioned you're new in town. How long have you been here in Summit County?"

"Only since the beginning of May."

"Where is home?" Val was doing her best to make small talk with her pretty blond target.

"Chicago. How about you?"

"Love Chicago. Myself, I'm originally from Vermont. I came here from San Diego, though. I just love the mountains. The ocean is great, but I'm a high altitude kinda girl."

Andi smiled cordially at her, then eyed the starting line in hopes of catching a glimpse of Julianna.

Val noticed Andi's attention wandering and tried to reel her back in. "So, Andi, will you be staying for the get-together after the run? It's always a good time."

Andi looked down at her notebook. "No, unfortunately, I have another commitment this evening." She didn't really have a commitment; she simply wanted to keep Val at bay.

Val looked mildly dejected. "That's too bad. I was going to offer to buy you a welcome to town drink."

"That's very nice of you. Maybe some other time." Andi spied Julianna in the crowd. She was close to Justin and wearing a serious expression on her face. She exchanged glances with Andi, then looked away quickly.

The booming voice from the loud speaker called for all runners to ready themselves at the start line.

Val touched Andi's arm. "Guess I better get going. It was nice to see you again, Andi, and I look forward to buying you that drink sometime."

"Have a good run, Val." Andi rolled her eyes as she walked away.

She seemed nice enough, but she held no interest for Andi. It was Julianna who had her so absorbed. Val was definitely flirting and the offer of a drink was most certainly a play for her attention. However, her infatuation over the girl with honey brown hair and the light blue shirt crowded the exchange with Val right out of her thoughts.

She joined Justin before the start of the run. "Once the last of the runners are off, we can go. I'll call Glen on his cell and have him meet us at my SUV when he's done."

Justin looked up from his camera and whispered, "Hey, did you know the chick in the blue shirt has been checking you out?"

She looked at him with reservation.

He turned sideways and casually pointed in Julianna's direction. "She watched you almost the entire time you were talking to that other girl in the green shirt with the short hair."

Andi gave him a sly grin. "That, my dear fellow, is our new client from Snow Cap marketing in the blue."

"No shit! That's the one you keep talking about?"

"I do not keep talking about her!"

He gave her a mocking grin. "No, of course, you don't. You just mention her every time you talk about Snow Cap. Nothing wrong with that, though, she's hot."

"Yeah, well, she's a client, and if I had to guess, she's very straight."

"Maybe, but she sure was eyeballing your every move there for a while."

Andi wondered if what Justin was saying had any validity or if it was just wishful thinking on her part.

Julianna counted down the minutes at the start line until the run got under way. She opened a bottle of water and casually looked back over at the tent where Andi stood. To her surprise, Val was by Andi's side and she was all smiles. Julianna knew what she was up to. She felt her face warm as she watched Val bat her eyes and flash enticing smiles at Andi.

She filled her mouth with water and held it before spitting it out. She knew her womanizing competitor would say anything to get what she was after and wished she could hear the lines she was feeding Andi. Irritation was brewing inside her as she continued to watch Val's flirtation.

At one point, she caught Andi's glance and held it briefly while Val continued to talk, but quickly shifted her gaze and moved away so Andi couldn't see her. The flush of her skin deepened over the entire scene and it alarmed her. Why would she care if Val made a move on Andi? Andi was an adult and more than capable of taking care of herself. Besides, she was free to see whomever she wanted regardless. It should be of no concern to her. But somehow it was, and she didn't understand why.

She shrugged it off and set the stopwatch on her Ironman, then focused on the trail run ahead of her.

The runners were off at the sound of the air horn blaring. Julianna pushed the button on her watch and jumped off the starting line.

Justin hung up his cell phone and grunted.

"What's wrong?" Andi asked.

He opened his camera case and fished out a large square battery. "Glen forgot to pack an extra battery for his camera. I have to get this over to him. His camera is about to die."

Andi took the battery from him. "Here, I'll take it to him. You stay and shoot."

"You sure?"

"Yeah, I got it. Where exactly is he?"

Justin pointed to the trail head about fifty feet from the last sponsor tent. "He said he was about a hundred yards in, give or take."

Andi headed in the direction of the trail at a brisk walk.

The last of the competitors passed by as Andi headed down

the winding trail. When she reached Glen, he took the fresh battery and said he was going to climb up a small ridge and get the runners as they crossed an open area of wildflowers. It would make for a nice shot with the sun setting in the distance. He would meet them back at the SUV in about twenty minutes or so.

Andi was about to make her way back to the road but was stopped by a teen boy who doubled back looking for help. He must have thought Andi was part of the coordinating team for the run. He called out, "Excuse me, there's a woman up ahead that needs help. I think she fell or something, anyway she can't walk."

Andi looked at him blankly. "Okay." Before she could say anything else, he was off in a full sprint. He had done his good deed and now he needed to make up for lost time.

Andi felt compelled to walk ahead and see what had happened. She had her cell phone in her pocket. She could at least call Justin and have him send the first aid team after the fallen runner.

She rounded a curve and carefully made her way down a sloping section of the path. She spotted someone at the bottom partially blocked by some brush. When she got closer, she recognized the ponytail and the blue shirt. Julianna was sitting on the side of the trail holding her right ankle and writhing in pain.

"Julianna, what happened?"

She grimaced when she looked up. "Andi? What are you doing out here?"

"I had to bring a battery out to my cameraman just up the trail. Some kid caught me before I headed back to the road and said there was a runner down. I thought I'd come see if I could help." She bent down to get a look at the injured ankle. "Let me see."

Julianna hesitantly let go and stretched her leg out. The joint was already the size of a tennis ball and turning purple.

"How did this happen?"

Julianna winced when she moved her leg. "I came down the slope too fast and stepped on an exposed tree root. My foot slipped and I rolled my ankle."

Andi stood back up and pulled her phone from her pocket. "I'll call Justin. He can send someone out to get you." She tried to dial out but got nothing. "Great!"

Julianna looked up with pain on her face.

"I have no bars on my phone. How can I have bars a hundred yards away and not here?"

"The connections get real weird out here once you get away from the populated areas."

"Do you think you can walk if I help you?"

"I don't know. I'll try."

Andi held a hand out to help Julianna up. Once she was off the ground, she leaned into Andi and tried to take a small step. As soon as she put the slightest weight on the injured ankle, her leg buckled and she moaned in pain.

"I'll never make it back to the road. I can't put any weight on it." She sat back down. "You can leave me here. When you get back to the road, send the first aid team to get me."

Andi looked around. The shadows were hanging heavy in the aspens and the temperature was dropping with the disappearance of the evening sunlight. "I can't leave you here." She looked at her phone again.

"You have to. I'll be all right."

Andi dropped the phone back in her pocket and extended her hand. "Come on, it's not that far. I'll carry you."

Julianna gave Andi a horrified look. "Are you crazy? You can't carry me back to the road."

Andi put her hands on her hips. "I most certainly can. You're not exactly a heavyweight. If I can carry camera equipment around, I can carry you."

Julianna turned away. "You're not going to carry me out of these woods."

"Look, by the time I get back and the first aid team gets here, it'll be dark. It will take twice the amount of time, besides you'll freeze out here in nothing but that T-shirt and shorts." The irritation was evident in her voice.

"Seriously, I'll be fine, just go." Julianna held on to her ankle and refused to look up.

"Hard head," Andi said to herself.

Julianna shot her a glare. "What did you say?"

"Nothing. Look, we're burning daylight here. I can do this."

"No, just go already."

Andi held out her hand once more and bent down so her face was directly in front of Julianna's. "Stop being so stubborn and trust me," she said, her temper flared.

Julianna looked up at her with surprise. She locked on to the steel points frozen in Andi's serious blue eyes. Her ankle was throbbing and it was making her nauseated. She didn't have it in her to argue with Andi anymore. She gave in and accepted her hand with a frown.

"Thank you for letting me help," Andi said with a congenial smile. The steel points softened to a bright twinkle.

Julianna got up on one leg with her support. Andi turned around and directed, "Put your arms around my shoulders."

Julianna hesitated.

"Do it," Andi said.

Julianna did as she was told. Andi wrapped her arms around Julianna's legs at mid-thigh and scooped her up on her back. She shifted Julianna slightly to adjust the weight and started up the slope toward the road.

Julianna tensed at first, but once they were at the top of the small hill in the path, she relaxed.

"You okay?" Andi asked.

"Yeah. My ankle really hurts."

"It won't take long. We're only a little over a hundred yards away."

Julianna rested her head on Andi's shoulder and took note of Andi's torso. The muscles in her back were hard and smooth, and her entire body moved unwaveringly as she kept a steady pace down the trail. She found comfort in Andi's strength and used it to contain her own weakness by not giving in to the tears from the pain.

"Almost there," Andi said. She looked down at Julianna's ankle. She knew the pain had to be excruciating with her leg hanging like it was. She quickened her pace and her breathing. The thin atmosphere had her gulping air as they went. A stream of sweat ran down her neck. Eventually, her muscles began to feel the effects of the thin air, as well. Her legs were burning with every step, making it difficult to maintain her pace. Her heart pounded as her arms and back fatigued from the weight of the body she carried.

She didn't see the rock in the path, and when she stepped on it, she stumbled. Julianna tightened her hold on Andi as she recovered her footing.

"Are you all right?" she asked.

"Yeah, I'm okay. I didn't see that rock sticking up in the path," she said, breathing heavy.

The faint sound of walkie talkies squelching in the distance signaled they were getting closer to the road.

They stepped out of the trees onto the pavement and were met by two volunteers. They helped Julianna to a chair and called for the medics.

Andi bent over to catch her breath. When the burning in her lungs subsided, she grabbed two bottles of water from a cooler under a tent.

"Here, you probably need this right about now." She was still breathing hard in the thin air.

Julianna gratefully accepted the bottle. After she swallowed a mouthful of water, she looked up at Andi apologetically. "I'm sorry for being so rude. You were only trying to help. Sometimes my independence turns to stubbornness," she admitted with sincerity.

Andi knelt next to her chair. "Apology accepted." She gave her a satisfied smile. "I'm just glad I didn't have to take you by force...that's a joke."

Help arrived to treat Julianna's ankle. One medic pulled a cold pack from his bag. He struck it with his fist to release the liquid activator, then shook it to mix the chemicals inside that created the cold. He placed it over Julianna's swollen ankle. She moaned in pain when he touched it.

"Do you need me to stay with you?" Andi asked with concern.

"I think I'll be all right now." Julianna grabbed Andi's hand. "Thank you, Andi...for everything." Her light brown eyes sparkled as she looked into Andi's eyes.

"You're welcome. I hope it isn't broken."

"I hope it's not broken, too. I shudder at the thought of surgery if it is." She released Andi's hand slowly.

"I better go. My camera guys are probably wondering what happened to me."

"Thanks again."

"Good luck. I hope you heal quickly."

Andi had a twinge of guilt walking away and leaving Julianna this way, but she was not her responsibility. She was merely a client. Someone who Andi barely knew. She tried to resolve her uneasiness by telling herself she had gone above and beyond by bringing her out of the woods and delivering her to the medics.

Justin was leaning against Andi's vehicle talking on his cell phone while Glen sat on his camera case eating a candy bar when she walked up.

Justin hung up the phone and looked at her. "Where have you been? We were worried that you got lost in the forest."

"I stopped to help a runner that fell. It took a little while to get down the trail with an injured ankle."

"Okay, Florence Nightingale," Justin said, "can we go back to the station now?"

"Ha ha." She tossed the keys at him. "Here, you drive. I'm still trying to catch my breath in this thin air."

The next morning, Andi dialed the marketing department at Snow Cap. She didn't know any other way to contact Julianna, but more than likely, Liz would be able to give her an update on her condition.

As expected, Liz was at the reception desk. "Good morning, Snow Cap marketing, this is Liz, how may I direct your call?"

"Liz, this is Andi Connelly."

"Andi, how are you today?"

"Good. I was calling to see how Julianna was doing. This is the only number I have to reach her."

"She's doing better. She took the rest of the week off. The doctor ordered her to stay off her ankle for a few days and keep it iced."

"So it's not broken?"

"No, just a bad sprain. I'm afraid her Summit Run Series is over for this year, though."

"I'm sorry that she's hurt but glad it's a sprain and not a break."

"Did Julianna thank you for carrying her back?" Liz asked.

Andi Laughed. "Yes, a few times, in fact."

"Good. She told me she gave you a hard time at first. She can be so pig-headed sometimes."

"I'll just say we had a lively exchange about how we were going to get her back to the road, but in the end, she was very cooperative."

"All in all, that was a very noble thing you did."

"I'm just glad I was out there to help. She might have been in the woods for quite a while in the cold if she had to wait for help to find her."

"You're too modest. She went on and on about you when I took her home last night. I think it's fair to say she's grateful for what you did."

"Liz, will you please let her know I called and tell her I hope she's feeling better soon? If there's anything I can do for her, have her call me."

"Will do, Andi. Have a great day."

"Thanks, Liz, you too. Bye now."

Andi hung up the phone at her desk. "Huh? She went on and on about me? Interesting."

"Who did?" Justin was standing in the door.

"No one." Andi was surprised to see him standing there.

He walked in and sat in the chair in front of her. "So who's talking about you?"

She gave him a look of annoyance. "You are so nosy."

"Yeah, and your point? Come on, spill it, who's talking about you?"

She showed some reluctance before she spoke. "All right, I just got off the phone with Liz over at Snow Cap. I called to see how Julianna was doing."

"What's wrong with her?"

"She's the runner I helped yesterday."

He was starting to get the big picture. "And why didn't you tell me this last night?"

She leaned on the desk. "Nothing to tell. It was all very innocent. She fell and I just happened to be out there, so I helped her get to the first aid people and because I knew you'd make more out of it than there was."

He shrugged his shoulders. "Not if that's the truth." He smiled at her dubiously.

She sat back and folded her arms. "Well, there's nothing more to it."

"And now she's talking about you because you helped her."

She had a strong feeling he would eventually hear what really happened. "Yeah, well, actually, I carried her back."

He gave her a loud disbelieving laugh. "Seriously?"

"Her ankle was huge and she couldn't walk. What was I supposed to do, leave her out there in the woods in the cold?"

"No, no, you did the right thing." He was still snickering. "I guess she would be talking about you. You're a hero, Ms. Connelly."

"Oh, please. You can quit with the hero business."

"So, did your crush fawn all over you for coming to her rescue?" He couldn't resist the opportunity to harass her.

She frowned at him. "She is not my crush and you may cease and desist with busting my chops, that's an order."

He got up from the chair. "Whatever you say, but I know the truth. You're sweet on that girl. It's written all over your face." He left her office still snickering.

Andi touched her face with both hands. She told herself he was just teasing. She wasn't that transparent, was she?

She shook his insinuations off and went back to work.

Chapter 8

William held the door open for Andi as they entered the building housing the marketing department in the newly constructed East Village at Snow Cap. Andi noticed the building had that new construction smell to it as they entered the elevator to take them to the third floor.

When the door opened, they stepped out to an open lobby with a large circular desk in the center of the room and two hallways opposite each other. The floor was nothing like the rest of the resort in its décor. Everything from paint to furniture to accent pieces that adorned the tables and shelves was contemporary. If it weren't for the view from the windows of the resort and mountains, one would think she was in a New York office.

The tall, thin, blonde at the desk greeted them. "Good afternoon, William, your meeting is in conference room two today."

Andi recognized the voice from her phone calls, it was Liz.

Liz looked at Andi and her deep brown eyes widened and a smile lit up her face. "You must be Andi."

Andi proceeded to offer her hand, but before she could say how do you do, Liz cut her off.

"Julianna was dead on with her description of you. It's nice to finally meet you after all the calls." She grabbed Andi's hand and shook it with enthusiasm.

"Yes, I'm pleased to finally meet you, too, Liz." Andi's

curiosity was fueled by what Liz had just said. Julianna had described her? Why? More than likely, there was nothing to it.

Liz motioned toward the conference room. "Help yourselves to the refreshments. Everyone will join you shortly. Their staff meeting should be about finished."

Andi set her portfolio on the large oval table in the middle of the room and helped herself to a chilled bottle of Pellegrino mineral water.

She stood at the window overlooking the center of the East Village. It was late June and the resort was almost empty. Only a few tourists here for summer activities strolled from shop to shop in the bright Colorado sunlight. Andi sipped the mineral water, trying to remedy the dry mouth caused by a mixture of anxieties, one being the presentation of the finished spots to her client, and the second of seeing Julianna for the first time since she carried her out of the woods several weeks earlier.

Andi was up to her neck in trying to get the morning show together and, at the same time, oversee the Snow Cap project. Once she received the go-ahead from William that everything was approved, she got to work.

In four weeks, the spots were complete, despite the interferences and complications created by Susan. Any business she had with Julianna, she was able to conduct over the phone or through William. Thankfully, Julianna managed to keep Susan out of the editing sessions by emphasizing to her boss the increase in production costs Susan had already generated while shooting.

Lost in thought, Andi didn't hear the marketing people enter the room. She did pick up on the scent of Julianna's perfume and turned to find her standing behind her. She looked smart in a royal blue mock turtleneck dress with the sleeves pushed up to her elbows, a wide black leather belt cinched at the waist, and matching flats. She looked amazingly attractive.

In the weeks since she last saw her, Julianna was well on her way to recovering from the ankle injury. She was still using crutches, but mostly, she was putting her weight on the afflicted leg. She had put on a few pounds from not being able to work out since the accident. Her face was fuller, the veins in her hands were not so pronounced, and she had a few curves in the right places; her overall appearance was softer and less gaunt. Andi was pleasantly stunned at the transformation. She was already enamored with the beautiful marketing exec, now she was truly having a hard time keeping her eyes off of her.

Julianna flashed an easy smile.

"Hi, Julianna, how are you?"

"Much better, thanks. I have to admit, though, I feel a bit like a slug. I haven't been able to work out since this injury."

Andi eyed her up and down. "Well, you look good for a slug."

"And you look nervous," Julianna said.

Nervous or a little freaked out at seeing Julianna again, Andi wasn't sure which was closer to the truth. "I'm fine…well, maybe a little." She tried to make light of her fidgetiness.

Julianna leaned in close. "You have nothing to worry about. My boss saw the rough cuts and loved them. I think the final versions will get even better reviews."

William motioned for Andi.

"Looks like my account manager is trying to get my attention."

"I think he wants to introduce you to my boss. Come on, I'll walk, or hobble, over with you."

Andi followed Julianna in the wake of her intoxicating scent.

"Andi, I want you to meet the director of marketing, Karen Birnbaum."

The director was a petite middle-aged woman with short black hair and a no-nonsense corporate look about her. Andi was surprised at how closely she resembled Susan. She thought they could be sisters. Same build, same hair color, the only difference was in the way they dressed. Karen was all business with her straight hair and brown suit, while Susan was more flamboyant and bohemian and her hair wavy.

She shook Andi's hand softly. "I'm happy to finally meet you, Andrea. You do very good work."

"Thank you, Ms. Birnbaum. May I call you Karen?"

"Please do. We're not that formal around here."

Julianna winked at Andi when she looked her way.

Once everyone was seated, William grabbed the portfolio and removed the DVD with the final cuts on it. He placed it in the DVD player and took his seat next to Andi.

Susan popped in at the last minute and took the empty seat next to Karen. The two huddled together as Susan whispered something to her. Karen's response was a vigorous shake of her head.

Julianna was across the table and at the opposite end, giving Andi a clear view of her as she watched the screen in front of her. Andi's gaze was glued to Julianna for most of the viewing. Twice she turned and looked back at her, and Andi had to quickly redirect her gaze so as not to get caught staring.

When the final spot was finished and the lights came up, the room was abuzz followed by a round of applause. Andi blushed. She looked first to Julianna for approval. She could see the delight in her expression. It was a gratifying moment for her. She had won the admiration of the woman with whom she was smitten. It felt good, even if it was only professional.

"They're perfect, Andi. I'm very pleased," Karen said. "I'd like to thank you and Susan and everyone involved for all your hard work and for giving this project all of your creativity." With that, Karen ordered everyone back to work.

"William, I think we may be ready to talk more about future projects. KCOR's production work is first rate and Ms. Connelly here is a real find. You'll let Thomas know that, won't you?" Karen patted William on the shoulder.

"I will definitely pass that on, but I think Thomas is well aware of the level of talent he has in Andrea." William gave Andi a favorable smile.

"Call me and we'll set up a meeting," Karen said as she left the room.

Julianna took Karen's place next to Andi. "I told you there was nothing to worry about."

Andi felt a huge weight lifted off her shoulders. "It's always nerve-wracking when you have people judging your work."

William retrieved the disc from the player. "I'll get these

worked into the programming schedule so they'll start running right away."

"I appreciate that, William, thank you for all your help." Julianna followed them out of the conference room. When they reached the lobby, Julianna grabbed hold of Andi's elbow. "Andi, do you have a minute? I'd like to talk to you about something."

She took Andi by surprise. "Yeah, sure."

She guided her over to two chairs opposite the elevator where they sat down. Julianna laid her crutches on the floor.

Liz watched from her desk with a cautious eye.

Andi focused on Julianna. "What's up?"

"I-I have a favor to ask of you." She winced as if she were about to inconvenience Andi.

"Okay. What can I do for you?"

"You know about the charity event we're hosting, right?"

"Yes, Thomas asked me to send a cameraman to cover it."

"Wonderful," Julianna said. "You know it's a wine sampling and silent auction?"

"Yes, I read the flier Thomas had in his office."

Julianna shifted in the chair and propped her recovering ankle up on a small table in front of them, revealing more of the bare skin of her lower leg. Andi's concentration was disrupted.

"I'm embarrassed to say that I know almost nothing about wine outside of there's red and white."

Andi focused again and recalled the night at the bar.

"Anyway, William told me your family owns a winery, so I did a Google search. When I saw your family's Web site, I guessed that you might know something about wine." She had a look of apprehension on her face. "You picked out such a good wine for me that night at The Bottom Dollar. I was hoping you might be able to help me learn the different wines so I don't look like such a dummy at the event. I mean, I'm a disaster, I don't even know the difference between a chardonnay and a cabernet and I'm chair of the event."

Andi wanted to laugh but held back. "You really are in trouble."

Julianna nodded and gave Andi a pouty look.

"So what you need is a wine 101, if you will, with maybe a few crib notes to get you through the evening?"

The pout changed to excitement. Julianna clapped and pointed at Andi. "Exactly! That's exactly what I need."

Andi rolled her eyes and jokingly looked annoyed. "I guess I can help you. We can't have the chair looking like an imbecile in front of all those potential donors, now can we?"

Julianna looked like she wanted to hug Andi, but she restrained herself. "Once again, you're a life saver. Thank you, thank you, thank you."

"When would you like to get together?" Andi asked.

Julianna thought about it. "Do you have time this weekend?"

"I think so, how about Saturday?"

Julianna called out to Liz. "Liz, am I free on Saturday?"

Liz looked at her computer screen. "You have a meeting in the afternoon to finalize the menu for the auction, then you're free, Jules."

She looked at Andi. "Saturday evening?"

"That'll be fine."

"You're sure? I don't want to interrupt anything."

"No, Saturday is fine. How about my place around six?"

"Six it is." Julianna's excitement was contagious.

Andi wrote out her address with simple directions and handed them to Julianna. She stood to go, but before she got on the elevator, she asked, "Just out of curiosity, what else did William tell you?"

"That's all." She turned on her crutches and started down the hall.

William was waiting downstairs in the main lobby for Andi. On the drive back to the office, they discussed the success of the commercials and the potential for future work. While they talked about work, Andi's mind was on another topic—Julianna and Saturday night.

Inside, she was conflicted. She wanted to shout with joy, but she also knew there was nothing more to this than what Julianna had asked for, a sharing of information. She wanted to call Desi, but she knew her friend would blow it out of proportion.

She couldn't deny that she wanted there to be more, but her common sense told her Julianna was a straight girl and didn't think of Andi in any way other than a business acquaintance and possibly a new friend. She was falling for this girl and falling hard.

Chapter 9

Andi looked at the clock hanging above the fireplace. It was 5:45. Julianna would arrive anytime. She adjusted the volume on the home theater system for the fourth time. Usually, the soft piano music was soothing, but that night, nothing was going to take the edge off her nerves.

The town house was spotless. She spent the day cleaning and arranging things so that everything was just right. Even Tinker got a bath and thorough brushing.

She tried to appear casual, dressed in a loose white cotton sweater and jeans and barefoot. Her makeup simple, her hair loose. She hoped it would hide the anxiety that jumped around in her stomach.

She poked at the fire burning in the fireplace while she waited. Tinker lay in the red chair half asleep. Her belly was full, she was clean, and she had not a care in the world.

Then the doorbell rang. The shepherd launched herself off the chair and ran for the door barking. Andi returned the poker to the stand, took a deep breath, then went to the door. The hinges made a small creaking noise when she opened the heavy wooden door. The smile on her face intensified at the sight of Julianna standing in the glow of the porch light minus the crutches.

Andi's gaze met Julianna's. "Hi."

"Hi," Julianna said with a smile, trying not to let her nerves show through. Her hair was tucked behind her ears and hung free.

She was lovely. She wore a pink pastel blouse under a black fleece jacket, with tight dark blue jeans that hugged her narrow hips and a pair of casual loafers. She carried a large Coach bag over her shoulder; Andi recognized it from Desi's collection of expensive bags.

"Welcome, come on in." Andi stepped to the side so Julianna could enter, and as she did, Julianna's perfume once again wrapped itself around her nose. Andi caught a glimpse of the black BMW SUV in the driveway as she closed the door. She tried not to think about what Leo said about Julianna's need for money and social status.

Tinker instantly went to Julianna with tail wagging, looking for attention.

"What a pretty puppy." She bent down to scratch Tinker's chin.

"Don't tell her she's pretty. Her head is already big enough."

"What's her name?" Julianna asked as she gave the canine lots of pets. Tinker returned the favor with a few licks to Julianna's hand, which helped her to relax.

"That's my guard dog, Tinker. Don't let that cute face fool you. She's a trained killer."

Julianna laughed as she stood. "I think she's sweet."

Tinker wagged her tail as she looked up at the two women.

Julianna gave the room a quick survey. The expression on her face was that of amazement. "Wow, how many roommates do you have?"

Andi wasn't sure how to answer. "Just one, the four-legged mooch right there." She pointed at Tinker as she returned to her place in the red chair. Andi stepped off the landing at the entrance and walked toward the kitchen.

"You mean you live here alone?" Julianna tried to take everything in as she followed Andi. The large painting hanging in the living room caught her attention right away.

Andi smiled. "Yeah, it's smaller than my flat in Chicago, but I'm getting used to it." Andi had no idea how expensive housing was for the locals. Thomas was charging her less in rent than she paid in Chicago, which to her was a real deal. She was oblivious to the fact that a lot of the locals shared small apartments with several others to live in the mountains. "What's your place like?"

Julianna set her bag on the kitchen counter. "I have a one-bedroom apartment in the Snow Cap Valley complex, across form the resort. It's employee housing. I was able to get it by myself because I'm considered administration and not operations." She looked a little embarrassed.

"That's cool." Andi sensed Julianna's discomfort with the subject, so she redirected the conversation. She did her best Vanna White and motioned to the table. "I have a few props to enhance your educational experience tonight."

Andi had laid out a dozen wine glasses, a tray of cut fruit, a few small chunks of chocolate, a piece of leather, a tablespoon of shredded tobacco, ground black pepper on a plate, vanilla extract, and a variety of cut flowers in a vase.

Julianna was intrigued. She looked over the items on the table and wondered what the odd assortment of stuff had to do with wine. She did notice there was something missing from the assortment—the wine itself. She removed her jacket and draped it on the back of a chair. "This looks like fun."

"I thought I would give you a hands-on lesson." Andi rubbed her hands together.

Julianna pulled a small notebook and pen from her bag. "Ready."

"First of all, remember wine is fun. Second, you want to get your senses involved. It requires a good sniffer, curious taste buds, and the use of a few brain cells." Andi's hands grew animated when she talked.

Julianna wrote in her notebook. "Have fun, got it." She looked amused.

"There's also a simple vocabulary that goes with the education of wine. Half the fun of tasting wine is talking about the many distinctions to it." Andi walked around the table. "Everything you see on the table is what you will smell in the different wines."

"That's the bouquet, right?"

"That's part of it. Some people refer to the nose of the wine, meaning the natural smell that comes from the fruit. The bouquet is the smell the wine develops from the aging process. But for simplicity's sake, we'll just call all of it smell."

Julianna nodded as she wrote.

Andi picked up an empty glass. "We'll start with the whites. Did you like the wine I ordered for you at the bar?"

"Yes, it was good, easy to drink."

Andi picked a slice of apple, a piece of melon, and a slice of pear from the platter of fruit and placed it in the glass. "What I ordered for you was a Riesling, a German grape that is picked when it's extra ripe, which makes it sweeter than other whites." Andi handled the glass by the stem. She put the rim to her nose. "You want to get your nose in the glass and take a good sniff." Andi demonstrated, then handed the glass to Julianna. "Close your eyes before you sniff and tell me the first thing you smell."

Julianna closed her eyes and put the glass to her nose as Andi had done.

She was lovely, Andi thought, as her mind wandered for a moment. Her long eyelashes, perfectly sloped nose, and full soft lips. Julianna's voice interrupted her daydream.

"I get a strong scent of apple, then the pear and the melon." Julianna was proud of herself.

"Good. The apple scent is a common denominator in whites. A chardonnay adds a tropical fruit like mango or pineapple scent, and if it's aged in an oak barrel, you might get a butter or coconut undertone." Andi picked up another glass and added an apple slice, pineapple chunk, and a small amount of shredded coconut together and handed it to Julianna.

She put it to her nose and closed her eyes. "Umm, this is a very different combination. I get the coconut after the apple, then the pineapple.

Andi cracked a big smile. "You learn quickly. Young wines are fairly straightforward. They have a simple, clean fruity smell that comes from the grape." She grabbed another glass and with the apple, she added a slice of grapefruit. "A Sauvignon blanc will be a bit citrus-y and may even have a slight grassy smell to it."

Julianna stuck her nose in the glass. "There's so much to know about wine. How do you remember all of this?"

Andi laughed. "You might say I was born into it. My grandfather has been in the wine business his entire life. In fact, I think his fingertips are permanently stained by the grapes. We were quite young when he began to educate my older brother and me. The nose to the glass method was how he taught us. He used to say…" She stood up straight and in her best imitation of his Irish accent said, "You children have to train your noses."

Julianna giggled at Andi's imitation.

Andi sat across from her. "We were always sticking our noses in things to sharpen our sense of smell. My grandfather would ask us to break it down and describe whatever it was we were sniffing."

Julianna wrinkled her nose. "Did your grandfather have you smell nasty stuff, too?"

"We put our noses to almost everything. Bad smells are some of the most complicated scents to dissect. The reason the smell is bad is because of chemical reactions. The smell of grass decaying, standing water that's undisturbed, old cheese, there's a lot going on that causes those odors to develop." Andi popped a chunk of pineapple into her mouth with a smile.

Julianna put her elbow on the table and propped her chin up with her hand as she watched Andi. She felt herself being drawn in by her exuberance. Something stirred inside her when she was near Andi. Something unlike any crush she had ever had. She felt it at the bar when she was pushed into her arms by the drunk. She found excitement and comfort in her touch that night, and tonight, she also found it in her voice.

They were becoming friends, that's all, Julianna told herself. To think there was anything more than that was just absurd and it frightened her to think how Andi would react if she knew. It terrified her to think of the repercussions if her thoughts became reality.

"So are you ready for the reds?" Andi grabbed another glass.

Julianna exhaled. "Let's do it."

"I'll try to make this as painless as possible. Reds are fruity also, but they're hearty fruits like berries." Andi added a few currants, blackberries, and a chunk of chocolate.

Julianna inhaled deeply from the glass. "I like that, but I like anything that has chocolate in it."

"That is an example of a merlot. Reds most often spend some time aging in oak barrels, too. It's the chemical changes that give it the unusual distinctions like vanilla, chocolate, tobacco, and sometimes coffee."

Julianna couldn't resist, she picked the chocolate out of the glass and ate it.

Andi smiled and shook her head. "A Syrah is a little spicier. You might notice black pepper and even flowers." She added a pinch of the pepper and some flower petals to the berries in a glass.

Julianna sniffed each glass several times and made notes as she went. She looked at the items on the table and pointed to the piece of leather. "What about the leather?"

"That's another nuance that oak aging can create." She held the leather up to Julianna's nose.

"It smells like the old books my dad has in his study back home."

"Usually, this will come from well-aged wine made from very ripe grapes. Some connoisseurs call it nostalgic." Andi put the leather to her own nose. "Okay, what do you say we try some of the stuff we've been talking about?" She went to the pantry and returned with four bottles of wine—two reds and two whites.

"I'll open all four of these so we can practice." She removed the corks and set four glasses out, pouring a different wine in each glass. "Now remember the idea is to get all your senses involved. First, you want to do a visual examination. Is the wine clear or opaque? Second, you want to get your nose in the glass and get a good sniff. I find it's helpful to sniff with my eyes closed. It will help focus your attention. And then taste. Hold the wine in your mouth and swish it around. When you do this, you're testing not only the taste, but the weight and texture of the wine or the body of the wine."

Julianna wrote down all of Andi's instruction. She was

fascinated by her enthusiasm and her depth of knowledge. She went step by step when she sampled each of the wines and, for the most part, picked up on the variety of aromas from each glass. She was happy that she was able to please Andi with how quickly she caught on.

"See how easy it is? And fun. You'll dazzle everyone Saturday night," Andi said.

Julianna was humbled. "I doubt that I'll dazzle anyone, but I sure won't look like a pinhead."

"Well, you've dazzled me." Andi paused. "With your zeal." She really wanted to say she was dazzled by Julianna's beauty and sweetness, but that was something she would keep to herself. "Now that class is over, how about a glass of wine?"

"I would enjoy that very much." Julianna's nerves were starting to come back.

"Which shall I pour for you?"

She chose the Riesling. Andi chose the merlot.

They walked into the living room. Andi added another log to the fire while Julianna curiously looked around.

"Would you like the ten-cent tour?"

"Sure. I love how you've decorated."

"Thanks. I've been collecting original works of art since my college days. I started by swapping pieces with my fellow students."

Julianna stopped in front of the large painting on the wall. Her eyes widened when she saw the signature at the bottom. "You're very talented, Andi." She pointed at the painting as she continued to examine the canvas.

Andi smiled. "Thank you. I was blessed with a gift."

Julianna turned to face Andi. "Did you show your work in Chicago?"

"I did, once upon a time, but it's been a while since I've had the drive or the time to start a canvas."

"You mean you don't paint anymore? With talent like this, why would you stop?" Julianna looked confused.

"Let's just say life has a way of getting in the way. Full-time job with long hours and a relationship that demanded attention but failed in the end anyway."

"I'm sorry." She watched Andi closely.

Andi set her glass on the table. "I've been thinking about painting again, but the inspiration is slow in coming."

"I'm sure you'll find it again. There's so much beauty here in the mountains, it's hard not to find inspiration."

There was a tremendous beauty standing right in front of her, Andi thought. "Let me show you the rest of the place."

Julianna followed Andi from room to room and back to the sofa in front of the fireplace. "This is a really nice place. It's so comfortable and warm and I love that bathtub."

Andi sat on the sofa and imagined Julianna naked and covered in suds. She watched her as she moved from picture to picture displayed around the room. "Those are all my family."

"I recognize them from the Web site. You have a beautiful family." She sat on the opposite end of the sofa. "I didn't see any pictures of you on the Web site."

"I don't really have any part in the business. I designed some of the labels for the bottles, but that's all." She ran her finger around the rim of her glass. "Once I left my hometown for college, I didn't return. I stayed in Chicago and went to work. I know the wine business just because I grew up in it, but my first love has always been art."

"You must miss your family."

"I do. I'm not there for birthdays and most holidays, but what I really miss is the everyday interaction. My niece and nephew are growing so fast and I'm missing it." She sighed. "But this is the life I chose."

Julianna recognized the gravity of the subject. "So tell me about you. Why did you move to the mountains? Why television? Do you have a boyfriend back in Chicago?"

"I graduated from the Art Institute of Chicago and, at the insistence of my parents, went on to Loyola and got an MBA before I entered the work force. I moved here for the job. I was looking for advancement and a challenge. Thomas gave me an opportunity and made me an offer I couldn't resist. Besides, I needed to get out of Chicago, you know, time for a change. Television because a girl has to eat. I'd love to be a full-time artist, but there's no security or benefits. As for the boyfriend, the last one I had was when I was six."

Julianna gave her a puzzled look.

"My last girlfriend left me seven months ago." Andi waited for a response.

Julianna caught on quickly. "Oh. Oh! So you're, you're..."

"Gay." Andi finished for her.

"It's okay. Really, I'm okay with that." She took a drink.

"You look surprised. Are you sure you're okay?"

"Yes, I'm fine." Julianna looked serious. "Actually, you're the first person I've met that's been that candid about their sexuality."

"No reason to hide it. It's what I am and how I live." Andi sat back and relaxed.

Julianna played with her glass. "I admire your candor. It must have been hard to tell your parents. I mean, it must have taken a lot of courage to tell them something like that."

Andi curled her bottom lip out and shook her head. "There really wasn't much to it. I think they knew all along, they were just waiting for me to realize it."

"When did you know?"

"It was the summer between my junior and senior year of high school. My brother had this friend, a fellow chemistry major from the university that he brought home to work in the vineyard that summer. She said she was interested in the winemaking process. We hit it off from the start, and one thing led to another. One afternoon, we went down to the wine cellar to escape the heat, and that's when she kissed me for the first time."

Julianna listened intently.

"It was that kiss that changed my life. I had always secretly been more interested in girls than boys. I thought there was something wrong with me because I had those feelings for other girls. Renee changed my life with just one kiss."

"How did it change?"

"It confirmed that I wasn't the only girl with those feelings, and when she kissed me, it just felt right. It was very natural."

"Did your parents see you together? What did you tell them?"

"No, I didn't say anything about Renee until long after she left. They could tell I was different, even at a young age. I liked hanging out with the guys, but I didn't fawn over them. Don't get me wrong, I like men, they make for great family and friends, but I just don't care to date them." She gave Julianna an apologetic smile. "The night I finally told my mom, we were sitting on the porch swing, and I felt like I was going to burst if I wasn't honest with her."

"What did she say?"

"She put her arm around me and told me that she and my father loved me no matter what and just wanted me to be happy. She also told me she was sure that one day I would find someone that would love me for the special person that I am."

"Your parents are very open-minded. Mine would have blown a gasket and disowned me. They're so unbelievably conservative."

Andi propped her feet up on the coffee table. "My parents were student activists in their younger days. I call them ex-hippies. My mom is a political science professor and my dad's a lawyer. They've always been very open-minded about things and allowed us kids to grow into the people we wanted to be, pursue our own interests."

"I wish my parents thought like that. They were thrilled when I agreed to go to Penn State, my dad's alma mater. They even let me pick my own major, but when they saw how serious I was about earning the marketing degree, they were less than thrilled."

"Why is that? Surely they wanted you to be successful."

"They did, in a way." Julianna looked uncomfortable. "If my dad had his way, I would be married to some frat boy with an MBA who would be working for him. We would have a couple of kids and I'd be an active member of the Junior League like my mother." She paused. "I wasn't interested in an MRS degree and they really took offense when I refused to join a sorority, especially my mom."

Andi was stunned. "Wow, I can't imagine my parents plotting everything out like that."

"I think my parents had everything planned for me and my older brother starting with the day we were born. We were both C-section babies." She snickered. "They made all the decisions for us, what private schools we would attend, the musical instruments we would learn, the after-school activities we participated in. It wasn't until I was a senior in high school that I became mildly rebellious. I had to draw the line when they tried to set me up on dates with the sons of their country club friends." She finished the wine in her glass.

Andi got up to retrieve the wine and refilled their glasses. "There would have been some serious fights in my house if my parents had been so manipulative. The three of us would have tag-teamed them with our insurgence." She held her hands up like a boxer.

Julianna laughed. "I never would have gotten any help from my brother. He fell right in line with my father and his plans. He went to Penn State also and now he works for my father. He's a junior partner at his financial management firm. He married his college girlfriend and they're raising their son the same way."

Andi just sat quiet for a while and drank her wine. Then she asked, "What instrument do you play?"

"Piano, of course."

They both laughed.

"Where is home?" Andi asked.

"Philadelphia."

"How did a proper girl from the Northeast end up here?" Andi sounded surprised.

"It's a long story, but I'll give you the condensed version. I came out here with a few friends for vacation seven years ago and met this guy who worked for the ski patrol. We stayed in touch, and six months later, I moved out here." She laughed.

"My parents were furious when I left. They were already frustrated that I was working full time and not married. When I informed them of what I was doing, my father told me not to look to them for any help. If I was going to throw my life away on a ski bum, they were not about to finance it." She set her glass on the table.

"Anyway, I got a job at the resort as a reservationist and moved in with the guy, but the relationship didn't work out. When we broke up, I moved in with Liz and eventually an assistant position in the marketing department opened up. From there, I worked my way up."

"Were your parents expecting you to come home with your tail between your legs?"

"I think my dad was, but my mom changed. She had this newfound respect for me and what I was doing with my life. I think secretly she was happy that I was out making my own life and not working off my father's agenda or his checkbook."

"They have every reason to be proud of you. I'd say you've made a success of your life. You are your own woman."

"Thanks. I think they're proud of me. At least my father is talking to me again. We went through a period when my mom would only talk to me when my father wasn't at home. That was when things were at their worst. Now I know they're there for me if I need them. If I want to make them completely happy, I need to find a husband and have children." Julianna made a face.

"Is that what you want?" Andi asked in earnest.

"Honestly, I don't know. I'm happy with my life. I've got a job I love. Good friends. I suppose if the right person came along, I might be open to a commitment." Julianna held back any mention of her current boyfriend, though she couldn't explain to herself why.

A sleeping Tinker interrupted the conversation with a growl as she rolled over on her back with her legs in the air. Both women laughed at the dog.

"Silly dog. See what I have to live with."

Julianna picked up a book Andi had left out on the table and read the title. "Jane Austen's Persuasion, I don't believe I know this one."

"She's one of the great romantics. I fell in love with her work the semester I took English lit," Andi said. "Persuasion is the last story she wrote before she died at forty-two. The story itself is somewhat autobiographical in that she loved and lost because her family didn't approve of the relationship, just like the main characters in the story."

Julianna opened to the page where Andi had left her bookmark and read, "I can listen no longer in silence. I must speak to you by such means as are within my reach." She stopped and looked up at Andi, then continued. "Tell me not that I am too late, that such precious feelings are gone forever." She stopped again and scanned the page. "A word, a look, will be enough..."

"Beautiful words, aren't they?" Andi asked.

"Yes, they are." Julianna looked up at the clock over the fireplace. "I really should go. I can't tell you how much I appreciate this, Andi. I had a good time. I enjoy talking to you."

"It was my pleasure, and it's been great spending time with you. I plan to have a dinner party soon. I'll put you on the guest list."

"Sounds great."

Andi walked outside with Julianna and got a better look at the BMW. She whistled. "You're doing well for yourself."

"It's not what you think. I was driving a ten-year-old Ford Explorer until an ex of mine drove it into a ditch and totaled it. This was my dad's." She patted the hood. "He wanted to be like his golf buddies, so he traded his sedan for the bigger X5 and ended up hating it. When I told my parents about the wreck, my dad offered this up, actually he insisted I take it. I think he used me as justification to go buy himself another seven hundred series sedan."

"I'd call that sweet justice for you."

Julianna laughed. "You're funny, Andi Connelly." She held her arms up for a hug.

Andi hesitated for a split second. To touch this woman could be a deleterious action Andi would regret. She was already far too attracted to Julianna, and it made her uncomfortable.

Julianna wrapped her arms around Andi's neck and squeezed her tight. Andi responded by lightly holding Julianna around the waist. She tried not to feel anything, but the explosion deep inside her detonated on its own. It was a quick and intense embrace.

Julianna felt something, too. She allowed herself to enjoy the feel of her body pressed against another woman, but not just any woman, one she wanted to get closer to, and it was blurring her conscious.

She let go of Andi and jumped into the black BMW. Before she closed the door, she asked, "You will be at the auction next weekend, won't you?"

Andi hesitated again. "Well, I-I..." She looked at Julianna's sweet face and couldn't think fast enough to come up with an excuse.

"Oh, please, you just have to be there." Julianna tried another tactic. "It's for a good cause. We want this year's ski camp to be bigger and better for the disabled kids."

Andi tried to look into her eyes, but Julianna's gaze was shallow and distracted while her smile remained engaging.

She caved. "Yeah, okay, I'll show."

"Wonderful. It's at the Old Miners Mountain House at the top of Snow Cap. It'll be a good time, you'll see." She gave Andi a quick smile and closed the door.

As she pulled out of the driveway, Andi gave her a subtle wave. She waved back, then she was gone.

Chapter 10

Andi knocked on Thomas's open door. He cradled the receiver of the phone between his ear and shoulder while he waved her in and pointed at the chair in front of his desk. She sat and waited for him to finish his call. When he was done, he tossed his pen on the desk and rubbed his eyes. "Andi, did you ever have one of those weeks where it feels like everyone wants a piece of you?"

"I've had many weeks like that throughout my career. The trick is to give everybody enough of you to satisfy their needs without spreading yourself too thin."

"That is a trick, isn't it?"

"Indeed."

"How are you doing? Everything okay?"

"Yes, in fact, I'm ahead of schedule on my own show reconstruction plan. Barring any major setbacks, I think we're going to have one hell of a new morning show."

"Good, I'm glad to hear about some progress."

Andi changed the subject. "Are you and Wendy still going to the charity auction Saturday night?"

"As far as I know, yes. Wendy's shop is a sponsor this year. I think she donated a ski outfit or something. You're not thinking of skipping the party, are you?"

Andi squirmed in her chair like a little girl. "No, I'm just… these formal events are—"

"Let me reassure you it's not formal or I'd be the one trying to get out of going. It's just a casual event. It'll give you the chance to mingle."

"I know, but I'm still very new here, and it's hard to be social with a crowd of people when you don't know any of them."

"Relax, Wendy and I will be there. You should know some of the folks from Snow Cap, and I know Julianna will be there. William said you two hit it off like old friends."

William talks too much, Andi thought.

"You wouldn't happen to have a date for this, would you?" Thomas asked sheepishly.

Andi looked mildly surprised. "No, no, I haven't had the time to really get out and meet anyone yet."

"Well, you should make some time. It might help relieve some of the social anxiety you're feeling." Thomas looked at Andi. There was something else bothering her. "Andi, are you okay? You don't seem to be yourself."

"Everything's good. I'm still adjusting to being in a new place with new people, that's all."

"Okay, well, if there's anything I can do for you, let me know."

Andi got up from the chair and started out the door. "Thanks, Thomas, I'll be all right."

Saturday arrived quickly. After a long day of hiking with Tinker, Andi got ready for Julianna's charity event. She looked at the clock as she buttoned her white silk blouse—6:50. The party started at seven, but she was in no hurry. She really wanted to skip the whole thing, but she told Julianna she would be there. She was tired from being outside most of the day and her bum knee was sore.

Every reason that rolled through her head was just an excuse to cover up the real reason she wanted to stay home. She contemplated her feelings for Julianna as she tucked her blouse in her black linen slacks. The more she saw of Julianna, the more of her heart she lost to the girl with the honey brown hair, and it was pointless. There was no use in falling for a woman she could never have. Why couldn't she get that to stick in her head?

Andi slipped her leather jacket with the standup collar on and checked herself in the mirror. She was dressy but casual. She gave herself a spray of perfume before she grabbed her handbag and turned out the lights in the bedroom.

Downstairs, Tinker was looking out into the night from the sliding glass doors. When she heard Andi in the living room, she came running in.

"I thought I'd find you asleep in the chair, little girl."

Tinker wagged her tail at Andi's voice.

Andi picked up her keys from the end table. "I won't be gone long. I just have to make an appearance." She gave the shepherd a hug and a kiss.

Andi parked the Escape under the yellow light of a lamp post and took her time walking to the gondola house in the brisk night air. Her nerves threatened to get the best of her, but the retired couple from Denver with whom she shared the gondola helped ease her fretfulness as they chatted casually on the way up to the mountain house. The couple was impressed by Andi and her position and promised to watch the new morning show when it started.

Once the gondola arrived at the top of the mountain, a courteous attendant in a blue resort jacket and khaki pants helped them out, then pointed them to the walkway that would take them to the house. Andi immediately spotted Justin with his camera near a side entrance as she entered the large hall of the house.

He greeted her when she walked up. "Hey, boss. Aren't you the little hottie tonight?"

Andi blushed. "You're only saying that so I'll keep giving you all the gravy assignments." She rapidly scanned the enormous room in search of a first look at Julianna.

He snickered as he checked the light on his camera. "If you look to the far end of the room, just to the left of that enormous flower arrangement, I think you'll find what you're looking for."

"What? What are you talking about?"

He leaned closer to her. "Julianna, that's who you're looking for, right?"

"No, actually, I was looking for…" She paused. "Thomas and Wendy."

He rolled his eyes at her. "Sure you were." He chuckled. "Andi, please, it's me. I sat in those meetings with you and Julianna. You couldn't keep your eyes off her. And if I'm not mistaken, she was the same way."

She looked at him with more surprise, but before she could respond to his accusations, she felt an arm wrap around hers, and the fragrant scent of Julianna's perfume filled her senses.

Julianna squeezed Andi's arm and leaned into her side. "I was afraid you might not show."

Andi turned to see Julianna's beautiful smile and twinkling brown eyes gazing back at her. "Me a no-show? I'm true to my word and here I am." She smiled back at Julianna.

"I'm so happy you're here. Thanks for coming." She squeezed Andi's arm again.

"I'm happy to be here and doing my part for a better ski camp." Andi was struggling to breathe with Julianna leaning against her.

"I have some things I need to go check on before the bidding begins, but let's have a glass of wine later, okay?" She let go of Andi's arm slowly.

"Sounds good. You get to pick the vintage." Andi winked at her.

Justin, who was listening to the flirtatious exchange between the two women, just shook his head.

"The pressure is on." Julianna made a face like she was scared as she started to walk away. "I'll catch up with you later."

Andi got a better look at Julianna as she walked away. She was wearing a sleeveless, scoop neck, black cocktail dress that hugged her body, with a hemline cut just above mid-thigh. She finished the outfit with silk stockings and black pumps. Her hair was back in a French-braided ponytail that followed the swing in her step as she walked through the crowd. She was pure sex in that dress, Andi thought. She fantasized about stripping it off as she kissed her way down Julianna's neck.

Justin interrupted the fantasy with a cough.

She turned and looked at him blankly.

He leaned on his tripod and asked, "Why don't you two just admit you want each other and get on with it?"

"Justin!"

"Don't act like you're shocked. It's so obvious."

Her face relaxed. "I'm afraid it's one-sided. Do you think it's that obvious to her?"

"Like I said, I don't see it as one-sided. There's at least some interest on her part."

"It's called straight girl curiosity, and it's a dangerous thing." She crossed her arms over her chest.

He put his arm around her shoulders. "I don't know anything about that, but I do know you have the look of love in your eyes and I'd hate to see you get hurt."

"That's why the whole straight girl thing is dangerous. Someone usually gets hurt." She sighed. "The tricky thing about dreams and wishes is knowing when to hang on and when to let go." She watched Julianna's head bob through the crowd. "I need to let go." She turned away from the sight of Julianna. "What do you say we get a drink?"

Justin stepped back. "I don't know, what if the boss finds out? I'm supposed to be working."

"I think it'll be okay. I know the boss, she's cool."

He laughed. "Then let's head for the bar."

She ordered a pale ale draft for Justin and a glass of fairly good red wine by her standards. She handed him the beer. "Cheers." They tapped glasses and, in unusual fashion, Andi downed the wine in one drink.

Justin watched as he sipped his ale. "Damn, girl, you can throw 'em back with the best."

She held her glass up to the bartender. "Not really. I just needed something to dull the edge a bit."

The bartender replaced the empty glass with a fresh one.

Justin patted her on the back. "Relax, will you? You're smart, funny, and attractive, what's not to like? I've been chasing girls a long time. If they're interested, let them act like fools to get your attention. You just be yourself."

She sipped her wine and gave him a suspicious look.

Thomas and Wendy arrived as Andi and Justin were finishing their drinks. Justin said hello, then got to work with his camera. Thomas and his wife insisted on escorting Andi around the room and introducing her to everyone they knew. She was slightly buzzed by the wine and feeling a little less overwhelmed by so many new faces. She liked the people she met. They were more her age and education level and their conversation more stimulating. Andi's only exposure to the locals thus far had been Thursday nights at The Bottom Dollar, which consisted mostly of the younger population and folks out for some fun.

Most of the participants at the auction were older established men and women, more like the crowd Andi found at art gallery parties. She was enjoying the night, even though she thought she wouldn't.

She headed toward the auction display to get a look at the items up for bid when she crossed paths with Liz.

"Andi, hi." She was wearing a sundress made of a pale yellow cotton material with a large white flower print.

"Good evening, Liz, it's good to see you."

"Good to see you, too." She was holding the hand of a tall gentleman who looked uncomfortable in the shirt and tie he was wearing. His brown hair was neatly combed to one side and he had a small red spot on his jaw he kept rubbing that looked like a nick from a razor. "Andi, I want you to meet my husband, Buddy McCray." She turned to Buddy. "Honey, this is Andi Connelly. She's the one that works for KCOR I told you about."

Buddy stuck his hand out to Andi with a crooked smile. "Nice to meet you, ma'am."

"It's nice to meet you, too, Buddy, and please call me Andi."

"Well all right, Andi, I sure will," he said with a Southern drawl.

"McCray? Are you by chance related to Charlie McCray?"

"That's my older brother."

"What a small world. Rachel introduced us. Very nice man."

"Yep, my brother's one of the best."

"Andi, will you be at Rachel's surprise party?" Liz asked.

"Yes, I wouldn't miss it. Charlie e-mailed the invitation so I could send it to everyone at the office. So far, I think it's been kept secret from her, which is a very hard thing to do."

The wheels were turning in Liz's head. She had her suspicions about Andi and Julianna. She would have to make sure Julianna was there, too.

"What do you do, Buddy?" Andi asked.

"I work for the resort. I'm one of the trail masters at the stables."

"I love horses. Unfortunately, they don't love me. My uncle tried to teach me to barrel race as a kid one summer. You might say I had a conflict of interest with a particularly stubborn quarter horse my uncle prized."

He chuckled. "The trick is to let 'em know up front who the boss is."

She laughed. "I think he knew quite well who the boss was, and I have the scar to prove it."

"Have you seen Jules?" Liz asked.

"Yes, she came by and said hello. I think we're going to have a drink together later if she's not too busy."

"I think she'll have time." Liz looked as if she knew something she wasn't willing to share.

Liz saw Julianna head toward them and excused herself and her husband on their way to the bar.

Julianna approached her with a slim well-dressed woman of about fifty. "Andi, there you are. I want you to meet Beverly Tillman."

Andi shook hands with the attractive woman. "Ms. Tillman, it's nice to meet you."

"Beverly is the wife of our executive chef at the ranch and the owner of Tillman Galleries."

Andi was caught off-guard by the introduction.

"I'm pleased to meet you too, Andi. Julianna has told me all about your work. I'd be very interested in seeing what you have if you think you might like to show again. I'm always looking for fresh new talent." Beverly gave her an easy smile.

Andi looked at Julianna. "Yes, well, I haven't done much recently with the move from Chicago and shift in jobs, but I am indeed ready to get back to work with my painting."

Beverly handed Andi her business card. "Here's my card, call me when you have something ready."

"Thank you, Ms. Tillman, I'll keep this handy." Andi held the card up.

"I look forward to seeing your work, young lady." Beverly excused herself and returned to her table.

"How exciting," Julianna said and slipped her arm around Andi's.

Andi wished Julianna would stop touching her the way she did. She made it hard for her to remain platonic with her thoughts. "It's very exciting, but you know I haven't got anything to show but some old charcoal drawings, and they're better off left in their portfolio case."

Julianna looked at Andi earnestly. "I know you don't have much right now, but you said you were looking for inspiration. I thought the idea of a gallery show might help motivate you into trying to paint again. I knew as soon as I told Beverly about your painting of the two women, she'd be interested."

She was so sweet and thoughtful. No one but Andi's family had showed such concern for her talent. She continued to endear herself to Andi's heart whether she meant to or not.

"Thank you for the introduction. I must say it does give me reason to try."

"Well, there you go!" Julianna flashed a sweet smile of accomplishment. "If you'll excuse me, I'll catch up with you in a bit. I have to go get the auction started." She strolled off into the crowd with Andi's gaze glued to her once again.

Andi moved on to the auction tables and looked over the donated items. She placed a bid on several just for fun so she could in good conscience tell Julianna she had participated.

Eventually, she found her way to the wine sampling tables. There she found ten restaurants participating with twenty-five wines. She was impressed with the selection of award-winning vintages the sommeliers chose. For a little competition, the chefs paired their wines with appetizers.

While she enjoyed the samplings, she stole a glance at Julianna, who was doing her best to talk wine with the people around her. She followed Andi's instructions to the letter on tasting and put forth an excellent display of technique.

Around ten o'clock, Andi wandered out to the deck overlooking the top of the mountain. The night was cool and beautiful, with the full moon above casting long shadows from the towering Colorado pines and aspens over the rough open ground of the barren ski runs. She walked to the far side of the deck and leaned on the wooden rail looking up at the star-filled night. She was lost in thought and didn't hear the footsteps that approached. She caught the movement of something white in the corner of her eye and turned her head. It was Julianna, wrapped loosely in a white cashmere cloak. She was carrying two glasses of white wine.

Andi's heart beat faster when she saw her. "Hey, you."

"Hey, yourself. I do believe I owe you a glass of wine." She extended a glass and a smile to Andi. "And I believe you said it was my choice."

"I think you're right." Andi accepted the glass and tried to look into Julianna's eyes, but she looked away.

"And what do we have here?" Andi held the glass up to check the color and consistency in the light, then she put it to her nose. "Let's see…I get apple and some pear. There's a nut, could be almond. And the citrus is definitely lemon. I believe what we have is a pinot grigio."

"You are correct, but then I knew you and your nose would figure it out. Care to guess where it's from?" Julianna was putting her to the test.

"I'll go with the Benton-Lane from Willamette Valley."

Julianna put her hand on her hip. "I don't know how you do it! You're right."

"Like I said, I've had my nose in a lot of wine over the years." Andi offered up her glass for a toast. "And I happened to sample it earlier."

They clanged their glasses together and laughed.

Julianna took a drink and leaned down on the rail next to Andi. "I read Jane Austen's Persuasion."

"And what did you think?"

She pulled her cloak tautly around her frame, breathed in the crisp mountain air, and looked out into the dark of the night. "I thought it was sad. I mean, you have two people who deeply love each other, but because of some ridiculous class barrier, Ann is convinced by Lady Russell that Captain Wentworth isn't good enough for her, and they waste eight years pining for each other." She turned and looked at Andi. "If two people feel that strongly, how could it be so wrong?"

Andi shrugged her shoulders. "The story was written in a time when social status was everything for people with land and money. It just wasn't acceptable to get involved with someone thought to be in a class beneath your own." Andi turned toward Julianna. "It does have a happy ending. Wentworth makes his fortune, and he and Ann do finally declare their love for each other, despite the objections of her family, and live happily ever after."

"Yes, but it shouldn't be that complicated. We love who we love."

"I couldn't agree with you more. If it were only that simple, even in the world we live in today." Andi took a slow drink from her glass.

Julianna looked at her solemnly. "I guess you must understand that better than anyone."

An awkward silence lingered between them.

Andi changed the subject. "How did you do with the auction?"

Julianna breathed a happy sigh. "We won't know the total amount until Monday. Personally, I'm glad it's over. It's for a great cause, but so much work and planning goes into it, at times it's exhausting if not overwhelming."

"I think you did a great job. I enjoyed myself very much tonight, and I think everybody here did, too."

Julianna moved in closer to Andi and leaned against her. She could feel her shiver occasionally from the chill in the night air. She hoped Andi didn't notice her own shakiness, not from the atmosphere, but from the proximity of her body to Andi's.

They stood together in silence simply enjoying each other's

company and finished their wine. When they were done, Andi led Julianna back into the hall.

"Thank you for the drink, the pinot grigio was very good. You're a good student."

She held Andi by the arm. "You're a good teacher. I'd like to pick your brain again sometime. I think I'd like to learn more."

The tension she unknowingly created with every touch was almost too much for Andi. She wanted badly to put her arms around her when they were out on the deck but knew she couldn't. Her scent, the feel of her warm body pressed against Andi's side, her hand on her arm. This girl was torturing her and wasn't even aware of the power she held.

Andi looked at her watch. "I hate to leave such good company, but I should probably go."

"If you can give me a minute, I'll grab my stuff and ride down with you."

"I'll meet you at the door." Andi went to say good night to Thomas and Wendy, who were sitting with friends. She bid good night to Justin, who was packing his gear. Then she made her way through the remaining crowd to the door leading to the gondola for the ride down the mountain.

The two women strolled down the walk to the gondola. The attendant held the door open as they entered the bubble-shaped car and it lifted off on its cable down the mountain. Julianna took the seat next to Andi rather than on the bench across from her. She tried to pull the cloak down to cover her legs from the chill. "This dress is great for a party, but it's not much for warmth."

Andi silently agreed the dress was great, especially on Julianna.

"The sky is magnificent with all the stars," Andi said, looking up into the night.

Julianna pointed toward the silhouette of the mountain ridge in the distance. "I love the way the moonlight bounces off the mountains. You sure don't get those views in the city."

Andi agreed.

Julianna stole a glimpse of Andi while she was admiring the nighttime scenery. The moonlight illuminated the square jaw and perfect nose of Andi's profile and highlighted the soft, smooth skin of her neck. It gave Julianna a surge she didn't expect.

Andi struggled to chat casually during the ride down to the East Village. Every cell of her body yearned for Julianna's touch. When they arrived, the attendant helped them out of the car and they walked to the bridge.

Julianna stopped and turned to face Andi. "I want to thank you again for helping me. I really enjoyed this evening so much more because of what you taught me."

"You're welcome, and it was fun for me, too. I enjoy talking wine whenever I get the chance. I could easily bore you to tears with it."

"I doubt that you would bore me with anything you talked about."

In awkward silence, the two stood in the shadows of the pines.

Julianna broke the silence. "I shouldn't keep you." She approached Andi with an uneasy smile and draped her arms around her neck like she did that night as she was leaving the town house. This time was different, though. This time, she held Andi close, and as she began to let go, her cheek stayed pressed to Andi's. Her lips barely brushed against the edge of her earlobe. Julianna's breath on Andi's neck gave her goose bumps and caused every muscle in her body to go rigid.

Julianna trembled in Andi's arms. A flood of heat burst within her. She slowly brushed her cheek down Andi's jaw line until she was face to face with her. She felt Andi's chest rise and fall faster and faster against her own. She didn't know what she was doing, and she was helpless to stop it. Her brain screamed to her, this is another woman, but something deep inside wouldn't listen. She liked having Andi's arms around her. She felt her own heart beat hard and her breath come fast; no one had ever made her feel like this.

Andi's entire body was in overdrive and her head was spinning. The energy created by Julianna's body pressed into her own shot right to her spine. She couldn't stop the overpowering urge to kiss the beautiful woman in her arms this time. She softly brushed her lips over Julianna's. When she didn't retreat from her, Andi slowly closed her mouth around Julianna's.

At first Julianna was still, but then with surprising desire, she kissed Andi back. She allowed Andi to explore the corners of her mouth and tease her with her tongue. Julianna released a gentle sigh and tightened her hold on Andi. Their bodies fit together perfectly.

Julianna was lost in the moment, feeling as if all that mattered was here and now. She kissed Andi hard and deep. It wasn't until Andi began to move her hands up Julianna's back that she suddenly stiffened, grabbed Andi's shoulders, and held her at arm's length. Her face was covered with fear and her eyes were glassy with tears. Andi was paralyzed by Julianna's expression.

"I have to go," Julianna whispered. She let go of Andi and hurried across the footbridge, disappearing into the dark of the village.

Andi stood motionless. The woman she was so hopelessly in love with was repulsed by her. She smacked herself in the forehead with the palm of her hand and growled, "Stupid!"

She quickly made her way down the sidewalk to the parking lot and found her vehicle. She unlocked the door, tossed her bag in the passenger seat, jumped in, and slammed the door behind her. She grabbed the steering wheel of the Escape with both hands and banged her head against the top. "How could I have been so stupid? If I had just kept my feelings in check…"

She snatched up her handbag and fumbled around for her phone. When she found it, she speed dialed Desi.

A sleepy voice answered. "Girl, do you know what time it is here?"

"Desi, I fucked up!" There was desperation in her voice.

Desi woke up quickly. "Whoa, whoa, what happened? You all right? Where are you?"

Andi's voice relaxed. "I'm all right. I'm in my SUV. I just left that charity party of Julianna's." Andi ran her hand through her hair.

"What exactly did you fuck up?"

"Des, I kissed her." Andi covered her face with her hand.

"Who?"

"Julianna, Des, I kissed Julianna."

Desi laughed. "Why is that so horrible? That's great. You've been goofy over that chick ever since you met her." Desi held back a snicker. "So did she slap you or what?"

"No, nothing like that." Andi paused. "Surprisingly, she was into it at first, but then everything went to hell in a hand basket. She pushed me away and ran off." Andi rubbed her forehead with her fingertips. "Desi, you should have seen the look on her face. She was horrified."

"Was she drunk?"

"Desi! I would never take advantage of someone like that."

"Were you drunk?"

"No. We both had a few drinks, but neither one of us was drunk."

"I'm just asking."

Andi took a deep breath. "She knew what she was doing. It just freaked her out."

"Listen, she kissed you back, right?"

"Yeah."

"Okay. If she wasn't drunk, then she must have some kind of feelings for you. Doesn't sound to me like she goes around kissing just any pretty girl that comes her way."

Andi calmed down and started to think. "I guess you could be right." She held her head up with her hand. "I'm so stupid. I know better than to mess with straight girls. It always ends badly."

"Andi, baby, hold up. Stop beating yourself up. You're not stupid and I know I'm right about this girl. If you ask me, the ball is in her court."

"How so?"

"She sent you signals and you responded, you kissed her. I think your intentions are clear, you're interested. Now it's her turn to let you know yea or nay."

Andi sank down in her seat. "From the look on her face, I'd have to go with nay."

"Give it some time. The girl needs to let it sink in, then she'll let you know."

"Desi, how are you so sure about all this?"

"Call it intuition."

"Intuition my ass."

"Listen, girl, you got to pick yourself up, dust yourself off, and go on."

"I'm getting tired of dusting myself off."

"Please don't dwell on this."

"I can't promise I won't." Andi hung up the phone and tossed it in her bag. She sat in the cold SUV thinking about what Desi said and trying to make it fit with the encounter at the bridge. She could still feel Julianna's mouth on her own and taste her lipstick on her lips. She lifted her fingertips to her lips and traced them lightly.

She looked at her reflection in the rearview mirror. "I won't do this to myself. I can't get caught up in someone's games again." She started the Ford and drove off into the night.

Chapter 11

Wednesday morning, Julianna returned to her office from a meeting. She closed the door behind her and walked around her desk, dropping her legal pad on top. She stood and looked around her office. It appeared smaller than it really was because of the amount of materials she had accumulated since taking over the marketing responsibilities for the resort's restaurants.

She barely had room for the desk and two chairs, two file cabinets, and two shelves hanging on the wall. Surrounding the furniture were stacks of mocked-up menus and art boards for the restaurants. The shelves were piled with file folders filled with past and present project information, old binders jam-packed with color slides, and newspaper clippings and articles from an array of publications, all pertaining to the food and beverages offered by the resort.

She had very few personal items displayed. On the desk next to the computer was a picture of her family and on a shelf were two pictures of her with friends and coworkers. On the wall was a single piece of artwork, a poster from the Taste of Snow Cap, the first event she organized when she took over restaurant marketing. It was matted and framed along with an article on the event from the local paper. And in one corner, a pair of skis and poles stood upright.

She thought about how nice it would be to have an office the size of Andi's. Once again, Andi had found her way back into the forefront of Julianna's mind, regardless of how hard she tried to fend her off. Andi was even beginning to inhabit such innocuous thoughts as office space.

She turned and faced the large window behind her desk that looked out over the base of Snow Cap Mountain at the East Village. From her office, she could see the gondola house at the base of the mountain. Summer visitors with their bicycles were being transported to the top of the mountain for an easy ride down along roads that crisscrossed the snowless ski runs. To the far left of her view, she could see the walkway from the gondola house and the edge of the footbridge where just a few nights before she had kissed Andi.

She leaned her head against the glass and closed her eyes as she lavished the intimate moment with Andi in her mind. She recalled the sweet sensual fragrance of her skin, the softness of her warm moist lips, and the lingering passion of her kiss. She could almost feel her all over again. Tears escaped her eyes and dampened her eyelashes when Andi's enchanting blue eyes flashed in her memory.

Her mood immediately turned sour. It was all a mistake. She couldn't be in love with another woman. Was it really love or forbidden lust that excited her? She could lose everyone and everything in her life if she were to pursue these feelings that stirred deep inside her.

She had never felt this way about anyone before. It was all so confusing. She asked herself, could she be running away from the very thing she had been running toward all along? Was this really who she had been looking for? She had no answers, it was all too complex.

She was so lost in her thoughts that she didn't hear the knock on the door. When she didn't answer, the door opened slightly and the voice in the hall announced, "Mail call." It was Liz. She opened the door farther and saw the back of Julianna's head. "Jules, do you want your mail?"

Julianna spun around when she heard Liz and tried to hide her wet, red eyes.

Liz stepped in and closed the door. "Hey, are you okay?" She dropped the mail on the desk and sat in the chair in front of the desk.

Julianna tried to clear the lump in her throat. "Yes, I'm fine."

Liz looked skeptical. "I think you're feeding me a line of crap." She sat back and crossed her legs. "You didn't return my calls on Sunday. Yesterday, you quarantined yourself in your office all day, now I find you staring out the window in tears. That doesn't sound fine to me. Is it David?"

Julianna sat at her desk. "No, it has nothing to do with him. He's fine, he's still out of town," she said nonchalantly and wiped her eyes. "I guess I'm just feeling a little overwhelmed."

"Overwhelmed?"

"Yeah, I've had a lot going on lately." She leaned on the desk. "I over-trained for the trail run and at the same time put in long hours to get the auction together. It was all very time-consuming and stressful."

Liz wasn't buying Julianna's excuse. She had seen her more deeply involved with work and multitasking in the past, and it didn't get to her like this. In fact, she seemed to thrive on it. "Jules, I don't want you to take this the wrong way, but I have to ask." She paused. "Is there something going on between you and Andi Connelly?"

Julianna's brow tensed and she pursed her lips. "I don't know what you're talking about, Liz. We worked together, that's all."

"Come on, Jules, it's me, your best friend. I think I know you better than anyone. Whatever is going on, I'm here for you."

Julianna's face went blank. She was dying to get the emotional weight off her shoulders, but she chose to keep it locked inside.

Liz tried again. "Jules, I saw you two on the deck at the mountain house the other night. You were very cozy, and if I'm not mistaken, you left together."

"We were only talking, and I was cold standing out there in that little cocktail dress."

"You also act differently when Andi's around, almost giddy." Liz continued to make her case. "And while you were working with her, that's all you talked about. It was Andi this and Andi that."

Her brow narrowed again. "Liz, what are you trying to say?"

Liz threw her hands up. "Something's bothering you and you won't tell me, but I have a pretty good idea what it is. I just wanna help."

Julianna looked her in the eyes and sat silent for a moment, then dropped her head down. "All right, yes, something happened between me and Andi." She raised her head slowly. "We kissed," she said softly, then covered her face with her hands, afraid of Liz's reaction.

"And?" Liz asked calmly.

Julianna dropped her hands on the desk and raised her eyebrows. "And? And it's wrong, Liz! I don't even know how it happened. We rode down in the gondola together, and I thanked her for the wine lessons. The next thing I know, we're standing at the bridge in a lip lock. Then I panicked and ran away like a scared little girl."

"Who kissed who first?"

She sat back in her chair. "Does it really matter?" she asked in a flustered tone.

"Yes, it does."

"I think she kissed me first, but I kissed her back, and the worst part is I enjoyed it!"

Liz grinned at her friend.

"What? Why do you look like the cat that just ate the canary?"

Liz threw her arms in the air again. "Thank God you finally feel something for somebody."

Julianna was bewildered by Liz's display. "Would you care to explain that?"

"Jules, since you and David have been together, you just seem to go through the motions, it's like you just settled for someone." She pointed at the pictures on the shelf. "My God, you don't even have a picture of him in your office. You have one of me, but not of him." Liz took a deep breath. "And before David, look at how many guys you dated, or should I say auditioned? Not one ever turned out to be good enough for you, and you've been out with some exceptional men, I might add."

"David is exceptional," Julianna said weakly. "He's handsome, well educated, and has a good job. Some women would say he's perfect."

"Yeah, perfect for your father."

She frowned at Liz's sarcasm.

"He's exactly the kind of guy your father would have you marry. He fits the description to a T. And I think you've settled on a frat boy to make your parents happy."

Julianna stood and put her hands on the desk. "Liz, how can you say that? I don't live my life seeking my parents' approval. You of all people should know that."

"Maybe not, but the point is your head keeps shopping for someone that will please everyone, and your heart keeps returning them because they're the wrong fit." Liz was proud of her analogy. "You always have an excuse for dumping the guys you date. I imagine you eventually will with David, too."

"And that makes me a lesbian?"

"Not necessarily, but I get the impression that deep down you want something different than what's expected of you."

"Well, that certainly would be different."

"You get this curious little glimmer in your eyes when something grabs your attention, and boy does it jump when you look at Andi. Admit it, you have feelings for her. I'm guessing they're starting to run pretty deep if they're weighing that heavy on your mind and causing you tears."

Julianna sat back down and rubbed her forehead with the palms of her hands. "Honestly, I don't know what I have for her." She looked over at Liz. "I've never felt this way about anybody. I'm happier when I'm with her than I am with the man I'm dating, or anyone else for that matter. It's so damned confusing because I'm not supposed to feel this way about a woman." She put her head facedown on the desk.

"How does she feel?"

"I don't know. She kissed me like she was interested."

"Have you talked to her since Saturday?"

Julianna got up from her chair and looked out the window. "No. She may not wanna talk to me after the way I treated her.

She probably thinks I'm a freak. Anyway, I wouldn't know what to say."

"How about the truth?"

She spun around. "How can I tell her the truth when I'm not even sure what the truth is? Hell, I haven't even been honest with her about David. As far as I know, she thinks I'm single. When she finds out about him, I'm sure it won't sit well."

"Then you should decide what it is you want. If it's not David, then you need to be truthful with him and let him go. When you're free, you'll be able to sort your feelings out with a clear mind."

"And if it's Andi, then what?" Tears welled in her eyes again.

"I think that telling her you feel something but are confused is a start. I'm sure she'll understand that." Liz handed her a tissue. "I can see the pain this is causing you. You have to make your decisions for you and no one else." Liz got up and hugged her.

"What if this is all just a game to her? What if after she gets what she wants, she throws me aside?"

"I don't think she's that type. If she were, she would have been on the phone to you already trying to make her move. I think if she has feelings for you, they're genuine and she probably knows you're struggling with this. Maybe she's waiting for you to make the next move."

Julianna folded her arms and thought about Liz's analysis. "She has been very gracious and unassuming around me. She doesn't act like she's on the hunt. You know, like she's playing games to get me in bed." A small surge spiked in her chest at the thought of being in bed with Andi.

"Maybe she should. It worked like a charm for Buddy and now look at me, I'm an old married woman." Liz winked at her.

Julianna smiled back.

"Seriously, Liz, this whole thing could turn my life into a house of cards. My family would permanently disown me. It would be ten times worse than what they did to me when I moved out here. I don't think I could handle that. And how would the people here treat me? You said it yourself. They all think I'm a man-eating machine. How messed up would I look?"

"You worry too much about what everybody else thinks. It's your life and you only get to live it once. You've heard all the clichés, live life to its fullest, et cetera, et cetera." Liz got up from the chair. "You should think about how Andi feels, too. If she's interested, and I think she is, she's not going to play the fool and wait around forever for you to decide if you wanna take a chance."

"I would never try to make her look like a fool."

"I know you wouldn't, you have a good heart." Liz walked to the door.

Julianna sat back in her chair. "Thanks, I guess I did need a little therapy."

"I'm glad you decided to let me help. Call Andi," Liz said on her way out the door.

Julianna tapped her pen on the desk. "I'll think about it."

All day long, Julianna tried to get some work done, but she couldn't stop thinking about the turmoil in her life. She knew she owed it to Andi to talk to her. She still didn't know what to say, but she thought maybe Liz was right, start with the truth, regardless of how ambiguous or screwed up it seemed.

Around three o'clock, she finally picked up her cell phone. The call would be quick, no in-depth conversation. She would ask Andi if she would like to meet somewhere to talk.

She took a deep breath and hit the call button. On the second ring, Andi answered.

"Julianna, how are you?" Her voice was cheerful but tentative.

"Hi, Andi. I'm fine. How is your day going?"

"It's busy, as usual. What's up?"

"I was wondering if you might like to get together and... talk. I think we need to discuss some things, you know, kind of clear the air. I mean, I just don't feel right leaving this hanging..."

"That's fine, I don't have a lot of time, but I'll be in Breckenridge this evening if you wanna meet me at the Rec Center after work." Andi's tone was cool.

"Okay, I'll come right from the office. I'll see you then." She hung up and wanted to crawl under her desk in a ball.

She put her hand over her mouth. "What does she think of me? I kiss her, then I run from her. What kind of adolescent game must she think I'm playing?" She glanced at her watch. "You have exactly two hours and fifty minutes to come up with something to say to her that won't make you sound like you're totally confused or a scared little girl."

She managed to make up an outline in her head of things she wanted to say. She would start by telling her that the kiss was a mix of excitement and fear. Then she would explain that she wasn't sure where this was going, but she wanted—no needed—to find out. She also wanted to reassure Andi that she didn't play games. She would tell her about David and that she would put an end to the relationship so they could start with a clean slate. She couldn't guarantee anything as far as the future goes, but she would be honest with her. This was too important not to try.

At 4:30, she gathered her things and walked to the lobby to see Liz before she drove to Breckenridge. Her insides were in knots.

"Did you call her?" Liz asked in a low tone.

"Yes. I'm on my way to Breck to meet her."

Liz's face lit up with excitement. "What did you say?"

"Not much over the phone. I told her we needed to talk and asked if she would meet me."

Liz clapped her hands together quietly. "Good. Do you know what you're going to tell her?"

Julianna tightened her grip on her bag. "Sort of. The only thing I have is the truth, like you suggested, and perhaps she might give me some time. I just hope I don't lose my nerve...Liz, I'm not rushing this, am I?"

"Jules, I think you already knew what you wanted Saturday night. Now you just have to go after it. Take your time. Things will work themselves out."

Julianna took a deep breath. "I'd better go. I don't want to keep her waiting." She walked toward the elevator.

"Call me later."

"I will," she said as she stepped onto the elevator.

Julianna pulled into the parking lot of the Rec Center a little before five and spotted Andi sitting on the stone wall near the entrance. She was playing with an iPod. Julianna's heart pounded. Andi was so cute in her blue workout pants and long-sleeved white T-shirt. Her blond hair was down and she had one side tucked behind an ear. Just seeing her made Julianna smile.

Andi put the iPod away and greeted Julianna as she sat next to her. "Hi."

"Hi, thanks for meeting me."

"I'm glad you called." Andi nervously played with the shoulder strap on her gym bag.

Julianna sat quietly, concentrating on what she wanted to say. The wind blew her hair gently across her face while she sat.

Andi wanted to reach over and brush it back but remained motionless.

Julianna spoke slowly. "I think we need to talk about what happened at the bridge Saturday night. I've been thinking about it all week and still don't know how it happened." She stole a glance at Andi from the corner of her eye, looking for a reaction.

Andi's face was serious.

"I enjoy talking to you, and that night at your place was a lot of fun. You also made work on the commercials seem easy, despite Susan's demands and temper tantrums." She felt herself starting to ramble.

"I enjoy your company, too, Julianna, but you can cut to the chase with this. Neither one of us expected that kiss to happen, but it did. We can't change that." Her mood was growing dismal, but she tried to hide the hurt inside. It didn't help that she already had the preconceived idea that Julianna had come there to reject her and she was dreading the speech.

Julianna turned to faced her. "You're right." She saw the pain beginning to burn in Andi's eyes. It unnerved her and her thoughts became scrambled. She wished she had written down the points she wanted to make.

"Andi, I...." She started to stutter. "I-I..." Andi's eyes sharpened and it caused her to choke on her words. "Andi,

Saturday night was…I mean, I'm not." She stopped. Her thoughts were running together and she couldn't seem to complete a sentence. "Oh, God." She wiped her forehead with her hand. "Andi, I don't…I can't…"

Andi had heard enough. She got up and grabbed her bag. "Let me fill in the blanks for you, Julianna, I've heard this speech before. Saturday night was a mistake. You're not like that." Her voice cracked. "We had a few drinks and got caught up in the moment, that's all." Her chest heaved when she took a breath. "You don't want to hurt me, but you can't do this." Andi stopped and looked at her. "Is that what you're trying to say?" Her words were cold and filled with pain.

Tears welled in Julianna's eyes and she tried to stop her bottom lip from trembling by holding it in her teeth. The best she could muster was, "Andi, please let me—"

"Hey, it's all right." She draped the gym bag over her shoulder. "Don't worry about it. I've been through this before. It was one curious kiss, so we'll just leave it at that." The hurt raging inside her intensified with Julianna's tears. She wanted this woman more than she ever wanted anyone, and she was mad at herself for letting it get this bad. She hurried up the walk and disappeared inside the building.

Julianna wanted to follow her inside and explain to her she was all wrong, but she couldn't pull herself together enough not to make a scene inside the busy gym. Instead, she wiped her tears as she hurried back to the BMW and left the lot.

Chapter 12

Andi sat across the table from Justin at Griffin's Bakery on an overcast Thursday morning, rotating the paper cup containing a vanilla latte. Bo's parents recently added a coffee bar to the shop to keep pace with the likes of Starbucks and Dunkin' Donuts. For the shop, it was proving to be a boon in business. For Bo, as she described it, it was a pain in her ass, just one more thing for the customers to complain about.

Her confrontation with Julianna at the Rec Center was all but gone from Andi's mind. At first, it occupied her thoughts continuously, but with the debut of the morning show growing closer, she forced herself to focus on the job and push Julianna far back in her memory banks.

"What are you going to do about Chip and his mouth?" Justin asked. "He hasn't even met the new co-host you and Thomas hired, and he's already spewing insults about her."

Andi swallowed a mouthful of latte. "I've tried to be sympathetic to his and Buster's situation. I know they've been the princes of 'Sunrise Summit' since its inception, but they don't seem to get it that the show is no longer a local cable access thing. They don't have carte blanche anymore, and it's killing them."

"I know those guys and they won't let up, at least Chip won't." Justin scooped a blob of whipped cream from the top of his café mocha with his finger and jammed it in his mouth.

"I run the show and I have the network and Thomas behind

me. They may find themselves unemployed before it's all over."

"Would you really do that?" He seemed surprised at Andi's hard line suggestion.

"If they continue to run their mouths and undermine my authority, they'll leave me no choice. I won't have them disrupting the rest of the crew and making me look like I don't have control." She looked Justin in the eyes. "This is just between us."

He put his hands up. "Hey, mum's the word for me. I love my job and I'm not about to jeopardize it for those two assholes. I don't get why you don't just dump them anyway and get all new blood."

"I had that discussion with the higher-ups, but they wanted to retain the flavor of the show. Assholes they may be, but they have recognition with the locals and returning tourists." Andi looked out the front window. "I plan to talk to them separately one last time. If attitudes don't change and they can't work with Brenda Fernandez, they're out."

"And it would be justified," Justin said. He noticed the change in Andi's demeanor. She seemed distracted at times and her sense of humor was thin. He brushed it off as the stress of everything catching up to her. "Hey, let's change the subject. Are you going to William's dog and pony show over in Vail?"

Andi wrinkled her nose. "I have to. He's got a couple of corporate executives coming in from New York to back him up with his sales pitch, and Thomas plans to introduce me to the PR and marketing people that will be there. I'd rather just go home and soak in my Jacuzzi." She leaned her elbows on the table. "Thomas did give me a pass on the cocktail party after, though."

"You're gonna pass up free food and booze? That's a shame." He shook his head.

"It's been a long week, and I just want some quiet time." She rubbed the back of her neck.

"Just stay long enough to have a drink with me." He put his hands together like he was praying. "Please, please, say you'll stay for the cocktail party?"

Andi gave him a disapproving look. "You're as bad as my brother, Tim. You think you can bat those long lashes at me, with that big goofy grin, and I'll just melt right in front of you." She sat up straight. "You only want me there so I can be your designated driver."

He batted his eyes again at her.

She laughed. "Oh, for Pete's sake, stop it! I'll stay for a drink, but that's all."

He pumped his fist in the air. "Yes!"

Andi folded her arms in front of her. "Wendy's been after me to get out and socialize more, and I guess I should start getting familiar with the other resorts and businesses in the area. Snow Cap is not the only one out there."

"Yes, but Julianna doesn't work for any of the others." Justin leaned back in anticipation of a strike.

Andi looked at him with total surprise. "What does she have to do with anything?"

"Really, Andi, work is just an excuse for you to keep yourself locked up in the office. You're afraid you'll run into Julianna, that's why you haven't been going out."

She looked at him blankly.

He gave her a devilish grin. "I knew something was going on with you two."

"There's nothing going on with us two," Andi said. "She made that abundantly clear to me." She looked at him hesitantly.

Justin's eyes opened wide and he rubbed his hands together. "This sounds like a scandalous bit of information. Tell Dr. Barnes all about it."

She threw a napkin at him. "It's not funny." She leaned over the table and lowered her voice. "This...thing...happened between us. And I think I scared her. And she sort of told me how she felt about it. And the moral of the story is...I'm an idiot."

"What happened?"

Andi hesitated again. "This goes no further than right here." She tapped the table with her finger. "I don't want rumors circulating about her because of me."

He nodded in agreement.

"The night of the auction, we got kind of close. On the ride down in the gondola, I thought I was picking up vibes from her that led me to think maybe she was interested in me. So I took the next step and I kissed her. A few days later, she tried to give me the I'm-not-gay-I-can't-do-this speech. And that's that."

He cringed. "That's tough. I really thought she was into you."

A voice spoke from behind Andi. "Straight girls always get cold feet when you get too close." Bo walked up with a tub of dirty dishes tucked under her arm. "Or they go on a rejection rampage if they think somebody might find out about their sexual escapades."

Andi looked surprised to hear Bo's voice.

Bo sat in the empty chair at the table with them. "Sorry, I didn't mean to eavesdrop. I overheard the end of the conversation, and well, been there, done that, ya know?"

"It's all right."

Bo looked at Andi with delight. "Funny, I had a feeling you were family, but I wasn't sure until I saw you that night at The Bottom Dollar. Don't get me wrong, you were a hard one to figure out. The first time you walked in here, I certainly didn't pick you up on my gaydar."

Andi laughed. "I don't try to hide anything."

"Then you shouldn't hide from this girl. The next time you see this chick, give her a nod and move on. She'll get the message that it's cool and things are done and over."

"She's right," Justin said.

"Yeah, well, I have a job to do and no time to play games with her or any other woman for that matter." Andi looked at her watch. "I think we better get back to the office before Thomas notices we're missing."

They picked up their cups and headed for the door.

"See ya round, Bo." Andi patted her on the shoulder.

"What about tonight?" Bo asked.

Andi looked at her with uncertainty.

Bo picked up the tub from the table. "Locals' night? The Bottom Dollar?"

Andi frowned. "I...I don't think so, not tonight."

Behind her back, Justin gave Bo the okay sign that they would be there.

"Just come for one drink, I still owe you that beer I promised."

"I'll think about it." Andi gave her a not-so-encouraging smile.

Bo stood at the end of the pool table rubbing the tip of her pool cue with a blue cube of chalk. Her green eyes lit up when she caught sight of Andi and Justin coming through the back door. She lifted her hand and gave a wave with two fingers when they looked her way.

Andi walked over and squeezed Bo around the waist with one arm. "Hey, girl."

Bo squeezed her back and, being a head taller, rested her chin on the top of Andi's head. "Hey back. Thought you weren't coming tonight?"

Andi hopped up on an empty barstool. "There was no way Justin was going to let me stay home tonight. The man can be a real pest sometimes."

"And I happily resemble that remark," he said from behind her.

"You look really great," Bo said. "Hey, I want you to meet my girlfriend." She turned around and took the hand of the woman with the geisha tattoo encompassing her upper right arm. "Andi, this is Sabrina." She pointed at Andi. "Babe, you remember Andi? I introduced her out on the patio one night."

The dark-haired girl nodded with a small smile and held out her hand. "Nice to meet you again, Andi."

Andi shook her hand. "Nice to meet you, too, Sabrina."

Bo leaned her pool stick against the chair at the table. "Let me get a round of drinks. What'll ya have?"

They requested a beer, and Bo darted off to the bar.

She returned with four bottles in hand. She passed off one each to Andi and Justin and one to Sabrina for which she was rewarded with a small kiss. Bo put her arm around Sabrina's shoulders, held up her bottle, and said, "Cheers."

They returned the sentiment and drank.

Justin couldn't resist engaging Bo in a game of eight ball while Andi sat by and watched.

She raised her bottle to her mouth to take a drink but stopped when a female voice very close to her ear said, "You're looking especially beautiful tonight."

She looked in the direction of the voice; it was Val standing next to her in a tight gray T-shirt and faded jeans. Her hazel eyes had a sharp glint to them.

"Hi, Val. You're quite dapper yourself," Andi said with a smile.

Val moved closer. "So how goes it in TV land?"

"Everything's going great."

"Good, glad to hear it…and how are you adjusting to life in the mountains?"

"I lived through the altitude sickness, so it's all good."

"Nasty stuff." Her gaze roamed up and down Andi's form, stopping at the undone buttons of her navy and white-striped rugby shirt. "From what I see, you've recovery nicely."

Andi smirked at Val's blatant display of flirtation. "Thank you for the compliment…I think."

Val leaned an elbow on the rail next to Andi. "My pleasure, beautiful."

Andi pitched her a sardonic look.

Bo looked over at Val from across the pool table and acknowledged her with a nod. Val returned the nod. The exchange was less than cordial between the two women.

Val refocused her attention on Andi. "Looks like you could use another beer."

Andi set the empty bottle on the table next to her. "I think I'm all right for now."

Val held up her own bottle and looked through the dark brown glass. "Well, I certainly could use another one and I did promise to buy you a welcome to town drink. I'll go get us two more."

Before Andi could protest, Val was headed toward the bar.

Bo walked over after she finished her shot and wrapped her arm around Sabrina. "Ya know, Andi, I don't wanna get in your business, but a word of advice about that one." She leaned her pool stick in the direction of where Val had been standing. "She's a snake, to put it in no uncertain terms."

Sabrina agreed.

A knowing smile rose on Andi's face as she crossed her arms and leaned on the table. "Oh, I know her type. Chicago is full of them. When I've had enough, I'll cut her off," Andi said.

A crooked smile ran the width of Bo's mouth as she took a drink from her bottle. "Something tells me this is going to be good." Bo set her bottle down and walked back to the pool table to take her next shot.

"Here you go, little lady." Val set a fresh beer on the table next to Andi.

"Thank you, Val, that's very nice of you." She gave her a curt smile.

She picked up the bottle and held it to her mouth to take a long drink when Julianna appeared in her line of sight. She was looking directly at Andi from the bar. The expression on her face nearly broke Andi's heart. She looked forlorn and hurt, much like an abandoned child. Andi wanted to go to—no, she wanted to run to—Julianna's side. She wanted to wrap her arms around Julianna's small frame and take the pain from her face. Then she remembered their meeting outside the Rec Center and decided the abandoned child look was part of the game. Andi bolted from her then, and now she was attempting to draw her back in with a look of distress and hurt.

"So what do you think?" Val asked.

"Huh? What? I'm sorry, Val, I didn't hear what you asked me." She shook her head to clear her thoughts and looked at Val.

"I asked if you'd like to get out of here and go someplace where we can talk."

Andi looked back at the bar, but Julianna was gone. She quickly scanned the crowd, but she was nowhere in sight.

"You're wasting your time," Val said.

"What are you talking about?"

Val motioned toward the bar with her head. "Stevens. I saw you watching her. She's one angry straight girl, and she takes great offense at women making passes at her. Trust me, I know. I tried." She took a long drink from her beer.

"Do you hit on every woman you see?"

Val grinned slyly. "Let's just say I don't miss many opportunities." She shrugged her shoulders. "What can I say, I like the ladies, and I especially like you." She leaned in closer. "I'm sure we could be good together."

Andi had heard enough of Val's lines. She was particularly offended at her comments about Julianna. The thought of Val's hands on Julianna made her skin crawl.

"Val, I think you need to back off. I'm not interested in becoming your next conquest. I don't play here-today-gone-tomorrow, wham-bam-thank-you-ma'am, or any other games you have up your sleeve."

Val gave her a calculated grin. "Ah, a nester."

Andi's eyes narrowed. "Excuse me?"

"You know, a nester. A lesbian that looks for someone to nest with. The old lesbian urge to merge. I guess in Chicago you called them U-Haul lesbians. I'm sure you've heard the joke, what does a lesbian bring on a second date?"

"I am not, nor have I ever been, a U-Haul lesbian."

Val held her hands up. "Hey, I was just joking. It's okay if that's what you like. It's not my thing, but—"

"There's nothing wrong with wanting to settle down and have a home and a family with someone you love."

Val's gray eyes mellowed. "Is that what you want, Andi? A home and a family?"

Andi looked back at the place at the bar Julianna had occupied. "Yes, I do, very much."

Val's voice softened. "Then that's my wish for you." She touched Andi on the shoulder in a reassuring manner. "Just be careful who you crush on. Stevens is not one for you to play with."

Andi picked up on the warning in Val's eyes. "I know the golden rule…no straight girls."

Val patted Andi on the back. "Good luck." She extended her hand. "Friends?"

Andi took her hand. "Friends."

"Well, friend, I'm gonna wander over to the jukebox and see what kind of action awaits me over there." She raised her eyebrows.

Andi laughed. "Geez, you never let up."

"I'll let up when I'm dead," Val said as she strolled away.

Bo laughed. "I liked the wham-bam line."

Andi covered her mouth. "Did you guys hear that?"

"Yeah, you brought her down nicely. My hat is off to you." Bo bowed in front of Andi.

"Oh, quit already." Andi laughed and hopped off the barstool. "I think I'll visit the little girl's room." Something inside moved her to the spot where she had seen Julianna near the bar.

From there, she walked through the crowd slowly, looking from table to table, group to group. She had no idea what she would say or do if she did find her. That something inside just wanted to see her once more, but Julianna was nowhere to be found. She returned to her barstool when her head finally convinced her heart Julianna was gone.

From a booth in the corner, Julianna sat with a group of friends. She spotted Andi making her way through the room full of people. Her face was pensive and her beautiful light blue eyes searching.

Julianna's heart jumped in her chest at the thought of Andi pushing through the horde of customers in search of her. Reality interrupted her fantasy when the dark-haired man next to her slipped his arm around her and pulled her in tight. At that moment, she was thankful she was sitting in the corner and faced away from the bar.

Andi couldn't possibly see her unless she walked right up to the booth where they sat. The wonderful sensation she experienced when she saw Andi in the crowd was gone, replaced by a sinking feeling of hopelessness.

Chapter 13

Thomas and Andi sat in a booth at The Salt Creek Steakhouse in Breckenridge, enjoying lunch away from the office. Andi had been non-stop with work on the morning show and other projects William brought in for over a month, and Thomas thought by taking her out to lunch, she might relax a bit.

He appreciated all of her hard work and dedication but was beginning to worry that she was spending too much time in the office and neglecting her own life. When he suggested she take a day off, her only reply was that she would when "Sunrise Summit" was on the air and running smoothly.

Of course, Thomas knew that would be months down the road. He didn't dare mandate that she take a break because he knew it would fall on deaf ears, so he kept a close eye on her schedule and work load. If it got to be too much for her, he would step in, but for now, she seemed to be at her best when it looked like she was working in a pressure cooker.

"I'll have to remember this place. I think my family would enjoy having dinner here when they visit. The food is excellent and they'll be all over the wine list, it's huge." Andi finished off the last of her blackened prime rib sandwich.

"Wendy and I have a date night every Wednesday. This is one of her favorite places."

"I can see why. The food is awesome." She winked at him.

"Thomas," a husky male said from behind Andi. "I hope I'm

not interrupting. I just wanted to say hello."

"David, nice to see you. We missed you at the ski camp auction." Thomas shook the handsome man's hand.

"Sorry I missed it. Quarterly meets, don't you know, and in Cleveland of all places." He was casually dressed in tan slacks, a red and white-striped golf shirt, and brown loafers, and his thick dark hair was perfect.

Thomas looked at Andi. "David, I'd like you to meet Andrea Connelly, my executive producer. Andrea, this is David Gerhart, a golf buddy of mine."

David extended his hand to Andi. "Nice to meet you, Andrea."

Andi accepted his hand with an easy smile. "Hello, David, nice to meet you, too."

"David works for Morgan, Templeton, and Associates. They specialize in resort and community land development," Thomas said.

"How interesting. What are you working on, David?" she asked.

"At the moment, I'm tying up loose ends on the East Village expansion for Snow Cap. I'll be making a short trip to Alaska soon on a consulting assignment."

Andi dropped her smile at the mention of Snow Cap.

"David's fiancée is a client of ours," Thomas said as he placed his napkin on the table.

"Really?"

David spoke up. "Yes, well, she's not my fiancée yet. I can't seem to get her away from the office long enough to make the proposal. Julianna has mentioned your name many times. I think she enjoyed her time working with you immensely."

An unpleasant feeling spread over Andi, and she nearly choked on the iced tea she was drinking. After she cleared her throat, she spoke slowly, "She's very professional. The commercials were a big success, for which she gets a large part of the credit."

"She does work hard. I've been trying to get her to take a vacation, but she's been so busy these last couple of months, we haven't been able to find the time. Now we'll have to wait till I get back from Anchorage."

Andi forced a smile as the word fiancée rolled around in her head like a roulette ball. "I would imagine she'll be thrilled when you do get the chance to pop the question," she said flatly.

David smiled back. "I hope so." He turned to Thomas. "Well, I won't keep you. Again, I just wanted to say hello." He slapped Thomas on the shoulder. "Call me sometime, Thomas, and we'll get out and play eighteen."

"Will do. Take care, David."

He pointed at Andi. "Nice to meet you, Andrea." He made his way out the door with cockiness in his stride.

Andi was stunned. Never a word or a clue was given to make her think Julianna had someone in her life. Surprise quickly turned to resentment when she realized that Julianna's deceit was nothing more than game playing, and she was starting to feel like a fool.

Thomas's voice invaded her thoughts. "Shall we go?"

"Yes, I have a pile of things waiting for me on my desk."

"You really need to slow down, Andi. Take some time to yourself while the weather is good. It won't be long before the cold and the snow will set in up here."

"I have a job to do for you, Thomas, and that's what's important to me right now, but I'll consider what you said." She smiled at him in appreciation.

Chapter 14

Andi finally had her separate talks with Chip and Buster. She knew going in it would be a battle, but she was ready to throw down the pink slips if they persisted. Chip was first in right at nine. He started off defiant, as she expected, but when she informed him this was the end of the road and she was prepared to send him packing, his attitude quickly changed. He no longer resisted the addition of a female co-anchor and agreed the new format was long overdue.

Andi was feeling in control all morning and attributed her mood to the fact that she no longer cared if her decisions offended anyone. She was hired to do a job, and Thomas expected her to get it done using good judgment.

Buster showed up later and was obviously unnerved to find out Chip was not a part of the meeting. When he tried to regurgitate Chip's rants, Andi shot him down, and when the decision to terminate was presented, he crumbled.

He became so overwrought, he was close to tears. He begged Andi not to fire him and pledged full cooperation with everything she asked. He assured her there would be no further disruptions on his part. Andi could now check the two troublemakers off her list. If they relapsed, it would be instant termination.

She finally felt like the executive producer of the station. She looked every bit the part, as well, dressed in her best black Ralph Lauren suit. She wore it specifically for William's sales presentation in Vail later in the day, but it didn't hurt that she looked her professional best when she confronted her problem employees.

Justin appeared in her door shortly after Andi was finished with Buster.

"You must have really socked it to them. I just saw Buster leave the building with his tail between his legs."

Andi looked up from the papers on her desk. "I took care of business is all. They now know where I'm coming from." She paused. "And I hope they're on the same page with me."

"I'd be willing to bet you got through their thick skulls this time."

Andi continued shuffling the papers in her hands. "I hope so. It's very late in the game to have to go out and find new talent for this show."

Justin took a seat in front of her desk. "So will you let me buy you lunch before we head over to Vail?"

She put the papers down. "I was thinking of skipping lunch. I really want to get these reports off to New York before next week."

"Oh, come on, it's Friday, and I wanna show my appreciation for your chauffeuring services this afternoon."

She grinned at him. "You're insufferable."

"Possibly, but my mama did teach me to be considerate."

She shook her head. "Fine, but something simple and no Mexican. I don't want to smell like a taco around the corporate big wigs."

"Have you heard from Julianna lately?"

The smile left her face. "No, and I don't expect to."

He leaned on the desk. "Do you think she'll be there this afternoon?"

Andi looked at him seriously. "I can't imagine why she would. She already knows what we're capable of here, and I doubt she wants to be anywhere near me, too uncomfortable." Her eyes narrowed. "Did I tell you I met her boyfriend?"

His big brown eyes got even bigger. "What?"

She sat back in her chair and folded her hands in her lap.

"Yeah, a few weeks ago, Thomas and I had lunch over in Breck, and this tall dark-headed perfectly handsome guy named David comes to the table to say hello to Thomas." She shifted in her chair. "Thomas introduced him as a golf buddy, then he proceeds to tell me his girlfriend is a client."

"Wow! I'm assuming Julianna never told you about him."

"No, she didn't. I nearly choked on an ice cube when he said he was the boyfriend and, get this, trying to work his way up to fiancé. Oh, and how convenient for her that he just happened to be out of town at the time of our little incident at the bridge."

He rubbed his forehead. "I guess you were right about the straight girl games."

"Yeah, well, it's over and I have more important things to think about." She stood and turned her computer off. "Like lunch. Where are you taking me?"

He grinned as he got up from the chair. "I know just the place."

Andi walked into the meeting room at The Lodge at Vail with Justin right behind her.

He whistled. "Wow, no wonder corporate picked this place. High class all the way."

Andi looked around the large room. Some of the guests were already gathering. She spotted Thomas and William talking to a middle-aged man in a dark blue suit and a woman who looked to be in her fifties, conservatively dressed in a gray suit, at the front of the room. She guessed them to be the New York execs and walked over to meet them.

"Ah, Andi, you're here." Thomas put his hand on her shoulder. "I'd like to introduce you to our guest speakers from the New York office. This is Ron Meyer, director of sales, and Gail Neiman, vice president of development. Thomas looked at Andi. "And of course, this is Andrea Connelly, my executive producer of whom I've been bragging on."

Andi offered her hand with a firm grip. "I'm pleased to meet you both. Thank you for taking the time to help KCOR get off the ground."

Gail smiled. "I'm delighted to be here and I'm most impressed with your work on the morning show. Thomas has kept me up to date with the progress, and I must say I like what I see."

Andi was flattered. "Thank you, Ms. Neiman. I want this show to run like a well-oiled machine."

"I'm sure it will, young lady." She pointed at Brenda Fernandez, who entered the room. "And hiring Ms. Fernandez was an excellent executive decision. I had hoped she would fit in at some level with VPMG. She's a rising star in this business." She smiled at Andi. "I do believe you have yourself quite a future with Vantage Point if the show succeeds." She patted Andi on the shoulder as she walked over to talk with Brenda.

"Thank you again, Ms. Neiman, I'm flattered." Andi's mind wandered momentarily to a move up to the VBN Chicago satellite or possibly even the New York studios.

"Andi, you won't have to give a speech." Thomas's voice brought her back from her daydream. "I'll give the crowd a brief bio on your career, then I'll introduce you. So if you'll just stand and acknowledge the room, that will do." Thomas handed her a folder, then started toward the podium.

"Sure, thanks, boss, whatever you want," she said, having only heard half of what he said.

Justin stood behind Andi and whispered in her ear. "Don't turn around right now."

"Why not?" she whispered back as she looked through the folder containing the presentation outline Thomas had given her.

"Because I don't want you to get pissed off, then you won't be any fun the rest of the day."

Andi had a very good idea why he warned her. She turned slowly and looked over his shoulder. Julianna was standing with a group of people from Snow Cap at the back of the room. She was absolutely breathtaking in a simple white linen blouse and navy skirt with heels. Andi didn't realize what not seeing Julianna for so many weeks had done to her. She thought she was doing quite well at working the gorgeous woman out of her system, but it was just the opposite. One look and her heart and mind filled with desire. She wanted terribly just to be alone with Julianna.

"Damn, I was so sure she wouldn't be here," she said through clenched teeth.

Justin slipped his hands in the pockets of his slacks. "There's only one reason she's here…to see you." He raised his eyebrows when he looked at Andi.

She hugged the folder she was holding. "That's ridiculous. She is most definitely not here to see me."

"I'm serious, Andi. She gave you time to cool off and now she's back on neutral ground to see if you'll talk to her."

"God, Justin, where do you get these psychoanalytical ideations of yours?"

He raised his shoulders and grinned. "I was a psych major before I ended up in art school," he held up a finger, "and I know women."

She rolled her eyes at him. "You are so like my stupid brother."

"Think about it, Andi. You haven't seen or heard from her in over a month and, what a coincidence, she shows up without the boyfriend in tow...again."

"I'm not playing any more games with her, period. Let her call the boyfriend if she wants someone to chase her, I'm done." Andi turned away.

She was set on trying to talk more with Gail Neiman after the presentation. She couldn't allow Julianna to invade her conscience or she would lose her opportunity to lay the groundwork for the future of her career and ticket back to the big city. This was her time to do some networking and who better to schmooze than the VP of development.

Julianna nervously fumbled with the brochure in her hand. "I knew this was a bad idea, Liz."

Liz leaned closer so she could keep her voice low. "Jules, you haven't even been here five minutes. Relax."

"Did you see the look she gave me when she turned around?"

"No, but you don't know that it was meant to be a look aimed at you."

"Yes, I do. My heart about leaped right out of my month when David told me he introduced himself to Andi. She already thinks I'm confused, she probably thinks I'm a liar, as well, for never mentioning him."

"Look, David is gone. You broke up with him so the slate is clean. Isn't that what you wanted?"

"Yes, the breakup was inevitable. It still scares me how badly he reacted. He was so insulted and sarcastic."

"I wouldn't worry about him. He's in Alaska right now. We're here so you can try to get Andi off to the side after the presentation and explain everything to her, and I'm right here for you."

"I know that's the plan, but what if she won't listen? I mean, I'll just make things worse."

Liz faced Julianna and held her by the shoulders. "Stop with all the negativity. It's all going to get worked out, okay?"

Julianna swallowed hard. "Okay. You're right. I need to think positive thoughts."

"Good. Let's go sit down. This thing is going to start soon."

From her seat in the back, Julianna was unnoticeable in the large crowd that had gathered for the presentation. By leaning to the right and looking around the big wavy hair of the woman seated in front of her, she had an unobstructed view of Andi, who was sitting off to the side of the large screen at the front.

The big hair had its usefulness, it afforded Julianna cover should Andi look her way. When the lights dimmed and the video started, Julianna leaned to the right. She couldn't keep her gaze off Andi's profile. Her sweeping blond hair lay gently against her cheek, and when she tucked it behind her ear, her angular jaw line made Julianna weak.

When the lights went back up, she ducked behind the wavy hair and tried to listen to what was being said. She sank down in her seat when Andi stepped up on the platform and faced the audience for Thomas's introduction.

At the end of the KCOR sales pitch, Thomas invited everyone to a cocktail party outside on the patio of The Wildflower Restaurant.

Andi stood with Justin and Brenda while the crowd made its way out of the meeting room and on to the patio for drinks and hors d'oeuvres. The vibration of Andi's cell phone interrupted their conversation. She looked at the screen; it was Rachel. She excused herself and walked into the lobby to take the call. While she talked, she found her way to a sitting area out of the way of the people milling around the lobby.

"Thanks, Rach, if you'll leave the flowers on my desk, I'll get them when I drop Justin off…yeah, we'll be careful…bye now." Andi hung up smiling. "I can't believe those two knuckleheads sent me flowers."

She was about to find her way to the cocktail party when she heard an all-too-familiar voice call her name.

"Andi? Andi Connelly." The female voice was smooth.

She turned slowly. "Elisha." The surprise in her voice did not deflect the tall brunette from wrapping her arms around Andi's neck.

"What a surprise," Elisha said before planting a soft kiss on her cheek.

Andi noticed right away she looked tired, but as always, she hid it well with makeup.

She was casually dressed in a low-cut white V-neck cashmere sweater with tight jeans tucked in black riding boots. She enticed many a glance and stare in the lobby from men and women alike because of her natural beauty.

Andi gently pushed her away and stepped back. "What are you doing here?"

"I was going to ask you the same thing. You look wonderful." Elisha took her in. "You always looked so sharp in a black suit."

She ignored the compliments Elisha tried to pay her. "I live here in Colorado now."

"That explains why your phone was no longer in service when I tried to call a few months ago. When I called your office, they wouldn't tell me a thing."

"What are you doing out here, Elisha?" Andi felt a twinge of anger.

"My father summoned me out here for my cousin's wedding,"

she said dismally.

Andi looked around the lobby. "Where's Ariella?"

"She wasn't invited…purposely, but it doesn't matter, she wouldn't have come anyway. She doesn't enjoy family gatherings." Elisha sat on the edge of a leather sofa and turned the rings on her left hand while she stared out the window.

Andi guessed the diamond to be about five carats set in platinum with another band of the same encircled with a row of smaller diamonds. More than likely, the rings were paid for by Elisha's trust.

"But she's your wife," Andi said.

Elisha looked up at her with sadness in her eyes. "Yes, but my family doesn't like her, and they refuse to accept our marriage, especially my father. He believes she's only with me for the money. She's not like you, Andi. My family loved you, and they still talk about you."

The conversation was beginning to make her uncomfortable. "I'm sorry to hear they don't treat her the same, perhaps in time they'll change."

Elisha sighed. "Perhaps."

"So why did your father summon you to this wedding?"

Elisha had a look of embarrassment that quickly turned to frustration. "He called it an act of discipline. He wanted to discuss my trust fund." She held a handkerchief to her mouth for a moment, then spoke. "You see my expenses have increased since I moved in with Ariella. She buys what she needs with her money, but I've been left to take care of everything else. If I say anything about money, she tells me it shouldn't matter because we're married." She took a deep breath and continued. "In order to have the wedding we wanted, I had to pay for it all up front out of my trust because Ariella claimed she was still waiting for Vanity Fair to pay her for work she had done for them months ago." She sniffed back tears.

Andi didn't want to hear any more. In the back of her mind, she was thinking it was all deserved, but she was not the kind to say so.

Elisha continued with her tale of woe. "My father is upset

that my spending has escalated and is concerned that I'm out of control. He blames Ariella. Now he's threatening to suspend my trust privileges unless I put an end to the relationship."

"That hardly seems fair. It's your life. But if he cuts you off, you still have your salary from the cosmetics company, and Ariella has money, she can pay—"

"But she doesn't," Elisha said. "She's been lying to me since the beginning. I discovered a lot of things once I moved in with her that she didn't own up to until I confronted her about them."

Andi smiled slightly. "You mean like her real name?"

Elisha looked at her with surprise. "You knew?"

"Let's just say I have my sources." She delighted in the smug attitude that rose up inside her.

"Then you know her real background?"

"Uh-huh." Andi sat on the arm of an overstuffed chair and folded her arms.

Elisha looked toward the front entrance. "Oh, Andi, I never thought it would turn out like this. She told me she'd take care of me, but it's the other way around, and it's costing me dearly." Then with tears welling in her eyes, she looked back at Andi. "I'm sorry for the way I treated you. I let the wrong people influence me, and I wasn't thinking clearly about the future." She reached out her hand to Andi, but she refused to accept it. "I never meant to hurt you, honestly."

She gave her ex a hollow look of indifference. "The damage is done, Elisha, but I've mended." She stood to take her leave. "I have no need to relive the past and neither should you. As you can see, I've moved on with a new life and new priorities, just as you have."

Elisha stood and moved toward her, but Andi's body language stopped her from coming any closer. "I need to get back to my business meeting. If you'll excuse me…"

"Andi, I wish the best for you. I hope you find someone who can make you happy."

She looked at Elisha and gave her a slight smile. "Goodbye, Elisha, and good luck." Andi went on her way to the cocktail party. She had no residual emotion over her exchange with her ex, only numbness.

Liz watched Andi's every move while the crowd thinned out. When she saw her heading for the lobby with her phone, she grabbed Julianna's hand. "Now is your chance. She's out in the lobby on the phone. This is it, Jules, time for you to go to work on her."

"Liz, I'm terrified."

"It's now or never. The lobby is the perfect place to talk to her. When she's done with her call, walk right up to her and say we need to get some things straightened out." She corrected herself. "Maybe straight is not a good word to use, but you know what I'm saying." She gave Julianna a push toward the door. "Go." And fanned her away with the back of her hands.

Julianna walked cautiously toward the door to the lobby. When she reached the earth stone tile, she took a deep breath and crossed the threshold that divided the carpet of the meeting room from the tile of the lobby floor.

She made a quick scan of the lobby but didn't see Andi. She walked a little farther over the stone tile and there to the right of the front desk, in a partially secluded area, was Andi with her back to the activity in the lodge, the cell phone pressed to her ear with one hand and her other hand on her hip.

She stepped behind a potted palm tree and fixed her gaze on Andi's form. She was so elegant in the black suit, yet at the same time poised with athletic strength that started with her broad shoulders and ran down through her legs. Julianna was still perplexed by the feelings that ran so deep inside her for Andi, but she couldn't begin to sort them out until she told her exactly how she felt. She was the only one who could help her understand what was happening to her because it was Andi who stirred her emotions.

When Andi hung up, Julianna closed her eyes and said a quick prayer. When she opened them and took a step out of the shadows of the palm to confront the woman she longed for, she was stopped dead in her tracks. A tall, gorgeous brunette with long silky hair approached Andi and wrapped her arms around her shoulders. She muffled a small cry with her hand when she saw the woman kiss Andi's cheek.

Andi still had her back to Julianna so she couldn't see Andi's reaction to the woman, but it all looked rather intimate. Clearly, the two knew each other well. She was convinced that it was too late. She had squandered her chances with Andi and now she had moved on, leaving Julianna in the shadows with a broken heart.

She couldn't watch anymore. She backed away from the palm tree and retreated to the empty meeting room. From there, she hurried to the patio of The Wildflower in search of Liz. She was near panic when she found her at the bar.

"There you are. How did it go? Where's Andi? I thought I would see a happy couple coming to join the party." Liz's voice was filled with enthusiasm.

"Liz, we need to go."

"But I just ordered a margarita…"

She grabbed her by the sleeve. "Now, Liz, I need to go now. I feel like I can't breathe."

Liz's face grew serious. "Jules, what happened? You look like you've just witnessed a murder or something."

"Yeah, or something, like Andi with another woman."

"What? Where?"

"Out in the lobby. This tall completely gorgeous woman walked up and threw her arms around her and kissed her."

"Who is she? Do you know her?"

"I have no idea. I've never seen her before." Julianna began to cry. "You should have seen her, she was so beautiful. I could never compete with someone like that."

"Oh, honey, don't talk that way." Liz wiped Julianna's tears with a cocktail napkin. "Let's get you home. Everything's going to be all right." She wrapped one arm around Julianna's shoulders and they left out a side door.

Andi entered The Wildflower shortly after Julianna and Liz made their exit. She took note of Gail Neiman talking with Thomas at a table near the bar. She walked out to the patio and found Justin at a table near the pool with Brenda and several other employees from the station.

"That was some call, it took you long enough. Did Chip and Buster burn down the station?"

She made a face at him. "Ha-ha funny. Actually, Rachel was calling to let me know those two lunkheads sent me flowers. Then I ran into someone I knew from Chicago, and we had a little chat." She released a sigh. "And now I need a drink. Does anyone else need one?"

Justin followed her to the bar and ordered another round of drinks for their coworkers at the table.

She looked around the restaurant, but there was no sign of Julianna.

"She's not here." Justin reached for an olive and popped it in his mouth.

"Who's not here?" Andi asked.

He smiled. "Julianna, that's who you're looking for."

"I am not. I was just looking around to see how many had stayed after the show."

"Yeah, right. Look, Andi, you can lie to yourself all you want, but I know there's only one person who attended this thing today that you give a damn about."

She held up a hand. "All right, yes, I was looking for Julianna, but only so I would know what part of the room to avoid."

"That's better. At least you're only half lying now. Regardless, she's not here. She and Liz left a few minutes before you came in."

She couldn't hide her disappointment. "Just as well."

He picked up his drink and was about to take a sip. "Julianna was acting kind of strange, though, when she came in. Liz was at the end of the bar and Julianna damn near sprinted to her. She looked pissed off at first. I thought maybe you two had gotten into it out in the lobby."

"I didn't see her while I was out there."

"She spoke to Liz, then teared up. The next thing I know, they're heading out the side door and that's the last I saw of them."

She shook her head in bewilderment. "Who knows, maybe

she and David had a spat over the phone. I won't play her games anymore, so she's stuck playing with him," she said with a smirk as she picked up her drink.

Later, Andi wandered over to the table where Thomas sat with the execs from New York. When the men excused themselves from the table, she was able to sit with Gail for a short time and chat in private. She tried her best to lay the groundwork for a future rise within Vantage Point without coming off as too presumptive.

On the drive back to Frisco, she had a good feeling about her future and, in all likelihood, she would have a new contract in a new city once she proved herself with the success of "Sunrise Summit."

Chapter 15

Rachel hurried down the hall with her arms full of thick black plastic cases containing videotape. She stopped and stuck her head in the door of Andi's office as she passed. "Andi, William called for you while you were in rehearsals. He needs a favor and wants you to call him."

She set her notepad on the desk. "Thanks, Rach." She reached for the phone on her desk and dialed his cell.

"Hello, this is William."

"William, it's Andi. Rachel told me you called. You should have had her come and get me out of rehearsal."

"I didn't want to interrupt you. I just need a small favor."

"Yeah, sure. What can I do for you?"

"I have an appointment this afternoon to get the contract extension signed for Snow Cap's additional air time. Unfortunately, I'm not going to make it back from Aspen in time to make the appointment. Do you think you might have time to run the papers over to the marketing department so I don't have to reschedule?"

Andi's face went hot. "I...I, yes, I can take care of it for you," she said reluctantly. She would do her best to get in, have Karen sign the papers, and possibly get out without running into Julianna.

"Great. In my office, you'll find a FedEx envelope addressed and ready to be shipped to New York. The contract is inside. If you'll have Julianna sign all of the lines I highlighted and give the envelope to Rachel when you're done, I'll owe you a nice dinner."

She felt as if she'd just been struck in the chest with a sword at the mention of Julianna's name. "Sounds easy enough. What time is the appointment?"

"One thirty. Do you know where to find Julianna's office?"

"No, I've never been there."

"Stop at the reception desk and Liz will tell you where to go."

I just bet she will, Andi thought.

"Okay, consider it done, William. Talk to you later." Andi hung up and plopped down in her chair. The move was so sudden, Tinker jumped up from her pillow.

She propped her elbows on her desk and wiped her face with both hands. "Damn it," she said, gritting her teeth. She couldn't turn William down, that would be unprofessional, but why Julianna of all people? She looked at her watch, it was almost twelve. "Great, I have ninety minutes to think about this." She looked down at Tinker. "Today would be the perfect day for a three martini lunch, baby girl."

Tinker turned her head sideways, listening for a word she recognized.

Andi did everything she could to busy herself and to keep from thinking about her pending trip to Snow Cap. The agitation inside killed her appetite and she skipped lunch. When the clock approached one, she went to William's office and found the envelope. She pulled the papers out of the envelope and looked them over so she would know how many signatures were needed before she went. If she had to see Julianna, she was determined to keep it strictly business and make the visit as quick as possible.

She stopped at the front desk on her way out. "Rach, I have to run over to Snow Cap for a few minutes—"

"To have William's contracts signed. Yes, I know." She had a look of satisfaction on her face. "And, yes, I'll watch Tinker for you until you get back."

Andi laughed. "Ya know, sometimes you border on being creepy with all that mind-reading you do."

"Oh, it has nothing to do with reading one's mind. It's simply examination. People have a pattern to their behavior, and once you become familiar with their pattern, they're fairly easy to interpret, and I overheard part of your conversation." She looked at Andi sheepishly.

Andi leaned on the desk. "So what you're saying is I'm a creature of habit and you're an eavesdropper."

Rachel laughed. "Quite so, yes."

"Just the same, you missed your calling, Ms. Oliver. You should have been a psychotherapist or a sociologist, something that would require a keen sense of observation and analysis."

"You can find that in most any job. People say more about themselves with their behavior than they do with the words they speak, or as you Yanks like to say, actions speak louder than words." She winked at Andi.

Andi gave Tinker a kiss on the head. "I shouldn't be long." She grabbed her portfolio with William's envelope inside and went to the door.

"Andi, will you be all right with Ms. Stevens?"

Andi stopped with her hand on the door handle and looked back at Rachel with an apprehensive face. "I'm not sure, Rachel." She exited the building for the parking lot.

She pulled off Highway 9 into the entrance to the East Village at Snow Cap and followed the signs to the employee parking lot behind the building. Looking down the row of vehicles as she crossed to the entrance, she spotted Julianna's shiny black BMW. She blew a heavy burst of air from her lungs and walked into the building.

When the elevator doors opened and Andi stepped out into the lobby of the third floor, Liz couldn't believe her eyes. "Andi, good afternoon. What brings you to Snow Cap today?" She tried to hide her surprise by maintaining a professional tone.

Andi was taken aback by Liz's greeting. She fully expected a cold shoulder from Julianna's best friend, given the interactions she and Julianna had recently engaged in. "I'm filling in for William. He was held up in Aspen and asked me to bring the contracts over for Julianna."

"That's wonderful, I mean, nice of you to cover." She twirled about a quarter of a turn in her chair and pointed down the hallway. "I believe you'll find Julianna in the big conference room."

"Thanks, Liz," she said on her way past the desk.

Liz smiled. "My pleasure, Andi." She turned away and mumbled, "Hopefully, it will bring you pleasure, too."

She looked back at Liz as she walked down the hall, unsure if she heard her say anything more.

The door to the conference room was closed. Andi ran her hand over her hair, then knocked on the wooden door.

Julianna's sweet voice called, "Come in."

She grabbed the handle and pushed it down. The latch gave out a loud click and the door popped open, releasing a flood of daylight from the large window in the conference room that spilled into the hallway. She stepped in and closed the door behind her.

Julianna was leaning over the table littered with artwork and print material. She turned around expecting to see William but was shocked to see Andi standing there instead. She gripped the edge of the table to steady herself. "Andi. I was expecting William. It's nice to see you." She couldn't hide the surprise in her voice.

Andi stepped toward the table. "Yes, well, this was all unexpected for me, too. William was held up in Aspen and asked me to bring the contract over for you to sign," she said in a lifeless tone. She opened the portfolio and removed the envelope.

Julianna cleared a spot on the table and watched Andi's every move with astonishment, trying to grasp the reality that she was actually here in front of her. She thought how amazing she looked in her tailored dark green slacks and white polo shirt.

"I won't take up too much of your time. I believe you've read the contract and everything has been agreed on." Andi spoke with professionalism.

Julianna clasped her hands together uncomfortably. "Yes, I have my copies."

"Good, then let's get started. William highlighted the lines that need your signature."

Julianna signed the bright yellow areas on the papers in silence. When she was done, they both reached to gather the scattered papers on the table at the same time. Julianna accidentally grabbed Andi's hand and they both froze instantly. Andi's gaze locked on their loosely joined hands and her mouth fell open slightly. Julianna looked slowly up to Andi's face.

Andi's eyes did not divert from their hands.

Julianna looked back down, and spontaneity took over. Using her thumb, she caressed the top of Andi's hand. She looked back up at her face.

Andi's eyes were closed and her breathing appeared to quicken.

Julianna felt her tremble under her touch and went a step further. She ran her fingertips slowly over Andi's wrist and started up her forearm.

Andi kept her eyes closed, hoping the fire coursing through her body would stop. Before she could speak, the ring of the phone on the table intruded on their moment.

Julianna jumped away from Andi like a school girl being caught by the teacher and snatched up the receiver. "Hello?... Yes, Karen, I know…Okay I'll be right there." She returned the receiver to its resting place.

Andi kept her gaze focused at the portfolio on the table.

"Andi, I want—"

"I think our business is complete. Thank you for your time, Julianna." She picked up the portfolio and walked toward the door.

Julianna watched her walk out without saying another word. She returned to her small office and closed the door. She deposited the artwork in a bin next to the file cabinet and sat in her chair. She laid her head facedown on top of the desk and ran through what had just happened in the conference room. She made an attempt to connect with Andi and her boss ruined it. The worst part of it all was Andi wouldn't even look at her when she left the room. She had no idea what was going on inside Andi's head.

She got up to look out the window and focused on the edge of the bridge visible from her office. "You lost. It's over. Too many things keep getting in the way, which must be a sign that fate is trying to intervene, and this was not meant to be, Julianna," she said to herself.

Andi clutched the portfolio to her chest and retraced her steps back to the elevator. She said a silent thank you as she passed through the lobby and hurried by the empty chair at the reception desk. She considered herself lucky as the elevator doors closed that Liz was not around to ask questions.

She pulled out onto Highway 9 and drove back to Frisco with a knot in the pit of her stomach. The swing of emotion that rocked her to her core in the conference room was almost unbearable. She was only there to have a contract signed, and it turned into something she desperately wanted to avoid—yet another intimate brush with Julianna.

Her head was swimming. She had no doubt Julianna probably did feel something, but she wasn't about to open herself up to being a pawn in whatever game she was attempting to seduce her into. What was Julianna's game? Was she simply bored and looking for something a little dangerous to spice up her life? Andi was tired of trying to understand the complexity of their encounters. By the time she reached the parking lot at the station, her head hurt.

She walked in the front door and was immediately greeted by the gray and black shepherd jumping up on her. She reached down and gave her several scratches to her back.

Rachel could tell with one look that something wasn't right. "How did it go?" she asked with reservation.

Andi laid the FedEx envelope on the counter in front of her. "Signed, sealed, and delivered," she said impassively as she opened the door to the hallway. "I'll be in my office, and, Rach, if anyone calls, please take a message."

"Sure, Andi, no problem." Rachel moved her glasses from the top of her head to their proper place across the bridge of her nose. She wanted to ask Andi what happened but knew she was better to leave well enough alone.

Chapter 16

After a brisk morning walk on the trails around Frisco, Andi drove over to Breckenridge to pick up a birthday present for Rachel. She had admired a blue cashmere sweater Andi bought in Wendy's shop. Andi decided to get one for Rachel in a light green. It would accentuate her dark red hair perfectly. She had been a tremendous help to Andi since she arrived, and Andi felt she was well worth the price of the sweater.

The bell attached to the front door jingled softly when Andi entered the shop.

Wendy appeared from behind a rack of children's ski suits. "Andi, how are you? It's great to see you."

"Hi, Wendy." Andi walked around the display of T-shirts in the front.

"I have your sweater in the back. Wait one second and I'll go get it."

Andi smiled and looked over a table covered with stacks of designer blue jeans.

"Here you go, one cashmere sweater in lime green. I can gift wrap it for you if you like."

"Yes, please, that would be great." She followed the petite woman with shoulder-length hair to the counter and picked out a floral print wrapping paper. "Are you and Thomas going to Rachel's surprise party tonight?"

Wendy smiled as she laid out the paper and began to wrap the box. "Oh, yes, Thomas is quite fond of Rachel. She works hard and always with a smile." She ripped off a piece of tape from a dispenser. "Any idea what Charlie's big surprise is?"

"Beats me. Justin and I were joking that maybe Charlie hired a male stripper, but that is so not his style, and it would embarrass Rachel to death."

Wendy laughed. "That's for sure. I've never seen a girl who blushes so easily."

Andi paid for the gift and thanked Wendy on her way out. "See you tonight."

Wendy waved as Andi rang the bell again.

The rest of Saturday morning was spent doing chores around Andi's home. At lunchtime, the sky clouded up and it began to rain. Andi sought solace in her studio room with the even diffused light of the clouded day. She sat on her stool in front of the easel. Once again, she started with a quick, loose sketch of a human figure and went to work refining it.

Tinker lounged on the futon as she usually did when Andi worked on a drawing. Time flew when she was engrossed in her artwork. When she stopped at five o'clock to get ready for Rachel's party, the drawing was near completion. It was of a woman in a small, sleeveless dress. She was leaning against a rail, holding a cloak loosely around her shoulders. The only part left unfinished was the face. Andi couldn't bring herself to complete it knowing the only face to fill it was Julianna's.

She stopped and covered the large drawing with an old piece of canvas and went upstairs to get ready.

The evening was cold and damp. The rain that had fallen all afternoon turned into snow flurries as evening approached and the temperature dropped. Andi walked into the Breckenridge Brewery around 6:45. Charlie and Rachel would be there at seven. Charlie had several tables reserved around the pool table. When Andi walked in, there were already about a dozen people gathered. A small table off to the side displayed a beautifully decorated sheet cake with hearts and flowers and the words "Happy Birthday,

Rachel," emblazed in red icing across the center. Andi laid her present with the others next to the cake. She joined Thomas and Wendy, who were at a table with a group of people from the station, and ordered a vanilla porter from the beer list. Shortly after she arrived, Justin walked in with the new anchor Brenda Fernandez on his arm.

Brenda was undeniably a lovely girl in her late twenties with long dark hair and big dark eyes. She was smooth with her delivery of a story and Gail Neiman was right, she showed the talent of a promising career. Andi admitted to herself that Brenda and Justin made a handsome couple.

Andi rolled her eyes at him when Justin looked over at her. He definitely had a way with the ladies.

Right at seven, Charlie and Rachel made their entrance with Liz and Buddy, and a loud surprise was shouted, much to the shock of the birthday girl. Rachel never expected a party. Charlie had told her it was a casual dinner with Liz and Buddy and nothing more.

Andi sat with her back to the birthday girl and her entourage as they made their way to a table. When they passed by, Liz gave Justin a thumbs-up, and he smiled and tilted his chin in return. The conspiring conversation, set up by Rachel over the phone a few days earlier, set in motion a plan to get Andi and Julianna in the same location at the same time and possibly force them to speak once more. All involved had hopes that the two women would overcome their doubts and egos and realize what was so obvious to everyone else.

Charlie bought everyone a round of drinks while Rachel made her way around to say hello and thank you to everyone. When she got to Andi, she stopped and gave her a scolding look. "How on earth did you keep this from me? I know everything that goes on in that office, but I definitely didn't know about this."

"You don't know everything, missy. We can be a sneaky bunch when we want to be. Were you really surprised?"

"Oh, Lord, yes, I'll say. I made Charlie promise me he wouldn't make a big deal out of me birthday. He told me we were going to dinner with Liz and Buddy, that was all, then I walk into this." She made a gesture with her hands. "And the cake is absolutely lovely."

Andi gave her a hug and wished her happy birthday.

While Rachel continued to make it around the room, Andi picked at a plate of nachos on the table. She raised her glass to wash down the peppers and cheese when she caught sight of Julianna walking into the room.

Julianna looked equally surprised to see Andi. She stopped in her tracks and looked as though she wanted to retreat until Liz jumped up and called out, "Jules, over here."

Julianna looked away from Andi when Liz popped over. She grabbed Julianna and led her to the table where she and Buddy were sitting.

"You didn't say anything about a party. Or that she would be here," Julianna said through clenched teeth.

"I didn't know any other way to get you out. You can't stay locked up in your apartment forever, and so what if Andi's here. It's a public place, right?" Liz squeezed her shoulders and gave her a reassuring grin.

"Liz, it's still so awkward seeing her." Julianna sat at the table.

"Just relax. Have a drink and have some fun." Liz took her seat between Julianna and Buddy. "In case you haven't noticed, she's here alone."

"She's moved on. I told you about that girl in Vail." Julianna spoke in a low tone while slipping her jacket off. Underneath, she wore a white cap-sleeve blouse and dark form-fitting jeans with black cowboy boots. "If she's out alone, that's her business."

Liz looked Julianna over. "Well, you're certainly an eye catcher tonight. I doubt Andi would ignore you if you made an attempt to speak to her."

"I didn't dress this way hoping to run into her." Julianna sat up straight in her chair and adjusted her blouse.

"You got her attention nonetheless. She watched us walk to the table and she saw you take your jacket off. I still think she's interested."

"Please, Liz, can we just let it go and try to have a nice evening?"

"Whatever you want."

The waitress came around and took Julianna's drink order. Unfortunately for her, Liz sat her in a chair at the table where she had a direct view of Andi and no crowd between them.

Andi couldn't help but notice Julianna when she removed her jacket; she looked thinner, but she was radiant. Her hair was perfect the way it fell on her shoulders. She tried to take no notice of her, but as deeply rooted as she was in Andi's heart, it was next to impossible for her to divert her eyes.

When it looked as though everyone had finished eating and the pool table was in full swing, Charlie motioned for Liz. She went over to the cake and lit the number two and five candles on the cake. Charlie found Rachel and took her by the hand and led her to the cake.

With his big booming Texas voice, he silenced the room of friends. "Hey, y'all, can I have your attention please? Will y'all join me in singin' happy birthday to my sweetie since this is her day?"

Rachel stood next to him and blushed. Charlie started them off, and as the song neared its completion, tears formed in Rachel's eyes. She wiped them dry and kissed Charlie.

He smiled back at her and pointed at the cake. "Make a wish and blow out your candles, honey."

She did and the crowd applauded. She then sat down and opened the stack of gifts that her friends had brought. She thanked each one as she opened them. She received a combination of gag gifts and nice presents, all for which she was grateful.

When she was done, one of Charlie's buddies called out, "Hey, Charlie, where's your present, man? You afraid we'll all find out what a cheap bastard you really are?"

The crowd roared with laughter.

Charlie responded with, "You're a funny man, Chet." Then he turned to Rachel, got down on one knee, and reached into the front pocket of his jeans.

A low hum came from the people in the room along with a few whistles from Charlie's buddies.

Rachel covered her mouth with her hands in anticipation of what was to come.

"Honey, you know I love you, and it's been a whole lotta fun havin' you in my life, and I'd just like to make things more permanent for us by askin'." He paused to catch his breath. "Rachel Louise Oliver, will you marry me please?" He held out a small white box and opened the lid to reveal a two-carat pear-shaped solitaire diamond set in a gold band.

The crowd was silent waiting for her answer.

Rachel sniffed back tears and managed to answer, "You just gave me my wish. Yes, Charlie, I will marry you."

A smile covered his face as he placed the ring on her left hand. She threw her arms around his neck and he picked her up off her feet and kissed her. The crowd went wild.

Andi's mind drifted back to the deck at the top of Snow Cap Mountain. She fantasized about standing in the moonlight with Julianna, holding out her grandmother's engagement ring and making the same proposal to the woman who had stolen her heart but quickly erased it from her mind. It was not ever going to happen and especially not with Julianna.

She turned to Justin and said, "He said it was something special, and here we thought it was a male stripper."

Everyone at the table laughed.

The happy couple made their rounds and was congratulated by all while Rachel showed off the ring.

Andi saw Julianna get up to go to the ladies room. She thought this would be the perfect time to make an exit, so she grabbed her things and said good night to her friends, with the excuse that she needed to get home and let the dog out.

Liz watched with disappointment as Andi headed for the door. Justin looked over at Liz and threw his hands up in surrender.

Andi worked her way through the heavy crowd at the main bar of the brewery and was three steps away from the door when she crossed directly into Julianna's path. They bumped into each other and both froze with surprise.

"Andi, hi."

"Hi, Julianna." She moved toward the door, but Julianna

stepped in front of her.

"How are you?"

"I'm fine, and you?" Andi said awkwardly, still eyeing the door.

"I'm good. Leaving already?" Julianna asked, attempting to catch Andi's gaze.

"Yeah, I need to get home to my dog."

The tension between them was high, despite the people and noise surrounding them.

"Andi, do you think we could try to be friends?"

Andi's face turned serious and she locked gazes with Julianna. She took her by the arm and moved them aside so they were partially blocked from sight by a rack of T-shirts near the gift counter. "Friends, Julianna? I have an attraction to you that's still fresh in my head, and I can't just turn it off with a switch. That makes it a little hard for me to be friends with you right now."

"I just thought we might be able to work it out. I mean, we'll probably be working together again, and I don't want all this anxiety between us."

Andi's gaze roamed over the open buttons of Julianna's blouse. They exposed an elegant gold and sapphire necklace against soft skin that directed her vision down to a small amount of cleavage. She was so damned beautiful and Andi ached from wanting her so badly. "Not to worry. I'm up to my ears in the morning show right now. I'll see to it that one of my producers handles things for you," she said.

Julianna glanced at her and looked away again. "You did such a good job, I'm sure Karen will insist you handle our future projects."

"Chris and Simone are quite capable of putting together a production crew for you, and I'll be overseeing things from behind the scenes." She was growing annoyed with the conversation. "Look, Julianna, you'll have to work with them eventually, so you might as well start building a rapport now while I'm still around to supervise them."

Julianna was taken aback by Andi's words. "Still around? What do you mean by that?"

"I mean, I've only got a one-year contract with KCOR." Andi didn't want to discuss this right now and not with Julianna. "A lot can change in a year. Thomas may not offer me another contract, or I may get another offer somewhere else, who knows. Anyway, I've been thinking that maybe I made a mistake by coming here in the first place." Andi realized she had said too much.

Julianna put her hand on Andi's arm. "You shouldn't feel like you have to leave, Andi. What happened between us—"

"Don't flatter yourself," she snapped back and pulled her arm away. "I'm thinking about moving on at the end of my contract because I don't belong here. I made a mistake thinking I could move to a secluded part of the country and be happy. I've spent my entire adult life in a big city, and that's where I belong. It's what I know. It's my comfort zone."

Julianna crossed her arms over her chest. "I saw you in Vail and got the impression you had already moved on." She bit her lip; she didn't intend for that to slip out.

Andi's eyes narrowed. "What?"

"Nothing." Julianna hesitated. "I mean, I saw you with that woman in Vail."

Andi was astounded by her comment. "Woman?" Then it dawned on her who she was talking about. "The brunette in the lobby?"

Julianna put her hands on her hips. "Yes, the one with her arms wrapped around your neck. The one that kissed you," she said with irritation.

"That woman is very much my ex, and it was by chance that we ran into each other. She was in Vail for a cousin's wedding." Andi rubbed her forehead. "Why am I telling you this? I don't owe you an explanation."

"No, I suppose you don't." Julianna folded her arms again and leaned away.

It was Andi's turn to throw a barb. "Just like you don't owe me an explanation about David." She had a smug expression on her face.

Julianna's mouth dropped open. "Andi, you don't understand… I mean there's so much more to the story…It doesn't matter anyway, we broke up or I should say I broke up with him."

"You did?" Andi was surprised.

She felt a flicker of hope with Andi's surprise.

"That's great, but I don't understand you. You tell me you wanna be my straight friend, now you're jealous over another woman? Who, by the way, means nothing to me." She put her hands on her hips. "Which is it?"

Julianna's entire body told of her discomfort and she struggled to find the words to answer Andi's burning question.

"Now's the time to lay it all out, Julianna. If you've got something to say, then say it. No more games." Andi's voice was filled with frustration.

Julianna didn't know what to say, she just stood still with her gaze pointed toward the floor, occasionally looking up at Andi. Her hands were shaking and her words stuck in her throat. She knew she was about to see her last chance slip away.

Andi rolled her eyes and looked away, waiting for her to say something, anything. She looked back at Julianna, who still wouldn't look at her. "Yeah, okay, I get it. Goodbye, Julianna." Andi squeezed by a man the size of a linebacker to get to the door and left Julianna standing alone in the crowd.

Once she got out the door, she took a deep breath and headed for her vehicle. Her head and her heart were stinging over her confrontation with the only person she had ever loved so deeply and the one person she was convinced she couldn't have.

She was halfway to her vehicle when Julianna shouted, "Andi, stop. You're not running out on me this time. At least not until you hear what I have to say."

Andi stopped and dropped her head back. Looking up to the cloud-filled night sky, she asked quietly, "Why me, Lord?" She turned around and found Julianna standing about two car lengths away.

"What do you want from me?"

"We're not done with this. There's still too much that's been left unspoken. I can't just let you go this time. Not until you know how I feel." She stopped and took a deep breath. Her heart was beating like it would pound right through her chest and her legs were shaking. "I think we need to deal with what's happening between us." Her voice cracked as she spoke.

Andi took a few steps toward her and held up a hand. "I'm not interested in games or being a part of your curiosity." She took a deep breath. "I don't want to be just another footnote in someone's life. I want what everyone else wants, to settle down and make a life together. I want to grow old with someone." Snowflakes were starting to fall around them. "Go find somebody that still enjoys playing games with straight women." Andi was done with the conversation and turned to walk away.

Julianna was desperate for something that would make Andi understand how she felt before it was too late. Then she remembered the words of someone that she knew Andi would listen to. With anguish in her voice, she started, "I must speak to you by such means as are within my reach. You pierce my soul. I am half agony, half hope."

Andi stopped and turned back around when she heard Julianna using Jane Austen's words.

"Tell me not that I am too late, that such precious feelings are gone forever." She stopped and looked at Andi with tear-filled eyes. She swallowed the lump in her throat and continued. "I offer myself to you again with a heart even more your own than when you almost broke it..." Her voice was heavy with emotion. "If you won't listen to my words, maybe you'll listen to someone else's that understands how I feel. I don't want to spend the rest of my life wondering what if just because I was too afraid to take a chance on a relationship I'm not familiar with. I don't know if I'm bi or gay, but I know I'm not playing games, Andi."

Tears of frustration rolled down Julianna's cheeks as the snow continued to fall faster. "And I know how I feel. No one has ever done the things you do to me. I hear your voice and my heart skips a beat. You touch me and I tremble. That's more than an infatuation, more than...than a curiosity. I tried to suppress these feelings for so many reasons, but they wouldn't go away, and I'm glad because I don't want them to."

Andi stood perfectly still, her face frozen with shock.

"You once asked me to stop being so stubborn and trust you,

now I'm asking you to do the same."

Julianna's voice calmed and she surrendered to her emotions. "I'm scared, too. I'm scared of what I feel for you, Andi, and I'm scared by how deep those feelings are. Forgive me for any pain I've caused you. It was never my intention to hurt you." She brushed the tears from her eyes. "You have no idea the price I'll pay for my precious feelings for you." Her bottom lip quivered. "I love you, Andi. God help me. I love you." She lowered her head and covered her eyes with her hand. Julianna was emotionally spent.

It was Andi's turn to be speechless. Frankly, she was stunned by Julianna's declaration. All along, she'd been reading her wrong and she couldn't think of an appropriate word to say.

The snow fell heavier as she walked back to Julianna and gently lifted her chin with her fingertips. Andi searched deep into Julianna's eyes and, for the first time, saw clarity through the tears that she had not seen before. Julianna had bared her soul and now stood before Andi offering up her heart.

Her pulse beat loudly in her ears. She tenderly wiped the tears from Julianna's face. "I am so, so sorry, Julianna. I had no idea, and even worse, I never gave you the chance to tell me."

"Andi, I don't know how this happened. How it got so messed up—"

"It doesn't matter." Andi smiled and brushed Julianna's hair from her face. "A friend of mine said we love who we love, it's that simple. You know, she's right."

Julianna managed a smile.

She slipped her arms around Julianna's waist and pulled her close. "You're shivering, we should go back inside."

"I'm okay." She cradled Andi's face with her hands. "I'm not about to let go of you now that I've finally caught you." The sparkle in her light brown eyes danced as she looked deep into Andi's eyes, then she covered Andi's mouth with her own and kissed her passionately.

When Andi moved her hand up Julianna's back, she didn't pull away this time, instead she leaned into her with a sigh.

The loud inebriated voices of a group of people leaving the

brewery intruded on their kiss.

Still holding Andi's face, Julianna whispered, "Take me home with you."

"Are you sure?"

"Yes, we need some time to be alone." She took a step back and held Andi's hands.

Andi smiled. "I couldn't agree more."

"I have to run inside and get my things. I'll meet you at your place. Is that all right?"

"Not a problem. You remember how to get there?"

"Not a problem," she repeated.

Andi brushed her lips over Julianna's, then they went their separate ways.

Inside the brewery, Julianna rushed back to the table with renewed energy to retrieve her things. Liz, of course, was curious what had taken her so long in the ladies room.

"There you are. I was starting to worry about you." Liz spoke before she noticed Julianna's damp hair and red eyes.

Julianna grabbed her jacket and bag. "I have to go, Liz."

"Wait, what happened to you? You're wet. And from the look of your eyes, you've been crying."

"I can't talk now. I have to go. I'll call you tomorrow." She hurried for the door.

"Jules, where are you going? Hey, did you see, Andi?"

Julianna didn't answer, she simply waved as she left the room.

Chapter 17

Andi walked into the town house and was immediately greeted by Tinker. She took her out back, and when they returned, she looked around to see if anything needed to be picked up. The place was in order. Andi's nerves were jumping. She couldn't believe what was happening. She paced around the room with Tinker watching astutely.

She went to her stack of CDs and found one that might help her calm down. She dropped the disc in the player and adjusted the volume. It was loud enough to hear but not distracting. The sound of a car engine came from outside; her guest had arrived.

Julianna entered through the door from the garage. "Hope you don't mind, I parked in the garage." She had a glow from the melting snow that highlighted her hair.

"That's perfect," Andi said. "Please, come in." Her heart was pounding as she walked over and hit the button on the wall to close the garage door. Julianna stepped lightly across the great room and laid her bag and jacket on the arm of the sofa.

Tinker trotted over and stood in front of Julianna and wagged her tail. Andi shook a finger at her. "You always have to upstage me don't you, Stinker-bell?"

Julianna bent down and scratched the dog's head. "She's the sweetest thing."

"Yes, she is, and she uses it to her advantage," Andi said. She wasn't sure what to do next. She wanted to touch Julianna, but her head told her to let Julianna make the first move.

Julianna smiled up at Andi. "She's a lot like her master."

Andi's cheeks reddened and she cleared her throat. "Would you like something to drink?"

Julianna stood. "No, thank you, I think I'm fine right now."

Andi slipped her hands into the pockets of her jeans and leaned her back against the wall next to the painting of the two women. "Jules, I know this is probably not the right time to ask, but I need to know." Andi pondered her next words. Everything was happening so fast, she needed reassurance that what she had heard was genuine. "Why did you break up with David?"

Julianna came closer and looked her in the eyes. "Because I'm in love with someone else, and I needed to be free to follow my heart."

"And where is your heart leading you?"

"Right here to you."

Andi returned a modest smile.

The music playing caught Julianna's attention. She stopped and listened to the soft sensual sound of the piano and synthesizer. "The music, it's beautiful. If love were something to be heard, it would sound like this."

"The title of the song is 'Childhood Hour' and I'm sure the composer Bernward Koch would appreciate your analogy."

She looked at Andi with amazement. "I was wrong about you when we first met."

Andi gave her a curious look.

"I said you were all business. I couldn't have been more wrong. You're all about the beauty that exists in this world." She pointed at the painting. "Your artwork, the music you listen to, it all expresses how full of passion and emotion you really are."

Andi extended a hand. "Dance with me?"

Julianna accepted the graceful hand in front of her. So strong and fluid, it was one of the first things she noticed about Andi the day their paths crossed for the first time in the grocery store.

Andi moved closer and wrapped her arm around Julianna's waist. Julianna leaned into Andi and rested her head at the nape of her neck. They moved slowly to the soft hypnotic melody of the piano as it blanketed them with dreamy ambience.

Andi pressed Julianna's hand gently to her chest just above her heart as they swayed back and forth to the rhythm. The rest of the world was shut out for now. There was only Andi and Julianna and the music that surrounded them.

As the song neared an end, Andi whispered, "Is this really what you want? Am I really what you want?" She brushed the back of her fingers over Julianna's cheek. Her skin was warm and soft.

Julianna kissed Andi long and deep. "I think those are questions that can be better answered by showing you." She looked up at the loft and the bedroom door.

"We don't have to do this if you're not ready. I mean, this is all happening so fast, and it's new for both of us. If you need time, I'm willing to wait."

Julianna put a finger to Andi's lips. "It's okay. Sex is not new to me. Granted, it has been a while. What is new to me is being with you. I don't want you to just hear my words. I want you to feel them and know that I mean them." She ran her fingers down Andi's arm. A flash of frustration surfaced on her face. "I'm not sure I know how to touch you, to please you. I've never…"

"We can take our time and work on that together." Andi pulled her closer. "I need to learn how to please you, too." She kissed her slowly.

Julianna's hands found their way down to Andi's backside and squeezed it gently. "I love a tight ass," she said as she nipped at Andi's earlobe.

Andi blushed.

"This just feels right, Andi. You and I," she whispered in her ear.

Andi ran her fingers through Julianna's soft locks. "Do you wanna go upstairs?"

"Lead the way."

Andi took her by the hand and led her to the bedroom.

Tinker made herself comfortable in the red chair downstairs.

When they reached the bedroom, Andi lit a candle on the dresser. The scent of lavender slowly spread through the room while the sound of the wind blowing against the windows echoed across the vaulted ceiling. Andi turned to Julianna, who sat at the foot of the bed removing her boots. She was mesmerizing in the flickering golden light of the candle flame. Andi's stomach muscles were tight with anticipation. She took Julianna by the hands and stood her up, then kissed the palm of her hand. "Are you okay?" Andi asked.

"A little nervous."

"Me too." She ran her fingers through Julianna's hair and kissed her soft full lips again.

Julianna pressed against Andi and tugged the shirt from her jeans so her hands could roam freely over her back. She stopped when she reached the waistband of her jeans.

Andi peeled her shirt off and tossed it aside, along with her bra, eliminating the obstacle between her body and Julianna's soft anxious hands. Julianna was overwhelmed with desire as her gaze panned down Andi's mostly naked torso. She reached out and slowly ran her fingers over Andi's breasts and around her ribs.

Andi kissed Julianna's cheek and ran her bottom lip down the length of her neck, starting behind her ear, lightly grazing her skin as she moved deliberately down to her shoulder. Andi's slow and steady breaths over her skin gave Julianna goose bumps. She moaned softly and grabbed Andi by the shoulders to steady herself. When Andi ran her tongue up Julianna's neck, she was so distracted she didn't notice Andi's fingers unbuttoning her blouse.

The blouse fell open and revealed well-rounded breasts covered by a simple white silk bra and a flat stomach. Andi found the clasp of the bra and released it. She felt her own excitement growing. She took a deep breath and let it out slowly. She didn't want their first experience together—Julianna's first with a woman—to be rushed.

Julianna's nerves were waning with each touch of Andi's lips and hands. Her touch was much different from the men she had been with. She experienced very little in the way of pleasure from the way men pawed at her flesh and squeezed her breasts with their rough, fumbling hands. They concentrated more on their own satisfaction than hers. Andi was different. Her hands were soft, her touch gentle and exciting, and she moved in ways that were purely feminine. Every touch felt like it was focused on pleasing Julianna.

Andi took a half step back and gazed at what the open blouse revealed. She locked gazes with Julianna and guided the blouse and bra from her shoulders and down her arms with her fingers.

Julianna caught her breath as her breasts were bared and the garments glided to the floor.

"You are so amazingly beautiful," Andi whispered. She wrapped her arms around her hips and lowered her mouth to Julianna's chest. She covered a nipple with her mouth and rolled the pink flesh with her tongue as she sucked gently.

Julianna reacted immediately to her mouth. Her nipples tightened to the point that she cried out, "Oh, God, Andi, don't stop." She closed her eyes, ran her fingers through Andi's hair, and threw her head back in pleasure.

Andi teased Julianna relentlessly with her mouth. At the same time, she undid her jeans and pushed them, along with her panties, down her hips till everything fell to the floor. She lowered Julianna onto the bed and slipped out of the rest of her own clothes, dropping them with the other articles of discarded clothing.

She then slid herself over the top of Julianna, placing kisses all the way up her stomach, to her breasts and her neck. She worked her hand down the length of Julianna's body and stopped at the inside of her thigh. She looked into Julianna's eyes for consent and found them heavy with pleasure. Holding her gaze, she brushed her fingertips up the inside of Julianna's thigh and touched her for the first time. Julianna's hips rose into Andi's as her fingers explored and excited her.

"Not yet, my love, take me further...with your mouth."

Andi did not disappoint.

Julianna could barely speak. "Oh, Andi, darling," she whispered and ran her fingers through Andi's hair.

Andi lifted herself up over Julianna and used her fingers to take her the rest of the way.

Julianna was breathless and her body in spasms from the

pressure of Andi's rhythmical movement. She moaned again and Andi molded her mouth around Julianna's, her sounds of pleasure reverberating in Andi's mouth.

When Julianna reached the point of release, Andi rose up on one elbow and watched her face.

Julianna's vision was clouded, but she managed to lock on to the bright blue of Andi's eyes just as the flood of orgasm broke through and filled her from head to toe. She closed her eyes for a moment and, when she opened them again, Andi's soft gaze was still focused on her. It was all like a wonderful dream. She cared about nothing at that moment but the feel of their bodies melded together.

She dug into Andi's flesh so hard with her fingers, she left deep red marks on her shoulder blades. Never before had she experienced such a rush. But it was more than the physicality of the sex; she was consumed by the feeling of connectedness with her new lover. From the moment her body clenched down on Andi, they became one in body and soul.

Andi brushed her lips over Julianna's and pressed her mouth to her ear. "I love you, Julianna."

Julianna smiled and wrapped her arms around Andi's neck, holding on like she never wanted to let go. When she had some strength, she pushed Andi onto her back and said, "My turn."

She pressed her thigh between Andi's legs and used her mouth to work her way down Andi's neck and quickly found her breasts. She was never the aggressor when it came to sex, but the need to take Andi was in control. She slowed her impulse to possess and became more focused when she realized Andi's body was reacting to her every touch. She held on tight to Andi's torso and raked her teeth over a taut nipple.

Andi groaned. "God, yes, Julianna. Don't stop." She dug her fingers into the sheets and pushed her chest up.

With the encouragement Andi gave her, she floated a hand over Andi's thigh and dipped her fingers between her legs.

Andi was overcome by Julianna's touch, and emotion flooded her brain. She could have easily reached orgasm but held back, wanting Julianna to touch her entire body. With her hips grinding against Julianna, she moaned again. "It's not going to take much…"

Julianna's fingers stopped Andi's thoughts as they massaged her. When she felt Andi's body begin to tremble, she lowered herself and covered Andi with her mouth. She pressed down with her tongue, tasting a woman for the first time, and gave an approving sigh. She felt the swell between Andi's legs, and in a matter of minutes, Andi was helpless to stop the rush of orgasm as it pulsed around Julianna's mouth. It was like nothing she had experienced before.

Andi held Julianna's head against her. "Dear God, what did you do to me?"

Julianna smiled and breathed against Andi, causing her to tremble once more. She lifted her weight back up onto Andi and kissed her neck. "I hope I did it right for you."

Andi laughed. "I think you should give yourself some credit. That was wonderful."

"Good." Julianna smiled and ran her fingers along Andi's jaw. "I think you have pleasantly exhausted me." She brushed back the sweat-drenched bangs from Andi's forehead.

"I think I can say the same for you," Andi said, still feeling the aftershock of orgasm working though her body.

They lay in each other's arms, quietly enjoying the closeness they had wished for from almost the first moment they met. When they finally drifted off to sleep, their bodies were tangled together and twisted in the sheets.

A few hours later, Julianna quietly rolled over on top of Andi and woke her with kisses to her neck. Andi lay beneath her with a smile and was almost immediately aroused.

Julianna whispered in her ear, "Make love to me again," and kissed her.

Andi rolled her over on her back and they made love, ending with a surge almost as powerful as the one before.

Andi collapsed next to Julianna, exhausted but feeling complete and satisfied. Once again, they gave in to sleep with Julianna's body nestled tightly to hers.

A little after six, Andi awoke to find herself pinned between

Julianna and Tinker. At some point during the night, the dog made her way onto the bed and curled up behind her knees. She managed to wiggle her way out from under the covers and left both dog and the beautiful Julianna asleep in the bed.

She went to the bathroom, and when she returned, she noticed the diffused morning light coming through the window of the loft. It formed a delicate halo of light around Julianna's face. The temptation was too much. Andi pulled on the jeans and T-shirt she left on the chair, grabbed a sketch pad and pencil from the top of the chest of drawers, and sat down to begin sketching.

Julianna eventually raised her head and looked up at Andi through sleepy eyes. "Good morning," she said with a smile.

Andi looked up from the sketch pad and returned a smile. "Good morning. Did you sleep well?"

Julianna hugged the pillow. "I can't remember the last time I slept so soundly, but then I was exhausted. You wore me out."

Andi moved to the edge of the bed and kissed her bare shoulder.

"What do you have there?" Julianna asked, reaching for the sketch pad.

Andi held up the paper. It was a drawing of Julianna with her hair draped around her face and shoulders, and she was wrapped in a sheet, sleeping.

"Oh, Andi, that's beautiful. I can't get over how talented you are. You make me look better than I really do."

Andi kissed her again. "On the contrary, it pales in comparison to your beauty."

Julianna blushed.

Andi got up from the bed and set the pad in the chair. "Do you prefer tea or coffee?"

Julianna sat up with the sheets barely covering her beautiful naked body and brushed her hair back with her hand. "Coffee please."

A burning sensation crawled over Andi's body at the sight of Julianna's tussled honey brown hair laying about her shoulders. She had a glow to her face and shoulders that made Andi feel good knowing it was of her making.

She sat back down on the bed. "I have so much to learn about you. I don't even know your favorite color," Andi said.

Julianna cradled her face with her hands and caressed her cheeks. "Won't we have fun discovering all of our likes and dislikes?" A flash of mischief crossed her liquid brown eyes. "And wants and desires."

Andi kissed her slowly.

When she moved away, Julianna lovingly brushed her thumb over Andi's bottom lip. It was still moist with her kiss. "Yellow," she whispered, "my favorite color is sunflower yellow." Looking deep into Andi's eyes, she added with a smile, "And my new favorite color is crystal blue."

Andi smiled. "Duly noted," she said as she left the room. "Coffee coming right up."

Tinker jumped off the bed and followed her downstairs.

A few minutes later, Julianna appeared in the kitchen wearing Andi's robe. "I hope you don't mind. I found it hanging on the back of the bathroom door."

"Not at all. You can even make an old terrycloth robe look sexy."

Julianna wrapped her arms around Andi's waist from behind. "You're just saying that so I'll let you peel it off of me later." She kissed her neck.

Andi laughed as she poured the water into the coffee maker. "Nothing gets past you."

"Especially you." She squeezed Andi tight and rested her head on her back. "Last night was too wonderful to put into words." She paused. "I want to be the best lover I can for you. I promise I'll learn."

Andi turned around and held Julianna's face in her hands. "You already are the best lover you can be for me." She tapped her chest above her heart. "The physical part will come." She grinned at Julianna. "And practice makes perfect is what I've always been told."

Julianna draped her arms around Andi's neck and laughed. "You are incorrigible."

Andi pointed at the cabinet above the sink. "Will you grab us a couple of mugs?"

Julianna retrieved the mugs, then leaned against the counter. "Do you have plans for tonight?"

Andi looked at her slyly. "What do you have in mind?"

"I'd like to take you to dinner."

"Why, Ms. Stevens, are you asking me out on a date?" She raised an eyebrow.

"Yes, silly, a date, like normal people."

"I would love to go on date with you."

"Good. I'll make the reservations for, say 5:30?"

"Sounds good. Where are we going?" She handed Julianna a mug of coffee.

Julianna kissed her cheek. "That, my dear, is my little surprise." She took a drink from the mug. "I will tell you this much, wear something dressy."

After returning to bed for several more hours, Julianna left Andi's place and promised she would be back around five.

Chapter 18

Andi and Tinker went out for an afternoon walk around Frisco. The light snow that had fallen the night before was melted, thanks to a half day's worth of full sun radiating out of a cloudless cobalt blue sky.

The days were getting colder and shorter as the calendar closed in on the end of another year. She had a spring in her step, thanks to Julianna, and she couldn't think of any place she would rather be. She stopped in at Griffin's for a lemonade and sat out on the bench in the brisk afternoon air. She watched the people going up and down Main Street and recalled the magnificent events of the night before. Eventually, she headed home to call her parents. She also needed to call Desi and fill her in on Julianna. It would be a long call, she told herself.

By 4:45, she was freshly showered with makeup done perfectly, and she wore her hair down and straight. She popped down the stairs in a sleeveless off-white stretch knit dress with a square-cut neck and black heels. She wore her grandmother's black pearls with matching earrings for the first time in several years.

Feeling the nerves of the coming evening, she stopped at the home theater system on her way to the kitchen and turned on some music. Sarah Brightman's voice filled the town house. As always, Tinker was right behind her.

She got a bottle of Perrier from the fridge and poured herself a glass. Tinker was not about to go unnoticed and pawed at her foot.

"I know, sweetheart, you want your dinner." She sang along with the music as she put Tinker's dinner together.

The dog watched with anticipation until something caught her attention at the front door. She walked toward the door and gave a low bark.

"What is it, little girl?" Andi looked at the clock. It couldn't be Julianna, it was too early. She turned the music off on her way to the door and looked out the side window. Leo was standing on the porch.

She opened the door and greeted him. "Hey, what's going on?"

He was rubbing his hands together with nervous tension. "Do you have any rosemary?"

Andi laughed. "You want fresh or dried?"

"Hell, I don't know the difference. Which one is more sophisticated?"

She waved him in on her way to the fridge. "Go with the fresh."

He took a good look at Andi. "Hey, look at you," he said and gave her a wolf whistle. "You look too good to be going to a work thing." He scratched his head and thought about it, then grinned big. "You've got a date."

She handed him the container of herbs. "So what are you cooking and why do you need to look sophisticated?"

"Don't change the subject. You've got a date. Out with it. Who is she?" He gave her a devilish grin.

"I can't say…at least not yet. I'm not sure she's ready to let the world know she's dating a woman."

He frowned. "Oh, come on, Andi. Do I know her?"

Andi cringed. "Yes, but please, Leo, keep this to yourself. She's so new to this, and I want her to move us along at a pace that makes her comfortable."

"I understand. You deserve to be happy with someone." He paused. "So who is she?"

Andi bit her bottom lip and mumbled out of the corner of her mouth, "Julianna."

He looked at her with surprise. "Excuse me, did you say Julianna?" He cupped his ear and leaned toward her.

Andi nodded silently.

He grabbed his head. "Wow! I gotta give you credit, girl. You got game."

She folded her hands together. "Not really. It was just something that caught us both by surprise." She smiled at him. "Okay, your turn. Why do you need rosemary to look sophisticated?"

He was still contemplating what he just heard when he answered. "I met this older chick a few weeks ago, and I really like her. So I thought if I told her I could cook, it might impress her."

"And how's it working for you so far?"

"Well, I haven't burnt anything yet, but I seem to have overlooked a key ingredient for the roasted chicken." He held up the rosemary. "Speaking of chicken, I better get back to the kitchen."

Andi raised her eyebrows. "Wow, you really must like this woman to go to so much trouble."

He backtracked to the door. "She's something special. If you're impressed, she should be, too."

"Good luck, man," she said as he closed the door. "Looks like we both found something special," she added with a smile.

Julianna was right on time and absolutely gorgeous in a dark crimson dress and the white cashmere cloak she wore the night of the auction with her hair draped around her shoulders.

When Julianna walked in and saw Andi, it took her breath away. She couldn't keep her eyes off her date and, for the first time, allowed herself to enjoy it completely.

She kissed Andi. "You look amazing."

"Thank you. Since this is our first official date, I wanted to look my best."

"You most certainly will turn heads at dinner."

"As will you, gorgeous." She brushed her lips over Julianna's. "Shall we go?"

Andi was very surprised when they drove up to the front door of the Log Cabin Club House at Snow Cap Valley Ranch. She knew it was extremely difficult to get a reservation for dinner since the dining room was usually booked months in advance.

When Andi asked how she was able to get a table on such short notice, Julianna winked at her and said, "I have a few connections. After all, I am the marketing manager for food and beverage, you know."

The valet took the keys to the BMW and they walked through the foyer of the clubhouse to the reservation desk at the entrance to the dining room.

The maitre d' recognized Julianna right away. "Good evening, Ms. Stevens, Ms. Connelly." He nodded.

Andi nodded back. She was surprised he knew who she was.

"Good evening, Paul," Julianna said.

"I'll have the table you requested ready in one moment." He motioned to the busboy to hurry.

"You requested a particular table?" Andi whispered.

Julianna smiled. "Only the most romantic table with the best view in the entire dining room."

Andi was amused and watched as the busboy and waiters hurried to put the finishing touches on their table.

Julianna was in heaven. She wanted to pinch herself to make sure she wasn't dreaming. She had been saving this table and this experience for that special someone. It was a date she thought would never happen, but she was here now with that someone and Andi made everything feel exciting.

The maitre d' led them to a candlelit table, complete with linen table cloth, silverware, and crystal wine glasses, near a picture window overlooking the golf course. Just outside the window, the water from a lighted fountain danced and scattered over the surface of the pond. Nearby a fireplace cracked with burning wood. The view was gorgeous as the sun set over the mountain ridge across the valley.

"Julianna, this is magnificent." Andi's face was radiant in the candlelight.

Julianna's heart beat rapidly when she looked into Andi's light blue eyes. She covered Andi's hand with her own. "Almost as magnificent as last night."

Andi blushed lightly and smiled.

"I've been saving this table for a special occasion."

"This is a special occasion?"

"Yes, it is. It's our first date and this will be our table from now on," Julianna said and gave Andi's hand a light squeeze.

When the waiter appeared at the table, Andi ordered a bottle of wine, an Australian white with a lean, fresh fruity bouquet.

Julianna held up her glass. "I would like to propose a toast. To no longer being afraid of my feelings and to the woman who fills my heart with joy. I love you, Andrea Connelly."

Andi touched her glass to Julianna's. "I love you, too, Julianna Stevens."

Julianna took a sip from her glass. "Once again, you've made the perfect choice."

"I couldn't agree more," she said with a wink.

Dinner was a superb four-course affair complete with an impressive wine list. Afterward, the ladies were treated to a tour of the wine cellar by the sommelier herself. To finish off their evening, they had coffee in the sitting room.

"You certainly know how to impress a girl on a first date," Andi said as she settled down on the couch next to Julianna with a Baileys and coffee.

"Thank you," Julianna said with a satisfied smile. "I do know something about fine dining and romance."

"I bet you do."

"Andi, can I say something about last night?"

Andi swallowed hard. "You can say anything to me."

"I want you to know that being with you last night was the best night of my life. For the first time, I felt like the person I was with was completely there with me and for me. I never thought it could be so good." Julianna felt tears trying to rise up. "You didn't even have to say I love you, I knew it the first time you touched me, but it meant everything that you did."

"I meant those words with all my heart."

"I know. I hope you know too that it is the same for me."

"The words you spoke in the parking lot couldn't have been more honest, and I know they came from your heart. It took a great deal of strength and courage for you to tell me how you truly felt. I only wish I would have let you say it to me before when you tried. I'm sorry that I was so self-absorbed and didn't listen. I promise I'll never let it happen again."

Julianna took Andi's hand. "It's behind us. The important thing is that we found each other through all the confusion, and I'm going to make sure you know every day how I feel."

"I promise you I'll do the same, my love."

Julianna looked at Andi with a sober expression. "Andi, can I ask you about something?"

"Anything."

Julianna gathered her thoughts. "The woman you were talking to in Vail, your ex, why did you break up with her?"

Andi saw that the subject of Elisha weighed heavy on Julianna's mind. She was more than willing to tell Julianna anything she wanted to know about her past; however, it was a wound that was still somewhat fresh, and she would have rather shied away from having it reopened again. Elisha represented the past and that's where Andi wanted her to stay.

"She walked out on me." Andi breathed a sigh. "Right after the New Year. I came home early one evening from work, completely exhausted, and found her bags sitting by the door. She tried to leave without having to confront me."

"You mean sneak out," Julianna said with disgust.

"That's how Elisha handled most things, through avoidance. She left me a note on the dresser. It only said that she was leaving me for another woman who understood her better, whose lifestyle was more compatible with her own, and that her leaving was the best thing for both of us." Andi laughed. "What she didn't know at the time was that the woman whose lifestyle she claimed was more compatible with her own was a phony. Elisha comes from old Chicago money, and her grandfather set her up nicely with a trust fund. The other woman really played her and all for the money. They even went so far as to get married in Massachusetts where gay marriage is legal."

"I'm sorry she did you that way," Julianna said.

"When you saw us together in Vail, she was crying on my shoulder about what a mess her life had become and how her family hated Ariella. Her father was demanding she put an end to the farce of a marriage or risk losing her trust fund."

Julianna took Andi's hand. "I must admit I'm not as sorry as I should be. Her loss is my gain, and for that, I'm truly happy."

"Me too, me too," Andi said with a smile.

"What was it about her that attracted you? I mean, besides the obvious that she's completely gorgeous."

"Well, yes, obviously, the outside had its appeal, but I would have to say what hooked me was Elisha's ability to make me feel as if I were the most important person in the world and that she really needed me." Andi stopped and took a drink from her cup. "She had a vulnerable side to her, or I thought she did, it spoke to me in a way that compelled me to want to take care of her, to protect her."

"And did she genuinely need you in that way?"

"In retrospect, I would have to say no, it was all a game to her. Once she won me over, the thrill was gone. I worked to keep her interested for a long time, but it wore me down doing and giving for her all the time. When I finally started doing some things for myself again and not putting her first every time, she went looking for someone that would." Andi looked away.

Julianna took Andi's hand, attempting to ease some of the anguish in her voice.

"She was persistent in her pursuit of me. I admit I enjoyed the attention, but the little voice in the back of my head kept telling me there was something about her that I wasn't going to like. I wish I had listened."

A man and woman who looked to be in their seventies sat across the room having their coffee. The woman's gaze was fixed on Andi and Julianna. When they noticed the woman staring, she smiled and winked at them.

"Do you know that couple over there?" Andi asked.

"No, I thought maybe you did."

Andi laughed. "I think we've just been made."

"That's fine by me. I want the world to know you're mine," Julianna said happily.

Andi stretcher her arms out and looked around the enormous room with the giant fireplace at one end. "It's beautiful here. I love the rustic look of the log cabin."

"Yes, it is. Liz and Buddy got married in this room at sunset in front of the old fireplace over there." She pointed at the huge two-story floor-to-ceiling river stone fireplace at the opposite end of the room. It faced a wall of windows that gave a view of the open grassland and mountain range.

"It must have been a beautiful ceremony. Were you in the bridal party?"

"Maid of honor," Julianna said proudly. "Liz kept everything simple, and that made it more beautiful. The reception was another matter all together. It was a barbeque at the stables. Jaynee, the trail cook, had some of the best food ever on her chuck wagon that night. And the champagne and beer flowed freely all night. I think we danced till two a.m."

"Sounds like it was a good time."

"Yes, it was. I thought I would eventually have my wedding here, too." She looked down at her coffee cup and twirled the spoon in the light brown liquid.

Andi put her arm around Julianna. "You never know...maybe one day you will."

Julianna looked up at Andi with wide eyes.

Andi smiled big. "Be careful what you wish for." She took a drink from her cup and pulled Julianna closer.

Chapter 19

Julianna guided the BMW off Highway 70 at exit 203 and North Summit Boulevard in Frisco. "It's pure hell traveling on a Friday, and the skier traffic coming out of the airport in Denver is crazy," she said as she drove.

Andi stretched her legs out in the floor board of the front seat as they came to a stop sign. "It sure is good to be home." She reached over with her left hand and massaged the back of Julianna's neck.

Julianna gave in to the pleasure of Andi's touch and smiled as she drove on. She had been five days without Andi while she was in New York on business. It was the longest amount of time they'd been apart since the start of their relationship, and she was happy and relieved to have Andi back home where she belonged. "It's good to have you home, baby. I can't even begin to tell you how much Tinker and I missed you."

Andi flashed a devilish grin. "I missed you, too, and I missed having you next to me in bed at night...and on top of me and under me..."

Julianna's cheeks colored. "Well, that's exactly where I plan to be tonight and every night thereafter."

"Did my little mutt behave herself?"

"She was perfect as always."

"How was work this week?"

"Busy. With ski season in full swing, it's wall-to-wall people around the resort." She stopped the BMW at a red light. "Karen actually paid me a very nice compliment. She said she was impressed and encouraged with the early reports of increased customer visits to the restaurants at the resort and she credited my marketing plan for the improvement."

The light turned green and Julianna followed traffic through the intersection at Main Street.

"Karen said that?"

"Yes, and in the weekly staff meeting of all places. She was very nice about it, too, not her usual stoic self. She told me to keep up the good work."

Andi brushed the back of her fingers over Julianna's cheek. "Nice work, love. I'm proud of you."

"She must be menopausal or something. I don't get it. Even Susan is being less ego and more friendly. It's actually kinda creepy, but who am I to question the boss and her mood swings."

"Exactly," Andi said.

"Are you excited about your meeting with Beverly on Monday?"

Andi rubbed her hands on her thighs. "More like nervous. It's been so long since I've had someone look at my artwork for a show. I just hope she likes what I have."

"I'm sure she will. Since it's a group show that should take some of the pressure off. I think it's very exciting that you're going to show at Tillman galleries."

"Let's not jump the gun yet. Beverly hasn't accepted my work yet."

Julianna patted Andi's arm. "Not to worry my love, I have a really good feeling about this."

They pulled into the driveway of Andi's town house. Leo and Vince were unloading snowboards from the top of Leo's Jeep. They waved as Julianna pulled into the garage.

When Andi walked through the door, Tinker almost knocked her down she was so excited to see her. She set her bags to the side and gave the dog plenty of pets and hugs.

Julianna dropped her keys on the table next to the red chair. "I thought we'd order pizza and I have a bottle of wine waiting for us. Are you ready for a glass?" she asked on her way into the kitchen.

"That sounds wonderful." Andi walked up behind Julianna and wrapped her arms around her waist and turned her around. "But first I want to give you a proper hello," she said, then pressed her lips to Julianna's.

Julianna circled Andi's neck with her arms and kissed her, then relaxed her lips and let Andi inside to explore the soft warmth of her mouth.

Andi pulled back only far enough to speak. "Can the wine wait? I'm thinking I need a shower. Care to join me?"

Julianna's knees went weak from Andi's breath on her ear when she spoke. "Sounds like heaven, but you may have to hold me up. You're making my legs tremble. See what happens to me when you're gone? I've lost all fortitude and completely surrendered to you with one kiss."

"Then let's go upstairs so I can give you something to really smile about." Andi took her by the hand and led her to the green marble shower. She turned on the water to warm the stall and started to strip out of her button-down shirt and jeans until Julianna stopped her.

"Let me."

Andi immediately gave way to the soft elegance of Julianna's hands. She worked slowly and purposely to touch Andi everywhere as she removed her clothes.

Andi closed her eyes and concentrated on the feel of Julianna's hands through the cloth of her shirt. When Julianna reached skin, Andi moaned with every breath.

Julianna watched Andi's face as she pushed her jeans to the floor. The look of pleasure that washed over Andi with her touch brought Julianna to full arousal, as well. Her legs were beginning to tremble again, and she leaned into Andi's naked body.

Andi held on to her with one arm and helped her remove her clothes with the other, then she guided her into the wide stall of the warm steamy shower.

Still holding tight to Julianna, Andi ran her tongue down Julianna's neck and cupped one of her breasts with her free hand as the warm water ran the length of their bodies.

"Oh, God, Andi," Julianna cried out when Andi rolled Julianna's already taut nipple with her thumb and forefinger. "I missed you so much, I'm nearly ready to explode and you've barely touched me." She gripped Andi by the shoulders for support.

"So I guess it wouldn't be nice of me to tease you for very long."

"I don't think I can hang on long enough for you to make me any more hot and wet than I already am." She pulled Andi in closer. "I want you now. Please, sweetheart, hurry."

Andi slid her hand down Julianna's wet torso to the inside of her thigh and found her hot and swollen. She wished she had more time to explore and excite Julianna, but she recognized her immediate need and wanted to satisfy it as best she could.

She buried her face in Julianna's wet hair, then moved her fingers in, and within a matter of four or five thrusts, Julianna burst in a flood of waves.

She pressed her lips to Andi's neck. "Oh, yes, baby, yes," she cried as her whole body pulsed from the inside.

Andi held her hand still until she felt Julianna relax. Still holding her up with one arm she whispered, "Are you okay, love?"

Julianna leaned back and cradled Andi's face. "Better than all right." She pulled Andi's mouth to hers and kissed her with urgency. Julianna pulled away and locked gazes with Andi. "Now, it's your turn," she said with a confident gleam in her sultry brown eyes. She gently pushed Andi against the wall of the shower stall.

Andi wasn't sure what was next. Julianna was slowly learning how to make love to her, but her confidence was still shaky, and she was still somewhat timid when she touched her. Andi had been a patient and gentle teacher for her as Julianna worked to learn what Andi liked and how to arouse her.

At this moment, Julianna looked as if she knew exactly what to do. She hungrily kissed Andi's neck while her hands roamed purposefully over her body. She made contact with all the right places, and in no time, Andi was feeling the need for Julianna to take her the rest of the way. There was no hesitation in her touch.

Julianna moved from Andi's neck to her breasts, using her mouth and tongue to tease her nipples until they were rock hard and Andi was breathless from the stimulation. Her hand finally glided down Andi's abdomen, and she cupped her between her legs. Andi was delightfully surprised. It was a move she hadn't tried on her before. Julianna worked in circles with her fingers to bring Andi to the edge.

Andi pushed Julianna's hand hard against her. "You've got me right at that edge, baby, take me the rest of the way."

Julianna didn't miss a beat. She pressed Andi into the wall with her body and kissed her hard and deep while her fingers worked rhythmically until Andi clamped down on her and her body stiffened with pleasure.

When she was finally able to speak, she said, "That was amazing, baby. You were amazing."

Julianna smiled. "I found a couple of books down in Denver and did some reading while you were gone."

"I applaud your astute enthusiasm. Books are a good thing."

"Pleasing you is a good thing."

When they were done in the shower, Andi stepped out and draped a towel around Julianna's shoulders as she got out.

"I'll go order the pizza. You've caused me to work up quite an appetite. Peppino's okay?"

"Yeah, that's great. Thin crust please." Julianna finished drying her body and slipped into Andi's old terrycloth robe.

Andi threw on a pair of jeans and a red tank top and sprang down the stairs.

Julianna came down just as Andi hung up. "Pizza will be here in about thirty minutes." Andi spread herself out on the couch.

"I'll get the wine." Julianna went to the kitchen.

She handed Andi a glass of her favorite red and sat next to her on the couch. "I'm so glad to have you home," she said, curling up under Andi's arm.

Andi laughed. "I kinda got that in the shower," she said as she took a drink from the glass.

Julianna elbowed her playfully. "It's more than that. Just having you with me makes my world complete. When you were gone, there was an uncomfortable emptiness I couldn't seem to shake."

"I know what you mean. When I got into that big bed at night at the hotel, I couldn't get comfortable. I didn't have you to snuggle with." Andi squeezed Julianna. "I'm sure I'll sleep very well tonight, though."

"I'm sure you will when I get done with you."

"Making up for lost time, are we?"

"Yes!"

Andi fingered Julianna's damp honey brown locks. "You are definitely the incorrigible one."

Julianna's face grew serious when she looked at Andi. "I talked to my parents this week."

Right away, Andi picked up on the angst in her otherwise sweet voice. "What did they have to say?"

"They want to come out for Thanksgiving."

Andi drew her closer. "How do you feel about that?"

She rested her head on Andi's shoulder. "Mixed feelings. I want to tell them about us and get everything out in the open, but I know how they'll react and it will be such a waste of a holiday."

Andi hesitated. "Would it be better if I weren't around while they're here? I mean if you're not ready to face them, I understand. I certainly don't want you to feel any pressure from me."

Julianna raised her head and locked gazes with Andi. "That's not even an option. You're the most important part of my life, and it's time they know about us." Her brow narrowed. "I just have to figure out how to tell them and make sure the timing is right."

Andi kissed her forehead. "I'm not sure there is a right time, baby. Their reaction will be the same regardless of when you tell them."

"Mom told me my brother just made deacon at the church. I can image what his pious reaction is going to be."

"Just remember I'm here for you. I'll stand by you no matter what. That's not going to change."

Julianna hugged Andi tight. "I know you will and I love you for that. Anyway, no plans have been made yet. Mom said Dad was anxious to get to their villa in Florida for the winter, he hates the cold."

The doorbell announced the arrival of pizza. Andi got up and answered the door. She handed the freckle-faced boy several bills and he in turn handed off the warm box and reached in to his pocket to make change.

Andi waved him off. "Keep it."

His eyes widened. "You sure?"

"Yeah. You have a good night."

"Yes, ma'am. Thank you, ma'am," the teen said with a huge smile. He bolted off the porch and headed for the old blue Chevy Silverado truck he left idling in the driveway.

Andi brought the box to the coffee table while Julianna retrieved napkins from the kitchen.

They both grabbed a slice of the pizza and sat back to enjoy it.

Julianna moved to the opposite end of the couch and laid her legs over Andi's so they faced each other while they ate.

"So you haven't told me how your breakfast meeting went with Gail Neiman this morning." She wiped a dripping of sauce from the corner of her mouth.

Andi swallowed the food in her mouth and washed it down with the wine. "It was nice. She was really impressed with our ratings. We were first in our market. She thinks KCOR could turn out to be one of the biggest components of Resort TV."

"Honey, that's wonderful. Thomas must be thrilled. I hope he realizes that hiring you was the smartest thing he ever did."

Andi's cheeks blushed lightly. "He was walking on air yesterday at the meetings."

"Was he at the meeting this morning with you?"

Andi finished her bite before she answered. "No, it was just Gail and me. She wanted to talk to me about future development."

Julianna's throat tightened. "But wouldn't that include Thomas?"

"Not necessarily. She wanted to talk about the future

development of my career."

Julianna set her food down. Suddenly, she lost her appetite. "What development does she have in mind?"

"She thinks I could potentially take over the VP spot for Resort TV if I want it. She offered to help groom me for the position by putting me in a junior executive spot under her in New York." Andi shoved the last bite of crust in her mouth.

Julianna looked as if her entire world were about to crumble. "Wow, that's quite an offer. I don't see how you could pass it up." A single tear escaped the corner of her eye.

Andi's face fell when she saw the alarm in Julianna's brown eyes. She was already assuming Andi's bags were packed. She wiped her mouth and tossed the napkin aside. Then she crawled over the couch and positioned herself over Julianna. She looked directly into Julianna's tear-filled eyes. "I told her no thank you."

Julianna sniffed back her tears. "You told her no? But...but that's what you were hoping for, a chance to move on, to get back to a big city."

Andi looked at her curiously. She had never said a word about wanting to advance. Once she and Julianna came together, all thoughts of moving on were gone. "Why do you say that?"

"You told me that the night of Rachel's party. You said you made a mistake coming here and that you belonged in a big city."

Andi's face softened and she wiped a tear from Julianna's cheek.

"Oh, sweetheart, don't you know everything has changed?" She brushed back loose strands of Julianna's bangs. "I'm happier and more settled in my life at this moment than I have ever been. You are my life now and I love you. That's all that matters." She slowly skimmed her lips over Julianna's. Then she leaned her forehead against Julianna's. "I have everything I need right here. So you're stuck with me because I'm not going anywhere."

Julianna leaned back and cradled Andi's face with her hands and brushed her thumb over her lips. She smiled and said, "Good, because I love you with all my heart and I have everything I want right here, too. My life is complete." She pulled Andi down on top of her and kissed her long and slow.

Andi sat back up and caressed Julianna's cheek. "I was thinking that after you tell your family and things are out in the open, maybe we could look for a place of our own, that is if you're ready."

Julianna's eyes flashed. "You mean like move in together?"

"Yes, like move in together." She rolled her eyes. "But we're going to need some place bigger than this with more closet space. I've seen your wardrobe."

"Very funny." Julianna held Andi's face again. "Yes, I'm ready, and I can't think of anything that would make me happier than to share a home with you."

"Let your clarity define you...in the end we will only just remember how it feels."

~ *Rob Thomas (2007)*

About the author

Jocelyn Powers is a native Missourian. She is a graduate of the art school at Washington University in St. Louis and worked for many years in advertising as a film and video producer. Wanting more from her career, Jocelyn turned to the health care field and redirected her path. For over a decade, she has enjoyed a successful and satisfying career in emergency medicine.

In recent years, Jocelyn has been drawn back to her creative roots. She has been writing stories in her head for years and credits longtime friend Robin Alexander for inspiring her to get them out of her gray matter and on to paper.

Jocelyn currently resides in St. Louis and shares a home with her beloved ninetypound Weimaraner (who thinks she's the size of a Chihuahua). Joce is an avid skier and loves to be outdoors whenever possible. She still dabbles with the visual arts and is an accomplished freelance digital video editor.

Jocelyn emphasizes she doesn't live a day without saying thank you for her family, good friends, good health, and an amazing life.

You may also enjoy...

Winds of Heaven
By Kate Sweeney
Release: September 2009

After the untimely death of a former lover, Casey Bennet receives a letter from Julie's lawyer, begging Casey to help Julie's partner, Liz Kennedy, and their adorable, yet precocious three-year old, Skye, who are now alone.

An avowed bachelorette, Casey has no idea what's in store when she grudgingly agrees to help Liz, who, by the way, is also pregnant and due in four months.

Casey, Liz, and little Skye find themselves in for a hilarious, tender ride that will change their lives forever.

Love's Someday
By Robin Alexander
Release: December 2009

Ashleigh Prather committed the sin of omission when she failed to reveal secrets of her past to her lover of five years. Her relationship becomes the casualty when the past and present collide. Erica Barrett's world is turned upside down when she is forced to watch Ashleigh confront old demons and become someone she doesn't recognize.

Is love worth fighting for when you realize that you never truly knew the person you've shared five years of your life with?

You can purchase other Intaglio
Publications books online at
www.bellabooks.com, www.scp-inc.biz, or at
your local book store.

Published by
Intaglio Publications
Walker, LA

Visit us on the web
www.intagliopub.com